Darcy vs. Bennet

A Pride and Prejudice Variation

Victoria Kincaid

ISBN: 978-0-9916681-8-2

Chapter One

"What could possibly go wrong?"

Elizabeth Bennet wished Louisa Green had not uttered those words. They almost guaranteed that something would go wrong.

They were standing at the edge of the Berwicks' formal gardens, which had been hung with Chinese lanterns and lit with torches. Elegantly dressed ladies and gentlemen mingled and laughed, taking glasses of wine from tray-bearing footmen. The annual midsummer masquerade ball at Tilbury Manor was well known among members of the *ton*. It started well before the sun set and would continue until the early hours of the morning.

Elizabeth and Louisa observed the activity from their vantage point behind a boxwood hedge. "Oh! It is so grand!" Louisa sighed. "I have been wanting to attend since I was but ten years of age."

"I cannot dissuade you?" Elizabeth asked once again.

"No. I must dance with Robert—or I will die!" she declaimed.

Elizabeth rolled her eyes. Her friend sounded like the overwrought heroine of a tawdry novel; perhaps Louisa's parents should add more poetry to their library. When Elizabeth had arrived for her annual summer visit to see Louisa at the Greens' estate, she had discovered that her friend was obsessed with the handsome oldest son of the neighboring estate. And Louisa was determined to attend the Berwicks' masquerade ball, which was the culmination of their summer house party. There was only one problem: Louisa had not been invited. Her family was respectable local gentry but not on a par with the elite society attending the ball.

Louisa had encountered Robert Berwick at a few local assemblies and was certain they were destined to be wed. Elizabeth was not convinced about the inevitability of the match, particularly since Louisa was seventeen and Mr. Berwick five and twenty.

Louisa had devised a plan to attend the ball, certain that no one would recognize her since she—like all the guests—would be wearing a mask. Elizabeth had tried in vain to dissuade her friend from a plan that was certain to end in disaster, but Louisa was ever stubborn and independently minded. In the end, Elizabeth decided to accompany her sometimes impulsive friend and hopefully stave off trouble. Admittedly, a small part of Elizabeth was excited about attending the sort of grand masked balls she had only read about. But her excitement was tempered by anxiety. What would they do if someone noticed they were uninvited?

"Enough observation!" Louisa whispered. "We must go!"

Before Elizabeth could raise any more objections, Louisa grabbed her hand and tugged her toward the center of the garden. Before they reached the circle of torchlight, Louisa dropped Elizabeth's hand and paused to smooth her dress and hair. Elizabeth followed her lead. Hopefully no one would guess they had walked nearly half a mile from the road to reach this event. She knew tightening the ribbons of the mask over her eyes was being excessively cautious, but she did not want it to slip off at the wrong moment.

The revelers were a riot of color. Women wore elegant, brightly colored silk gowns and feathers in their hair. Many of the men opted for basic black but often had masks of blue, red, or yellow covering their eyes. Moonlight streamed down from above, lending a cool light to the garden's central court. The Berwicks' servants had distributed enough standing candelabras that the scene was very well illuminated. Despite her misgivings, Elizabeth broke into a smile. Everything was so glittering and beautiful. This was the sort of party she had always hoped but never expected to attend.

"Oh, I see Robert!" Louisa whispered, and before Elizabeth could stop her, Louisa had disappeared into the crowd. Elizabeth attempted to follow, but throngs of people obstructed her path, and she quickly lost sight of her friend. Had Louisa run toward the fountain or the maze? Elizabeth threaded her way through the sumptuously attired merrymakers for the better part of fifteen minutes before she was forced to admit the truth.

She was alone at the masquerade.

***

Why had he felt even a twinge of excitement at the prospect of a masquerade? Perhaps he had hoped to meet some new people, Fitzwilliam Darcy mused. But most of the revelers were the same guests he had come to know during the two-week house party at Tilbury. The rest were members of the *ton* who lived close enough to visit for the day. And he knew them all. Despite the mask, Sir Richard Edgeworth was immediately recognizable by his laugh. The woman who was already unsteady on her feet was Lord Nightingale's daughter, Amelia. The plump couple that teased everyone about their identities was Mr. and Mrs. Graves.

Discerning identities was really not so difficult for Darcy although others seemed to find it challenging. After all, a mask did nothing to conceal hair color, the shape of a body, or the sound of a voice. Darcy was well aware he knew everyone at the ball —and he did not wish to speak with any of them. The affair was tedious beyond belief. He longed to check his watch and see how soon he could politely withdraw.

He should have invented business at Pemberley and departed a week ago. *Why did I attend this house party at all? Oh yes, I must find a wife.* He had hoped to meet someone new, but they were all the same beautiful, haughty ladies who talked of nothing but gossip and lace. He already knew them, and they were not what he was seeking.

This excursion had been an utter failure. He had not met a single woman he would consider for more than a minute. The thought of marrying any of these women made him shudder. Darcy could not explain precisely what he sought in a wife, but he would recognize it when he found it.

Laughter cut into Darcy's ruminations. Guiltily, he realized he had not been attending to the conversation around him. One of the men in his group was finishing up a story. "—and there Peter Brooks was—with his cravat flapping in the wind and an overturned curricle!" This last line provoked more laughter from his listeners, and Darcy joined in despite having missed most of the story. He glanced furtively at Robert Berwick, one of his oldest friends from his university days —who was already a little foxed—talking and gesturing expansively. Good. Perhaps he would not notice if Darcy simply slipped away.

He could retire to his bedchamber and read a nice book, or have a chat with Georgiana if she was still awake. His sister had been enjoying the house party but was too young for a ball and remained in the house with her companion. Perhaps Darcy could have their servants pack for a departure tomorrow. If only they could! It was a tempting fantasy.

As Darcy watched Robert, a woman he did not recognize rushed up to his friend. "You owe me a dance!" she insisted to Robert. Wearing a black silk mask, she was petite and blonde, quite coy in her manner.

"I-I-I what?" Robert spluttered.

"You owe me a dance, Mr. Berwick." The woman wrapped her hand around Robert's arm. "Do not tell me you have forgotten already!" Her flirtatious smile took the sting out of her words.

Had Darcy seen this woman before? How intriguing to think there was someone here he did not know. Her blue dress was simpler than most others at the ball, and her voice was unfamiliar. Was she one of the younger Fenton daughters? They had a prodigious number of children.

The woman was young, probably only recently out. And all of her attention was fixed on Robert. "It will be a great scandal if you do not keep your word!" She giggled. Darcy sighed. Giggling was not a feature he sought in a wife.

Robert, on the other hand, seemed simultaneously perplexed and charmed. "Do not say so! I cannot be forsworn, miss. I shall keep my oath!"

"I believe they are forming another set," the woman trilled, gesturing to the veranda where the dancing took place.

Robert bowed deeply. "Shall we, then?" He offered her his arm, and she consolidated her hold on it as they walked off. The other men who had congregated around Robert wandered off as well, and Darcy was abruptly alone.

Now would be an excellent time to sneak back into the house and his bedchamber. There were simply too many people at this ball. The constant movement of people and the press of bodies were fraying his nerves. And no one would notice his absence.

However, Darcy had barely taken three steps when he saw a vision. Clad in a pale yellow gown, the woman's figure was light and pleasing. Lush curls of dark hair were piled high on her head, intertwined with tiny flowers. Instantly, Darcy knew he had not encountered her before.

She was not moving or conversing with anyone; in fact, she seemed a bit lost.

When Darcy stepped toward her, her eyes flashed up to his, and his breath caught. Set off by the pale yellow mask, her eyes were a vibrant blue he had never seen before. There was something about her…as if he knew her already—which was ridiculous since he had never met her before. Without a conscious decision, Darcy took several more steps toward the mystery woman.

She had turned her face away and was now scanning the crowd. Seeking another man? He felt a twinge of unease, which was bizarre. He knew nothing about this woman.

A crease appeared between her eyes, and her mouth tightened. Was she in distress? "May I be of service, miss?" He bowed. "You appear uneasy." What a ludicrous thing to say! Surely he could think of a better way to introduce himself to this vision of loveliness.

She was biting her lower lip, and Darcy wanted more than anything to alleviate her anxiety. "I was looking for my friend." His surge of jealousy was instantly assuaged by her next words. "She is blonde and wears a blue dress."

"Ah, I believe she has accompanied my friend onto the veranda for a dance."

"Oh. So I *have* been abandoned." Her lips quirked into a half smile. *She sees her friend's abandonment as a cause for amusement rather than resentment,* Darcy noted.

"As have I. Perhaps we may be abandoned together." How did such flirtatious language emerge from his mouth? Usually he had no facility with words. Perhaps the mask offered him some kind of license? But her clear blue eyes held his in a captive gaze. No, it was her. Something about this woman stirred deep feelings so all he saw—all he could see—was her. The rest of the world simply fell away.

Her eyebrows tipped upward doubtfully. Was he being too forward with a woman he had just met? Darcy almost did not care. He would do anything, break any rules of propriety to stay with this enchanting creature. "Would you do me the honor of the next dance?"

She blinked rapidly and blushed, her gaze not meeting his. Was the request such a surprise to her? Of course, they had not been introduced, but a masquerade should allow them to dispense with such formalities. Then she gave him an arch look. "A stranger in a mask has just asked me to dance. What would my mother say I should do in this situation?"

Was she teasing him? He had seen other men engage in such banter, but it never happened to him. He cleared his throat. "I believe your mother would advise you to accept under the circumstances." He found himself smiling at her. "I assure you, miss, I am not a highwayman despite the mask."

She tapped her lips thoughtfully with her forefinger. "So you would have me believe you are a respectable gentleman? I would expect a highwayman to say so."

Darcy could not prevent a laugh from bursting forth. At the beginning of their conversation he had suspected she might be unaware of his identity, but now he was sure of it. No woman ever dared to banter with Fitzwilliam Darcy in such a way; they were too eager to compliment his figure, his features, his clothing, his horse…and anything else he possessed. Every exchange with a marriageable woman was colored by awareness of his fortune—except this one, and it was delightful. How had such a woman found her way into the Berwicks' masquerade?

He restrained an impulse to take the woman's hand; he did not know her. "Very well, will you promise to dance with me if I promise not to purloin your reticule or jewelry?" As he said this, he realized she possessed neither. How odd.

She laughed, a bright, silvery sound. He had made her laugh! "Yes, I thank you. But this set has just begun."

He glanced at the veranda where the couples had just begun their set. "Then perhaps we may take a stroll in the gardens before the next one commences." Where had he discovered this new fount of gallantry and ease? Robert often teased Darcy about being stiff and formal in company.

The woman took his proffered arm, and they slowly walked toward the formal gardens, which were less crowded than in the area around the court. He had so many questions about this enchanting woman that his throat felt clogged with them. "I pray you, tell me your name," he finally managed.

She slid him a sidelong glance. "It is a masquerade. Should not my identity remain hidden?"

He shrugged. "I do not wish to think of you as 'that woman in yellow' for the entire evening."

Her laugh was genuine, not the polite tittering allowed for a lady of the *ton*. "Very well, my name is Elizabeth."

Elizabeth. Darcy savored the taste of the name in his mind. It suited her: elegant but lively. She did not give her surname, but he supposed that was consistent with the spirit of a masquerade.

"And I am William," he responded.

She gave no sign of recognition although he was the only William at the masquerade. "I am pleased to meet you, William." Her smile illuminated the surrounding darkness.

"The pleasure is all mine," Darcy said, and he meant it.

The garden paths were lit by torches at regular intervals, but many areas remained swathed in shadows. In one such patch of darkness, a couple stood rather close as if they were about to kiss. A swift glance at Elizabeth showed her blushing at the sight, so he rushed them past it. *Fortunately, Georgiana is up in her bedchamber under the eye of Mrs. Younge!*

Darcy ceased worrying about Elizabeth's offended sensibilities when he heard her laugh. "Wearing a mask may sometimes become a license to behave more freely than one might ordinarily," she said.

This struck him as a rather astute observation. "Indeed. A mask gives the illusion of anonymity—as if you can be someone else." *Perhaps that is why I may approach this woman so boldly.*

"Are you saying you are not ordinarily a pleasant, gentlemanly fellow?" Elizabeth asked with an arch smile.

She was teasing him, and surprisingly, he loved it. "Indeed not!" He smiled. "As you have guessed, I am a highwayman—and usually quite proud and churlish. What think you of my thespian skills?"

Her laugh was warm and throaty. "You had me completely fooled, sir! You could rival the greatest actor in Covent Garden."

"And what of you, Miss Elizabeth? Are you also playing a role?"

"Oh, most definitely." Her smile was enigmatic.

"And will you tell me what it is?"

"Perhaps you may figure it out."

"I see." He smiled. "So you are playing the part of a conundrum."

He was thrilled to have provoked more laughter. "Yes, that is me."

"Miss Conundrum?"

"My mother would say so; I puzzle her exceedingly."

"In what way?" Darcy asked.

She shrugged and blushed faintly. "I read all the books in my father's library and prefer to take long walks rather than remain inside to discuss fashion with the other ladies."

Darcy experienced a jolt of something akin to recognition. He had not known it until that moment, but were those not qualities he would seek in an ideal wife? She had wit; he could attest to that after only a brief acquaintance. And now he found she loved reading and the outside.

This resulting surge of hope frightened him. He found himself envisioning a future with this woman although he knew nothing of her family or situation. Her family might be objectionable, or she might already be promised in marriage. But reciting these cautions to himself did nothing to extinguish the small ember of hope flaring to life in his heart.

"What do you read?" He strove to keep his voice casual. They had reached the edge of the formal gardens without having stopped to admire any of the foliage. Turning around, they strolled back toward the house.

She gestured expansively. "Anything! I read the papers daily. I believe it is important to know the latest news from the war and elsewhere. I read every travel book in my father's library; some of the places sound so fascinating!"

Hope was like the drumbeat of hooves in his chest. "And poetry?"

"Everything I can find. Although I am particularly fond of Wordsworth and Shakespeare. I do believe Lord Byron's talents to be overrated."

Darcy could have uttered those words himself. "I love Wordsworth and Shakespeare as well." Good. His voice was only moderately strangled.

She gazed on him with shining eyes. "Have you read Wordsworth's latest volume?"

"Yes. It was…magnificent."

She sighed. "I have not yet read it, but I hope to soon."

His copy was at Tilbury, in his room. "I—" Darcy could lend it to her, but they were not likely to see each other again. That reality was like a cold bucket of water.

Elizabeth waited for him to finish his sentence. He swallowed. "Um, where does your family reside?"

She shook her head and gave a playful smile. "Nay, if I reveal everything I cannot maintain the illusion of mystery."

"I would on no account deprive you of that pleasure," he said.

Their walk had led them back to the house. He led Elizabeth onto the wide stone veranda where couples gathered for the next set. But then he spied an all-too-familiar dress, easily identifying its owner despite her mask.

"I pray you, excuse me for a moment." He dropped Elizabeth's arm and walked purposefully toward the girl. She was tall, blonde, and quite pretty. Her hair was done in a simple style, with ribbons that matched her white dress. Waving her arms with animation, she conversed with Mrs. Beckett, an older lady with too many feathers in her hair.

Darcy took her elbow. "Please pardon us," he said to Mrs. Beckett as he drew the girl to an empty corner of the veranda. Dismay was written all over her face.

"Georgiana! You were expressly forbidden to attend this ball." He kept his voice low but could not disguise his anger.

His sister raised her chin defiantly. "Only because I have not yet made my debut, but with the mask, no one will know who I am. They would never guess I am not of age."

Darcy was forced to concede that point. His sister was blessed, or cursed, with a very womanly figure that, combined with her height, made her appear older than she was. Nevertheless… "I recognized you immediately!" he observed.

"You are my brother!" Exasperation tinged her voice. "You probably recognized my dress."

"The Berwicks would recognize you…and perhaps some of the other guests. What would they think?"

"I shall avoid them," she promised. Darcy scowled at her. "Please, William, I would like to see what a masquerade ball is really like. I have heard so much! I hate being confined to my room while others are enjoying themselves. Please, let me stay for a little while!"

"Where is Mrs. Younge?"

"Over there." Georgiana gestured to an older, plainly dressed woman who stood near the back of the veranda watching them. "She will be with me constantly!"

"Father would not like it," Darcy warned.

"Father is back at Pemberley." Georgiana bit her lip. "You will not tell him?"

Darcy shook his head. It was easy to predict what his father would say, and Darcy must avoid provoking any anger at Georgiana.

If only he could escort his sister around the party! But he glanced back at Elizabeth, waiting patiently where he had left her. He could not squander another minute with her. However, their father had selected Mrs. Younge, who had come very highly recommended.

Georgiana's eyes pleaded with him for understanding. He sighed. "Very well." He consulted his pocket watch. "You may stay until midnight but not a minute after. You must never be unescorted. And no dancing!"

She nodded eagerly, a broad smile on her face.

He gave Mrs. Younge a stern glance before striding back to Elizabeth and recapturing her arm. "I apologize." Elizabeth nodded but regarded him soberly. Darcy realized he should explain why he was whispering urgently to a young, attractive girl. "That is my sister, Georgiana. She was not supposed to attend the ball, but she begged me to allow it since her companion is with her."

Elizabeth's eyebrows raised. "Why was she not permitted?"

"She is not yet out. But she is headstrong and does not like to be told what to do."

Elizabeth laughed a bit. "Few people do. I would imagine *you* do not care for it."

Darcy thought about Georgiana's situation from this perspective; yes, he would chafe at those restrictions in her place.

Elizabeth continued. "It is hard on younger children when their elders may attend events that they are not yet permitted to attend."

"Do you speak from experience?" He wished to know everything about this woman.

She laughed. "Indeed, I do! I have an older sister and three younger ones."

Darcy sought to recall if he knew of any families with five daughters. "Did you resent your older sister?"

"No. She is a lovely creature, so patient that no one could possibly resent her. And we are so near in age that our parents brought us out together. But my younger sisters were very unhappy before they could come out."

Darcy then wondered at her age. She did not seem older than eighteen; her sisters would be rather young to already be out in society.

Darcy took Elizabeth by her gloved hand and led her to the dance floor; it was just as crowded as when he had left it. Elizabeth's face was aglow. "Oh, this is indeed very grand! Those candelabras are so elegant."

"But surely you have been here before?" he asked.

She blinked rapidly. "Of course, but only briefly when we first arrived. The garden is so much cooler."

Yet another piece of the puzzle. Who had she accompanied? Surely she and her young friend had not arrived alone. There were many things about this young woman that puzzled him. She was a conundrum he very much wanted to solve. "Shall we take our places for the next set?"

They took a place at the end of the line of dancers. As he faced her, Darcy had a moment of doubt. He knew nothing about this woman, not even her surname. How could he be so captivated? Perhaps he should maintain a polite distance. But then the music commenced, and Elizabeth immediately occupied all of Darcy's thoughts.

Chapter Two

Elizabeth dearly loved to dance but seldom had she found a partner as accomplished as William. They moved so well together that it was as if they had been dancing together for years. Already she regretted that they would not share another set. But she had sufficiently indulged her whims; she and Louisa would need to leave soon. What would Jane think if she knew Elizabeth had kept company with a masked man—without any sort of proper introduction? Elizabeth herself was a bit startled at her own temerity.

She had planned to observe Louisa from the shadows and avoid the other guests. But then Louisa had abandoned her, and William had appeared as if heaven sent. He had intrigued her at once. His clothes were almost all black—a common choice for men at a masquerade—and of the highest quality; they displayed his tall figure to great advantage. What she could see of his face suggested he was quite handsome. He was gentlemanly and solicitous in his manners. But what most struck Elizabeth was that the conversation between them flowed so effortlessly; it was as if they had known each other for years rather than minutes.

She had resolved many times to quit his presence but found herself instead agreeing with his every suggestion. When he had left her to speak with that other woman, she had felt a ridiculous twinge of jealousy—and accompanying relief when he revealed her identity. But even in the grip of such a turmoil of emotions, Elizabeth had eagerly awaited his return rather than take the opportunity to escape.

And now they were dancing. Each touch of his hand thrilled her upon contact—like a special gift reserved for her alone. Every touch felt so illicit, so naked; Elizabeth actually checked to ensure they were both wearing gloves. Although she knew it was wrong, she yearned for more contact with him—to touch his arms, his back, his face. Shivers traveled up and down her spine. She had danced with many men; why did this one affect her so?

Other women in the set were throwing William flirtatious glances, but he ignored them. Undoubtedly, they knew his identity. The quality of his clothes suggested his family had at least a moderate fortune, which was bound to attract feminine attention. *Why does he pay me any attention at all? He is too high in the instep for me.* Sharply she reminded herself it did not matter. There was no harm in enjoying his company for this one night, and she would never see him again.

The dance called for them to clasp hands and turn in a circle. His eyes caught and held her gaze as they turned. Despite his mask, she could discern he was a handsome man with a fine figure. But there was something else that stirred inside Elizabeth when she lost herself in his dark blue gaze—almost as if she were coming home to someone she had known all her life.

Then she gave a little shake of the head. *Stop this foolishness!* she admonished herself. *The warm air, the torchlight, and the scent of roses are simply casting a spell—enchanting my senses and encouraging flights of fancy.* At the conclusion of the dance, she would thank him, and they would go their separate ways. It was well past time for Elizabeth and Louisa to depart. The longer they remained, the greater the risk of detection.

Elizabeth ignored the pain in her chest. She could not possibly miss a man she had known for less than an hour. This was not a fairy tale or a popular novel.

He had simply sought her temporary companionship. Perhaps he was more handsome and charming than most...well, any other man she had met.

But no doubt he would forget her the moment they parted ways. And she would forget him as well…eventually.

The dance brought them very close for a moment, face to face, and he smiled at her, creating a tingle of excitement that spread into the very core of her body. The sensation was both exhilarating and frightening. Would she—could she—ever have these feelings for another man?

For the remainder of the set, Elizabeth tried not to think, deliberately focusing on dance steps rather than dwelling on the future—or lack of future—she faced with this gentleman.

At the end of the dance, he bowed, and she curtsied to him. When their eyes met, she could not stifle a gasp. His gaze was so intense that she thought she might go up in flames just from his eyes. *He feels it as well.* But in the next moment, he glanced into the crowd, and she could not be sure of what she had seen.

He took her hand and led her out toward the edge of the veranda where there was fewer people and cooler air. They stood by the balustrade, catching the evening breezes. "Thank you for the dance." William was a little breathless. "It was most enjoyable."

"Thank you for asking me. You are an excellent dancer!" She could not help smiling at him.

But his face was solemn, almost as if he was concentrating on something. Without taking his eyes from hers, he slowly brought her hand to his lips and kissed it, lingering far longer than was strictly polite. A shiver shot through Elizabeth's entire body. He did not relinquish his hold; he turned her hand over and bent his head to gently kiss her palm. *Thank goodness I am wearing gloves. If he were kissing my skin, I might burst into flames!*

"I must see you again, fair Elizabeth," he breathed. "Where can I find you so I might obtain permission from your father to court you?" His head was still bent over her hand, but he glanced up through his lashes.

Elizabeth could not quite stifle the thrill of excitement at the thought of being courted by a man such as this. But she forced herself to ignore the sensation. "I am afraid it is impossible, sir."

He straightened, regarding her with a frown. "Are you promised to another?" His voice had a new hoarseness.

"No, but—we are from different worlds."

The lines on his forehead deepened. "You are a gentleman's daughter?"

"Yes, yes, of course." She cast about for a reason that would not reveal her identity. "I am not from Sussex."

"Neither am I," he responded promptly. "My family has an estate in Derbyshire. Where do you reside?"

She opened her mouth to say "Hertfordshire" and only just remembered that she should not reveal *anything*. It was all too easy to forget herself in this man's presence!

"It matters not. It is in every way impossible. I am sorry."

He appeared so crestfallen that Elizabeth considered revealing the true reasons they could not meet again. But if the Berwicks discovered that Louisa Green and her friend had insinuated themselves into the ball, it would be a great scandal, risking both women's reputations—and likely earning William's disgust as well. It was best if she departed while he still thought well of her.

This is my fault! I was too enamored of the masquerade, and now I have disappointed William. She needed to find Louisa and depart immediately.

A glance over the balustrade to the garden below revealed a glimpse of Louisa's blue dress. She could collect her friend and be gone before the next set started. But William must not notice them leaving the estate.

Inspiration struck. "The dancing has made me very thirsty. Could you possibly obtain a glass of lemonade for me?"

He frowned, but she gave him her best imploring look. "Certainly, but I am not finished with this subject. I will convince you somehow." He turned and walked briskly toward the crush surrounding the lemonade table.

Elizabeth hated her small deception, but it was necessary. It also relieved her of the burden of bidding goodbye to William. She could pretend she might see him again.

Gathering her skirts in her hands, Elizabeth prepared for a swift descent into the garden. But where was Louisa's blue dress now? There was no sign of her friend. Elizabeth sighed; this would require a tedious search throughout the garden.

Then her gaze was arrested by a different sight. Not Louisa's blue dress but a white one—the one worn by William's sister. Yes, it was Georgiana—in a little area almost completely surrounded by tall hedges—and she embraced a young, brown-haired man of medium height. He pressed a row of kisses along the pale column of the girl's neck. The behavior was indiscreet in the extreme and unthinkable for a girl not yet out.

Elizabeth sought in vain for a glimpse of Georgiana's companion. Had the girl eluded her somehow? The couple's position in the garden would shield them from surrounding eyes; only someone in Elizabeth's position would notice them.

What was a girl of Georgiana's tender years about, embracing and kissing a man like that? Where was her companion? She was not yet out, so she could not be betrothed, and no one would embrace a relative in such a way. *I must do something or William's sister will soon be ruined!*

The easiest course of action would be to await William's return, but obtaining lemonade could take some time in a large crowd. It was why she had chosen that errand for him. By the time he returned, his sister's reputation could be damaged beyond repair.

And Elizabeth knew no one else at the ball, no one who might intervene.

Without a conscious decision, Elizabeth found herself hurrying across the veranda and down the steps to the garden. She sped along the garden paths, brushing against a couple of guests without apologies. How fortunate no one knew her identity. Finally, she reached the entrance of the small area she had observed before. She paused for a moment to collect herself and then turned the corner.

The couple remained in position, intimately drawn together. The man's hand was stroking Georgiana's hair while the other held her waist. She touched only the sleeve of his coat but gazed into his eyes with adoration. The man wore no mask, suggesting that he was also an uninvited guest.

"Georgiana! I have been looking all over creation for you!" Elizabeth spoke loudly in the hopes of attracting attention from other guests. She walked boldly toward the couple, ignoring the man and closing her hand around the girl's wrist. "I need your help desperately! Mama wants me to dance with this most dreadful man. He is fat and greasy, and he has the moistest hands in England. You can talk to her about it! She will listen to you."

She tugged a stunned Georgiana away from the man, who promptly released her and stepped back as if to pretend there had never been inappropriate contact.

"W-Who are you?" Georgiana stuttered.

"You don't know this chit?" the man demanded of Georgiana.

"We spoke at length at dinner last night. Pray, do not tell me you forgot already! I told you—" Elizabeth hoped a constant stream of chatter would drown out Georgiana's objections and the young man's questions.

A crease formed between Georgiana's brows. "I sat next to Lord Pippenworth last night."

Elizabeth shook her head impatiently. "Perhaps it was the night before. I cannot recall..."

"You need not go with her!" the man cried as he grabbed Georgiana's hand, pulling her in one direction while Elizabeth pulled in another.

"I do not know you!" Georgiana cried in dismay, trying to free her hand from Elizabeth's grasp.

Elizabeth talked over them, desperation making her bolder. "—and then when I was dancing with William, he spoke of—"

"William!" Georgiana and the young man said in unison. Georgiana seemed perplexed, but the man had blanched. No doubt he wished to avoid Georgiana's brother.

"Yes." Elizabeth pretended to be oblivious to their alarm. "He is an excellent dancer and cuts a fine figure..."

"Why, I thank you," said a voice behind her. She whirled to see William standing in the entrance, holding a small glass of lemonade. Had he always been so tall and imposing? Fortunately, his glare was not turned on Elizabeth but on the other man, whose face had drained of color.

"Wickham," William growled. "There can be no legitimate purpose for your presence here. You are no friend of the Berwicks. And the last time we spoke, I warned you to stay away from Georgiana!" He took a menacing step toward the brown-haired man, who cowered, pressing his back against the surrounding hedges.

"No, Brother!" Georgiana grabbed onto William's arm. "We are in love! He will take me to Gretna Green." Then her hand flew to her mouth as if to stifle words already spoken.

Elizabeth gaped. She knew nothing of Georgiana, but the girl was too young to make such a life-changing decision.

William trembled with the effort to keep his anger in check; a muscle in his jaw clenched rhythmically. But when he turned his attention to his sister, his expression was gentle. "No, dearest. He does not love you. He wishes to marry you for your dowry of thirty thousand."

Thirty thousand! Elizabeth barely stifled a gasp. William's family must be wealthy indeed.

William continued, taking his sister's hand gently in his. "He has many gambling debts and no means of supporting himself. Marrying you would solve many of his problems, but it would create many problems for you." By now there were tears gleaming in Georgiana's eyes.

"Gambling debts?" Georgiana turned to Mr. Wickham. "You said nothing to me of debts!"

"I knew you would form the wrong impression of me!" The man took a step toward the girl, but a glare from William arrested his progress. "The debts have nothing to do with us. I love you! I swear it."

"You told me you were enlisted in the army…" Her voice trembled, and her whole body shook. She looked wildly about, her eyes landing on Elizabeth as if hoping another woman might help her delve through the lies to find the truth. Elizabeth wrapped an arm around the girl's shoulders and handed her a handkerchief. "Now I do not know what to believe." Georgiana looked imploringly at Elizabeth.

How was I drawn into this drama? I do not know these people! But then Elizabeth realized she knew enough to form a judgment. She gave Georgiana a squeeze. "I believe that those we love—and who truly love us—are those we can trust. And they are the ones who will tell us the truth, even when it is painful."

Mr. Wickham scoffed. "This woman knows nothing about me or my life! Georgiana, I love you!"

Georgiana's gaze shot from Mr. Wickham to William and back. She cleared her throat. "William always tells me the exact truth, even when it is not what I want to hear. If he tells me you have debts and seek my dowry, I have no reason to disbelieve him."

Mr. Wickham scowled, but William nodded and opened his arms. His sister rushed into them, burying her face in his shoulder and sobbing in earnest.

Over Georgiana's head, William glared at Mr. Wickham. "I have forgiven you because of your ties to my family. But you have gone too far this time! If you come near Georgiana again, I will destroy you." The steel in his tone told Elizabeth he meant every word.

"You can try," Mr. Wickham sneered.

William released Georgiana and stalked toward the other man. Grabbing Mr. Wickham's arm, he pulled him toward the alcove's entrance. But the other man drew back his fist and punched William in the jaw. William fell to his knee, clutching his face. "This isn't over, Fitzwilliam Darcy!" Wickham shouted as he ran through the entrance. In seconds he was swallowed by the darkness of the gardens.

Elizabeth bent to help William to his feet, but he was already standing, brushing dirt from his clothing. He glared in the direction that Wickham had run, but his sister shook her head. "Let him go," she said wearily. "I am in no danger from him now, and I would rather everyone not know what a fool I was."

"Oh, dearest…" William enfolded his sister in an embrace.

Elizabeth smiled at the tender scene before her; William clearly cared for his sister very much. But something Wickham had said nudged at her consciousness. Something important.

26

Darcy. Wickham had called William "Fitzwilliam Darcy." And William lived in Derbyshire. Anxiety clenched her stomach. He must belong to the Darcy family of Pemberley. George Darcy's son and heir. Oh, Good Lord! Of all of the men she could have met that night, he was the worst possible choice. Elizabeth would have been better off dancing with Mr. Wickham.

I must leave at once. Before he discovers who I am. She had not even realized she nurtured a faint ember of hope for a future with William until it was extinguished. In its ashes remained fear and bitter regret.

Slowly, Elizabeth backed away from the brother and sister in tight embrace, shuffling her feet in the grass so they would make no sound. The Darcys were so focused on each other that they might not notice her departure. She must flee immediately, even if she must walk alone all the way to the Greens' estate.

One step. Two. Three. A couple more and she could safely turn and flee. Four. Five.

"Elizabeth!" William raised his head and stared directly at her. She froze like a terrified fawn.

He released his sister and strode toward her. "I cannot thank you enough!" His arms were raised as if he would embrace her as well, but Elizabeth backed further away, and he dropped them awkwardly. "If you had not seen her and gone to her. And if I had not followed you—" He shuddered but did not finish his thought. "You saved a girl who was a stranger to you and confronted a man who could easily have proved dangerous. I am in your debt."

No, no. She did not want Fitzwilliam Darcy in her debt. She did not want Fitzwilliam Darcy to ever think of her again! Swallowing, she managed to find her voice. "It is what any decent person would have done."

Mr. Darcy gave a mirthless laugh. "I am afraid you are wrong there. Very few would bother to intervene." Stepping closer to her, he shook his head in amazement.

"You are even more extraordinary than I originally realized." He brushed his fingertips over her cheek; she realized that her mask had come dislodged during the activity and now hung around her neck. "And so beautiful…" he murmured.

She fought the urge to hide her face. There was no reason to believe he would recognize her. "I only wished to help. That man seemed to be taking advantage of Georgiana…"

"But you thwarted his plans all by yourself," Darcy said firmly. "You are extraordinary. Not a conundrum but a guardian angel."

"Yes, thank you so much." Georgiana's voice was little more than a whisper. "You prevented me from making a terrible mistake."

"You are welcome." Elizabeth's mind worked furiously. *How can I extricate myself?* It was bad enough when she faced William's admiration, but now she had the attention of both Darcys.

William—Mr. Darcy—stepped toward her. "Now more than ever it is imperative that you tell me your name and allow me to speak with your father."

She shook her head. Now more than ever it was imperative that he never know!

They were interrupted when Louisa and Mr. Berwick pushed their way into the tiny alcove.

"Darcy, what happened?" Mr. Berwick cried. "Someone said they heard a commotion."

"I merely had a difference of opinion with an uninvited guest." Running his fingers through his disheveled hair, Mr. Darcy did an admirable job of keeping his voice level. He seemed remarkably calm for a man who had just thwarted his sister's elopement, but he must not allow any suspicion of impropriety to fall on his sister. "I am afraid Georgiana found the conflict distressing."

Mr. Berwick turned his eyes to Darcy's sister for the first time. "I thought...where is your companion?"

"Yes, where is Mrs. Younge?" Mr. Darcy asked.

Miss Darcy blushed under the force of such scrutiny. "S-She said someone wished to meet me. And when I turned around, she was gone."

"She has done this in the past." It was not a question.

"Yes." Georgiana nodded miserably. Elizabeth was horrified to realize this meant the companion had allowed previous meetings between Georgiana and Mr. Wickham.

Mr. Darcy said something under his breath that might have been an oath. This was the start of a long disquisition on the subject of Mrs. Younge, how she had been hired, and how she would be turned out without a character reference. Georgiana pleaded on behalf of her companion while Mr. Berwick agreed with Mr. Darcy's every word.

Elizabeth took the opportunity to pull on Louisa's hand. "We must leave now!" she whispered in her friend's ear.

"But—" Louisa objected.

Elizabeth would not be convinced to stay one more minute. "No!" She hissed. "We must go immediately."

Her friend looked a bit startled by her vehemence. "Very well." Louisa took another longing look at Mr. Berwick but allowed Elizabeth to pull her out of the alcove. Before she turned away, Elizabeth snuck one last glimpse of William, wishing things could be different. But she might as well wish she could fly. There were enough hurdles between them to build an obstacle course.

She paused for a moment, wishing—despite everything—that he would glance up. However, William was engrossed in impugning Mrs. Younge's character and had all his attention fixed on Georgiana. *It is for the best. This way I need not bid him goodbye.*

She would not have expected a Darcy to be so amiable, but perhaps he was only pleasant on the surface— particularly when encountering young ladies at soirees. Most people were amiable in such a setting. But he displayed anger toward Mr. Wickham, with good cause. Nevertheless, perhaps his true character was proud and disagreeable. What a shame she would never know the truth. But she had no choice; there was no question of staying. As she watched, his dark head bent over his sister's blonde head, and he gently massaged her back comfortingly. *William, if only...*

If only they were two completely different people, then they might have a future. Elizabeth told herself she was being silly over a man she had known for only two hours. Gritting her teeth, she turned from the sight and rushed to catch up with Louisa, who had already reached the edge of the garden. Once they were past the circle of torchlight, they ran.

By midnight, Elizabeth was back in her bed in the Greens' guest chamber, and the whole adventure seemed like a wonderful, strange dream.

Chapter Three

Darcy watched as Colonel Fitzwilliam took a careful sip of Darcy House's excellent French brandy. "Thank you for trusting me with the story about Wickham and Georgiana. Now I may imagine creative ways to wring his neck should I ever encounter him."

They sat in two large chairs facing the study's fireplace, now dark in the heat of the summer. "I am happy someone else will be on guard against Wickham and protect Georgiana."

Richard glanced sidelong at his cousin. "What said your father about the incident?"

Darcy grimaced. "I have not been to Pemberley since then, but I wrote him a long account. Among other things, I needed to explain why I fired the companion he had hired. He did not respond. He never wishes to believe any stories about Wickham."

"He was always too quick to forgive the scoundrel." Richard shook his head and took another sip of brandy.

Darcy fought to keep the bitterness from his voice. "My sole concern is that the story be sufficient to have the man banned from Pemberley. I do not want Georgiana to stay at Pemberley if he might visit."

Richard gave a low whistle. "I would not wish to be present when you have that conversation with your father."

Darcy shrugged, leaning forward so his forearms rested on his knees. He hated being at odds with his father, but sometimes it was necessary. "I am not willing to sacrifice Georgiana's well-being. If necessary we will simply live in London all year round. The staff here knows not to admit Wickham. And my father rarely comes to Town."

Richard's eyebrows raised. "That would be quite a sacrifice. I know how much you both love Pemberley."

"*Someone* must act responsibly," Darcy growled as he took another swig of his brandy. Their father seemed unwilling to take the necessary measures, but Darcy would sacrifice far more to ensure Georgiana's safety.

Richard regarded him rather closely, making Darcy feel unaccountably irritable. "Otherwise, how was your sojourn in Sussex? Did you encounter any likely ladies?"

Excellent. Another subject he had no desire to discuss. Darcy's mouth drew into a thin line. "It was a pleasant visit. But no luck. I still have more than two years before my father's deadline."

Richard snorted. "He would never force you to marry Anne."

Darcy raised an eyebrow and locked eyes with his cousin. "You know my father; he is capable of almost anything." Finally, Richard's gaze shifted to the floor. "He thinks I should be grateful he has given me three years to find a 'suitable replacement' for Anne."

"Have you considered if you are perhaps too selective? There are many beautiful, well-bred ladies here in London."

Darcy's fingers tightened around his glass. "I want something more than beautiful and well-bred." *Although I did not know what until I met Elizabeth.* Damnation! Darcy drained his glass.

Richard shifted in his chair. "Georgiana told me there was one lady…the night of the masquerade ball—"

This was too much! Darcy shot to his feet and hurled his crystal glass into the fireplace where it shattered spectacularly. Richard recoiled, his eyes wide with shock. "Why does she insist—? There is no one who—! I do not wish to discuss it. There is nothing to discuss."

Darcy paced relentlessly between the fireplace and the far wall, feeling a bit like a trapped animal. He was acting like a fool but could not find it in himself to care.

Richard eyed the broken shards of crystal in the fireplace. "Your reaction does not suggest 'nothing.' It most definitely sounds like something." His voice was level, reasonable, and Darcy hated him for it.

"You would have made an excellent doctor," Darcy growled. "You know exactly where to poke at the wound and make it hurt!" Richard did not react; he simply watched as Darcy paced.

Darcy ran both his hands through his hair, completely disheveling it. "Yes! Yes, there *was* a woman at the masquerade. I danced *once* with her. If she had not noticed Wickham with Georgiana and prevented their elopement, I would have been too late. She was very compassionate with Georgiana. My sister was much taken with her."

"So you owe her a debt. What happened to this woman?" Richard asked.

"She disappeared," Darcy mumbled. "After Wickham escaped and while I was comforting Georgiana. She simply left—left us, left the ball, everything."

Richard rubbed his chin. "A woman ran away from Fitzwilliam Darcy?"

Darcy shot his cousin a quelling look, disliking this levity at his expense. "It is not as if there are many women running *to* me."

"There would be if you wanted them."

Darcy had no desire to have this conversation once more. He fell wearily into his chair. "I asked her if I could court her."

"What?" Richard leaned forward so abruptly, some of his brandy spilled on the floor. "Why, that is wonderful!"

"She said no."

Darcy's cousin blinked and then frowned. "Are you certain you understood her correctly, Cuz? You are the kind of man all women dream of."

Rather than being flattered, Darcy bristled at this compliment. "Apparently not *all*. She took the first opportunity to escape my company."

"Perhaps she misunderstood your intentions. If you visit her house…"

"I cannot," Darcy replied. "I know neither her surname nor where she lives." He levered himself out of his chair and poured himself more brandy at the sideboard. This conversation required more alcohol.

"No surname?" Richard exclaimed.

"It was a *masquerade*," Darcy ground out. "I expected to learn her identity at midnight, but she was gone by then."

"Surely your host could tell you—"

Darcy was already shaking his head. "There were three Elizabeths invited, but none were young and unmarried—with a headful of dark curls."

"She was uninvited?"

"Apparently. I care nothing for that. But I wish I knew her name…"

"Perhaps she was from a neighboring estate."

"I considered that as well. I questioned the Berwicks at length. No doubt they thought me unhinged. But they have no neighbors named Elizabeth who fit that description."

"Perhaps she gave you a false name."

"It is possible." Darcy thought about how the name seemed to suit her. He threw himself back into his chair, unconcerned about how his clothes would crease. "Why did she run? I cared not that she was uninvited. But she is the first woman I ever—" He stopped before revealing too much. Richard might be his best friend, but Darcy did not discuss his feelings with anyone. He rubbed his face with his hands. "She did not know my name or that I am the heir of Pemberley, and yet she liked me. I swear she liked me!"

"Perhaps something else caused her to flee," Richard suggested.

Darcy stared moodily into his brandy glass. "Such as?"

"She might be a member of a notorious smuggling ring...or perhaps a French spy. Or maybe she ran off to join the gypsies." Richard grinned.

Darcy snorted. Under other circumstances he might have laughed.

Richard made an expansive gesture. "Now that you know what kind of woman you find attractive, you may look for—"

Darcy's teeth ground together. "There are no other women like her! Do you know how many women I have met in this quest for a wife? Hundreds! They all simper and agree with everything I say."

"And Elizabeth did not?"

Darcy paused to think how he would describe her. "No...she...teased me. Challenged me. I do not know why I find that appealing."

A smile quirked one side of Richard's mouth. "Perhaps because no other woman does so?"

"Perhaps." Darcy stood again, leaning an arm against the mantel. "She likes Wordsworth and dislikes Byron."

Richard's eyebrow arched. "You have rather specific requirements for a wife."

Darcy ignored this; it was good to tell someone about Elizabeth even though he would never see her again. "And she reads the papers—knew the latest happenings on the Peninsula. She has read every travel book in her father's library; I am sure she longs to travel."

"Was she pretty?"

"Lovely! The finest eyes I have ever beheld. Dark curls of hair. A light and pleasing figure. I saw her for only a moment without her mask, but I will never forget..." He rubbed a hand over his face. "I will never find another like her."

"Perhaps you will encounter her again. In our circles there are many Elizabeths—"

Darcy shook his head; he had given this matter a great deal of thought. "She is not a woman of the *ton*, I am certain. She had none of that languid affectation—and listed walking as one of her preferred occupations."

Richard laughed. "No woman of the *ton* would admit to that."

"Her gown was a rather simple affair. I guess her family is of more humble origins. The daughter of some local squire perhaps. But not a squire from Sussex." He could not keep the bitterness from creeping into his voice.

Richard frowned. "Your father is unlikely to approve of a marriage to such a woman."

"If I could have such a woman, I would make him accept her." Darcy contemplated his empty brandy glass and considered if he wanted more.

"It would not be so easy," Richard countered.

Darcy poured more brandy into his glass. *No, nothing with his father was easy.* "It hardly matters since I will never see her again." He was weary of discussing his mystery woman, but Richard seemed full of questions. Time for a new subject.

"My father has evicted more tenants from Pemberley."

Richard gaped. "Why?"

Darcy shrugged. "Various reasons. Mostly because he can. Some of the families had been at Pemberley for generations. But instead of working at Pemberley, they had to find new places—mostly on Matlock lands."

"And who called my father's attention to their plight?" Richard gave Darcy a knowing grin.

Darcy sighed. "I only wish I could do more. Since my mother's death, my father has grown steadily worse. She was able to restrain his most egregious behavior, but now he listens to no one."

"Has it affected the estate's production?"

Darcy gave a bitter laugh. "Not much, yet. But it will—when he cannot attract new tenants."

"Did he ever resolve that feud with your neighbor?"

"The Chesters? In a manner of speaking. He wanted them gone from the neighborhood so he had someone spread rumors about Chester's daughter and a local farmer—up in the hayloft, you know." Richard made a noise of disgust. "Once the daughter's reputation was in tatters, the family finally fled Derbyshire." The memory prompted another gulp of brandy. "I do not visit Pemberley often. There is always a new story like that."

"Good Lord, Darcy! He *is* growing worse." Darcy could only nod. There was a pause. When Richard spoke again, his voice was low. "Have you considered what your father might do if you bestowed your affections on a woman he deemed unsuitable?"

Darcy felt the muscles of his jaw clench. "Oh yes. Fortunately, there does not seem to be much danger of that."

"Perhaps you should just pick some biddable girl who is honored to have the Darcy name. You need an heir. It will solidify your position with your father." Richard was very careful not to look at Darcy as he said this. But Darcy was not surprised at the suggestion. Richard had given this advice before.

Darcy conjured up the image of those fine eyes, the laughing mouth, the shining dark curls. It was difficult to surrender that dream. But Richard was right; he would never find her. It was time to forget his fantasy and focus his efforts on finding a suitable Mrs. Darcy.

Chapter Four

"Just think, five thousand a year!" Elizabeth's mother exclaimed for at least the sixth time that day. "Jane, you must be sure to smile at him."

"Yes, Mama," Jane said serenely—again.

"And be certain to have him dance with you. Lizzy's friend Louisa swore that it only took one dance with her Robert and he fell in love! Now she is married into the Berwick family as happy as can be!"

"Yes, Mama," Jane said.

Elizabeth exchanged an understanding smile with her elder sister. All week the family had been in an uproar over the arrival of Mr. Bingley at Netherfield Park. Her father had called on the man, and he had returned the call, but the Bennet daughters had yet to meet him.

Now, however, they were on their way to the Meryton Assembly, where Mr. Bingley was certain to be in attendance. Elizabeth winced as the carriage went over a particularly big bump, and she was jostled against Jane.

"And he may have other wealthy gentlemen with him!" her mother exclaimed. "I heard he was to bring twelve ladies and six gentlemen to the assembly."

"I heard it was seven ladies and four gentlemen," Lydia put in.

Her mother waved her handkerchief irritably. "In any case, he is likely to have other wealthy friends."

"I will be sure to smile at them!" Lydia exclaimed.

"Good for you!" Their mother smiled.

"I can smile at gentlemen, too!" Kitty whined.

"There is no doubt of that." Their father rolled his eyes.

"I do not believe it is appropriate to smile at men to whom we have not been properly introduced," Mary added.

Elizabeth massaged her temples. It was possible she would have a headache before they even arrived at the assembly.

"Do you think there will be any men in regimentals?" Lydia asked. This began a discussion of how dashing men appeared in a red coat, and Mr. Bingley's party of guests was temporarily forgotten.

Lady Lucas greeted the Bennet party at the entrance to the assembly with the information that Mr. Bingley had brought two gentlemen and two ladies. The ladies were his sisters, and one of the gentlemen was married to one of the sisters. The other gentleman was a friend of Mr. Bingley's who was rumored to be worth ten thousand pounds a year, but Lady Lucas had not caught his name.

At this news, Elizabeth's mother was in an even greater frenzy of excitement. "Oh, Jane! You must be sure to dance with both of them! Is the other gentleman well favored? He must be in want of a wife as well. Elizabeth, be sure to stand near him. Perhaps he would dance with you too!"

Elizabeth simply nodded; she knew from experience that any type of protest was futile and would only prolong her mother's inappropriate behavior.

Within a few minutes Mr. Bingley had made his way to their party, and Mr. Bennet introduced the newcomer to his wife and daughters, whereupon Mr. Bingley immediately invited Jane to dance. Lydia and Kitty ran off to join some of the other neighborhood girls, and Mary departed for a discussion with the local vicar.

Elizabeth stood awkwardly with her mother. The assembly hall was quite crowded and warm. The others in Mr. Bingley's party were well concealed by the crush of people, for Elizabeth noticed no strangers. However, Mrs. Long waded through the crowd to be at Mrs. Bennet's side. Her eager expression suggested she had some interesting gossip to impart.

"Have you heard about Mr. Bingley's guests?" she asked Elizabeth's mother.

"Indeed, I have! Ten thousand a year!" Mrs. Bennet exclaimed.

"Well, the man may have a fortune, but the man is proud and disagreeable!" Mrs. Long said. "He has refused to dance with anyone save the ladies in his party and stares at everyone with haughty disdain. I told Henry, 'Well, if that is how Mr. Darcy feels about Meryton, then Meryton does not—'"

Elizabeth and her mother gasped in unison, but Mrs. Bennet recovered first. "W-What is his name, Marianne?"

"Mr. Darcy. I believe his given name is Fitzwilliam. I am sure it must be a family name because who would choose to bestow such a name—"

Mrs. Bennet had turned white, and Elizabeth was sure her complexion looked no better. "Where does he reside?" Mrs. Bennet asked her friend.

"I believe his family is from an estate in Derbyshire."

Elizabeth's world went white for a moment at these words, so implausible and unwelcome, and she thought she might faint. *He* was here. There was no doubt it was *him*. In the two years since the masquerade ball, he had constantly invaded her thoughts. She could not help comparing every man she encountered to "William." But she had believed herself safe from another encounter.

Would he recognize her? Remember her? Was he angry at how she had fled the ball? Of course, he would know by now that she had not been invited. Did he think her terribly wanton? Perhaps he had forgotten her; that would be for the best.

Elizabeth attempted to quell her growing panic. *It hardly matters what Mr. Darcy thinks of me*, she reasoned. *Once he learns I am part of Thomas Bennet's family, he will be disgusted.* But the thought of seeing that look of disgust on his face ignited more panic. *I must leave before he sees me!*

Mrs. Bennet's face was gray with two spots of color on her cheeks. Elizabeth feared for a moment that they would need her mother's vinaigrette. But she quickly recovered enough to call shrilly for her husband. "Mr. Bennet! Mr. Bennet!"

As heads turned in their direction, Elizabeth whispered, "Mama, please!" But her mother gave no indication that she had heard. She plowed through the crowds with Elizabeth in her wake, snatching Mary by the collar on her way and dragging her along. They arrived in a corner of the room where her father was conversing with Sir William Lucas and Mr. Rufus Connell.

Mrs. Bennet was breathless and red-faced. "Mr. Bennet! The most terrible thing has happened!"

Her husband raised a skeptical eyebrow. "Has the cost of lace increased again? Or has Lydia lost a ribbon from her dress?"

At least Elizabeth's mother had the presence of mind to pull her husband to the side before she whispered to him. "It is far worse. Mr. Fitzwilliam Darcy is here! He is Mr. Bingley's friend."

The color drained quickly from her father's face. "Mr. Darcy from Derbyshire?" His wife nodded vigorously.

"We cannot escape the introduction!" Mrs. Bennet exclaimed.

"We should leave at once," Elizabeth suggested, her eyes darting around the room, alert for any sign of Mr. Darcy. If she departed immediately, perhaps she could avoid him for the rest of his time in Hertfordshire.

Mr. Bennet humphed. "No. I will not be rousted from a gathering in my own town by that man's son. We will simply avoid him."

Inwardly, Elizabeth quailed at these words. It was all very well for her father to make a stand, but encountering Mr. Darcy would cause more than unpleasantness for her. At a gathering of this size, she could not avoid him all night. "Papa, I have a headache. Might I return home—?"

"Oh, oh! I should warn Lydia and Kitty!" her mother interrupted. "They must stay away from that horrid man." She turned to Mary. "Fetch them immediately!" Then her horrified eyes met her husband's. "Jane is dancing with his friend! What should we do?"

Mr. Bennet rubbed a hand over his mouth. "Mr. Bingley is unlikely to mistreat Jane at a public assembly— even if he is a friend of a Darcy."

"Everything was going so well with Mr. Bingley!" her mother wailed.

Mary returned with a sulky Lydia and Kitty in tow. Mrs. Bennet whispered the dire news to them. They squealed in horror although their reaction seemed more excited than distressed.

Realizing the set had concluded, Elizabeth went in search of Jane. Her sister was red-cheeked and glowing with excitement. "Mr. Bingley is the most amiable man of my acquaintance, Lizzy! He is everything a gentleman should be." Oh, how Elizabeth wished she did not need to deliver such dreadful news!

"About Mr. Bingley—" Elizabeth caught her sister's arm and guided her toward their parents. Jane's attention was caught by something, and she glanced back over her shoulder. "Mr. Bingley is bringing his friend to meet us!" she exclaimed. "That is very good of him."

Elizabeth could barely hear for the pounding of blood in her ears. Escape was the only option. "I must leave—" She released Jane's arm, looking wildly about. Why were all the doors so far away?

But her well-meaning sister took her hand. "Lizzy, you are very pale. Are you ill—?" Elizabeth pulled her hand from Jane's grasp, but it was too late.

The sound of Mr. Bingley's voice behind her made Elizabeth shudder. "There they are! May I present Miss Jane Bennet and Miss Elizabeth Bennet?"

Too late. She was trapped.

Jane gazed beatifically at Mr. Bingley while Elizabeth turned around slowly. And found herself staring straight into the face of Mr. Darcy.

***

Darcy had not wanted to attend the Meryton Assembly. Upon his arrival at Netherfield the previous day, Bingley had talked incessantly about the neighborhood's charming families and the excitement of making their acquaintance—while Caroline Bingley rolled her eyes disdainfully. Darcy had simply stopped listening. Bingley could rhapsodize on a subject for hours. Sometimes Darcy found it charming, but yesterday it had been irritating.

However, saying no to Bingley sometimes felt like kicking a puppy, and this proved to be one of those times. Darcy could not possibly miss the assembly; he was certain to find Bingley's new neighbors as charming as he did. Darcy had finally conceded defeat despite knowing that it would be a dull, tedious occasion. Bingley had reacted with glee. "You will see, Darcy. It will do you good. You have been too sober and gloomy recently."

Darcy could not deny his dark mood although he doubted an assembly would help. His father's increasingly difficult behavior and his own failures to find a suitable wife were ever heavier burdens. He sometimes caught himself being short with Georgiana, and more than once he had needed to apologize for his temper to a servant.

However, recognition of his behavior did not seem to curb it. He had hoped a visit to Hertfordshire would help him set aside his worries, but a country dance surrounded by strangers would only increase his agitation.

Bingley had led Darcy all over the assembly, introducing him to the "charming" country neighbors, all of whom were uniformly dull. Perhaps the whole visit to Netherfield was a mistake; he could not weather weeks of such tedium. Although he did receive a brief respite from Bingley's enthusiasm when his friend danced with the pretty daughter of a local landowner.

When the set concluded, Bingley bounded over to Darcy once more. "Jane Bennet is an angel! Let me introduce you to her family. I met them earlier, and they are all quite charming."

Darcy simply nodded, wearily surrendering to Bingley's good mood. He followed Bingley across the room to where his "angel" was conversing with a dark-haired sister. "May I introduce Miss Jane Bennet and Miss Elizabeth Bennet?"

Jane Bennet smiled warmly at Darcy as she curtsied. "How do you do?" Her sister had her back to them and her head down longer than was strictly polite, but slowly she turned to face them.

At first Darcy could not believe what he saw. Had he finally fallen into madness? Or perhaps this entire evening had been a long, involved dream. Perhaps he was mistaken, as he had been so many times when glimpsing dark curls and blue eyes. He blinked. No, every detail fit his memory precisely, and her name was *Elizabeth*. It was *her*.

Chapter Five

"Elizabeth." Darcy breathed out. His eyes feasted on the sight he had desired for so long—her vibrant blue gaze, full lips, and glossy dark curls.

"You have met before?" Bingley asked.

Her eyes were wide and stricken, and she seemed poised for flight, like a rabbit facing a predator. "No!" Elizabeth said emphatically. "I do not believe we have met before. Perhaps I resemble someone else you know?"

Someone else who happens to be named Elizabeth?

But that rational objection was swallowed by the plummeting sense of dread in his stomach. He had no doubt she recognized him and was equally sure she was unhappy to see him. All of Darcy's visions of a happy reunion shattered in an instant. Why was she denying their previous acquaintance? Had she not enjoyed their evening together? All this time had she dreaded the thought of seeing him again?

But it did not matter. He would give her what she wanted, no matter the reason.

He ran a shaky hand over his face. "No. I was mistaken. My deepest apologies." He took her gloved hand and kissed the back, painfully reminded of the last time he had done so. He murmured, "I pray you, forgive my error."

Bingley gaped; belatedly, Darcy realized such gallantry was out of character after he had ignored the better part of the Meryton Assembly. Miss Bennet appeared bemused while Elizabeth …Elizabeth's face could have been carved from stone. Was she horrified at his presumption? Disgusted by his touch?

Perhaps he should leave. Darcy stumbled back a step. Bingley's eyes darted from Darcy to Elizabeth and back. He cleared his throat. "Er…perhaps I should introduce you to the rest of the Bennet family."

Darcy nodded, tearing his gaze from Elizabeth and allowing Bingley to guide him. The family they approached was conducting an animated discussion, which ceased the moment they appeared.

They were unexceptional. A plain man in his late fifties and his frowsy wife. Two girls who were pretty, albeit giggly, but much too young to be out at such an event and an older, sour-faced daughter.

Bingley gestured expansively. "May I introduce Mr. and Mrs. Thomas Bennet? And their daughters Miss Lydia Bennet, Miss Mary Bennet, and Miss Catherine Bennet. This is Mr. Fitzwilliam Darcy."

Darcy had provoked many reactions when introduced to strangers, but never had he provoked such expressions from complete strangers. The two younger girls regarded him with fright as if he were about to demand their purses at knifepoint while the third appeared to smell something rotten. Mrs. Bennet drew herself up to her full height as if she was about to deliver a tirade. Mr. Bennet's face was red with…rage? But it made no sense. Darcy had never met the man; how could he be enraged? It seemed to be his fate to elicit strange reactions from the entire Bennet family; only the eldest daughter had regarded him with common and indifferent courtesy.

No. I must be misinterpreting their behavior because of my encounter with Elizabeth. He made a brief bow, which the girls returned with curtsies. Then he extended a hand to Mr. Bennet, who regarded it as if Darcy were offering a poisonous snake. After a moment, Darcy let his hand drop. Bingley was wringing his hands by now.

"Pleased to make your acquaintance," he said to Mr. Bennet.

"The pleasure is all yours," Mr. Bennet responded coldly.

Why was he receiving such a frigid reception from complete strangers? Hastily, he searched his memory for an encounter with the Bennet family. Finally, he made the connection. Bennet. Hertfordshire. His stomach twisted with anxiety.

"Are you Thomas Bennet of Longbourn?" he asked.

"I am." Mr. Bennet bit off the two words.

"I see." Darcy's mouth went dry. Elizabeth's behavior suddenly made more sense. *She must have known since the night of the ball.* This was not the first time he had encountered someone wronged by his father. "I know that in the past you and my father had a... disagreement." Mr. Bennet snorted. "But I do not consider it to involve me. I am not my father."

Mr. Bennet's glare could have frozen water. "That remains to be seen."

This was damned uncomfortable. Why could he not have broken his leg before this farce of a social engagement? It would have been less painful.

Yet, this man was Elizabeth's father. Darcy wanted to find some common ground. "I only wish the best for you and your family."

Mr. Bennet stepped closer to Darcy, exuding quite a bit of menace for a man who was almost a head shorter. "You will stay away from my family."

Darcy bristled. Who was this man to give him orders? He met Mr. Bennet's gaze. "I will associate with whomever I want, wherever I want."

Mr. Bennet seemed to be gathering himself for a thunderous response but was interrupted by Bingley. He placed his hand on Darcy's arm. "I believe Hurst wishes to speak with you."

Darcy allowed himself to be led away but could feel Mr. Bennet's glare following him. They arrived at a corner near the door where the Hursts and Miss Bingley had sequestered themselves from the rest of the "rabble."

Mr. Hurst was more awake than usual and not eating for once. No doubt he was husbanding his resources for a renewed attack on the refreshments. "I say, Darcy, is that Thomas Bennet of Longbourn? The one your father quarreled with all those years ago?" Darcy nodded in the affirmative. Although labeling it a "quarrel" was akin to saying the French Revolution was a "bit of trouble." Darcy did not know the reason for their disagreement, only that his father hated Mr. Bennet.

Hurst was longstanding friend of George Darcy's, one of many reasons Darcy did not care for the man. Of course, he knew who Thomas Bennet was. Darcy's father was liable to complain about the man when he was in his cups.

"I knew there was something wrong about that family!" Miss Bingley cried triumphantly. "How dare they show their faces here?"

"Hertfordshire is their home," Bingley pointed out.

Miss Bingley merely sniffed. "They are particularly ill-bred."

Bingley frowned at his sister. "Well, I think they are perfectly pleasant." Those were not the words Darcy would have used to describe his encounter with the Bennets, but Bingley did seem to be partial to the eldest daughter.

"They are not the type of people with whom we should associate," his sister warned. No doubt she was readying herself to argue against Bingley's interest in the eldest Bennet daughter.

Bingley looked imploringly at Darcy. Damnation! Sometimes he wished his friend would fight his own battles. "I do not see any harm in Jane Bennet. She seems a sweet girl," Darcy conceded cautiously.

Bingley grinned, but Hurst and Miss Bingley both scowled. Belatedly, Darcy realized he had endorsed a member of the Bennet family. Such disloyalty might be reported in Hurst's next letter to George Darcy; the man had informed on Darcy before. Blast! If he did anything to reveal his partiality for Elizabeth… The thought made him shudder.

"However, the rest of the family is insufferable," Darcy added and was relieved to see Hurst smile.

"I believe we have stayed a sufficient amount of time," Miss Bingley declared.

Bingley frowned. "I would be pleased to dance some more. And Miss Bennet has promised me the next set. Come, Darcy." Darcy followed his friend, eager to support any demonstration of backbone. But once Bingley started stealing covert glances at Miss Jane Bennet, Darcy experienced misgivings.

"Mr. Bennet may not care for your attentions to his daughter," Darcy murmured in Bingley's ear.

Bingley set his jaw. "He did not tell *me* to stay away from his family. I like Miss Bennet and will stand up with her again." Darcy had never seen his friend quite so insistent about a lady; what an inconvenient time for him to be so determined.

"You should stand up with someone as well," Bingley told his friend. "There are many uncommonly pretty girls here."

From the corner of his eye, Darcy glimpsed the Hursts and Miss Bingley approaching. Did they intend to eavesdrop? He must avoid even the slightest hint of partiality toward Elizabeth. Anything he said would be repeated to his father.

"You are dancing with the only pretty woman in the room." Darcy hoped he could be forgiven for uttering such sacrilege

"There is her sister, Elizabeth. She is very pretty, too. It is a shame she seems to dislike you," Bingley responded.

Darcy restrained an urge to groan as Bingley unknowingly pressed on a tender spot. If only he *could* ask Elizabeth to dance with him! Instead he was trapped into pretending his dislike. Darcy rolled his eyes at Bingley. "She is tolerable, I suppose, but not handsome enough to tempt me."

"I would not be as fastidious as you for all the world, Darcy!" Bingley laughed.

He hoped the Good Lord could forgive him for the rank blasphemy that had fallen from his lips, but he must protect Elizabeth at all costs. Thank goodness she could not hear him.

Had Hurst and Miss Bingley heard the exchange? Darcy turned his head slightly to see them but realized to his horror that Elizabeth stood immediately behind him. *I thought her safely on the other side of the room!* Had she heard? He allowed his eyes to briefly skim over her features. Her face was blank, lacking its usual animation. Was that because she had overheard his awful words, or was she merely unhappy at his presence? Damnation! Mere minutes after rediscovering the woman who inhabited all of his dreams, he contrived to insult her.

Before he could say anything, she hurried across the room toward a plain woman in a blue dress. If only he could get her alone and explain! But he noticed Mr. Bennet watching him from across the room while Caroline Bingley and Hurst observed him from a closer distance. Any attempt to approach Elizabeth would merely add fuel to everyone's suspicions. Darcy sighed.

He must give up any thoughts of speaking to Elizabeth; there were too many dangers. Somehow the prospect of his sojourn in Hertfordshire had become even bleaker.

***

The rest of the evening passed in a haze for Elizabeth. Initially she had regretted the lack of male partners, but now she was glad for it. She had not the disposition for dancing that evening.

Seeing Mr. Darcy again had been horribly awkward; the memory of the encounter still made her cheeks warm. At first he seemed pleased to see her, but when she had denied their previous acquaintance, he had grown so cold. She could hardly blame him; nevertheless, it saddened her. And then her father had treated the poor man like a common thief, mortifying her further.

Still, she never expected him to say such insulting things about her—particularly at a public gathering. *It is my fault. I injured his pride by pretending not to know him, and now he hates me.* Or perhaps his negative opinion of her had been formed two years ago when he discovered she was not invited to the ball. Tears pricked her eyes. She treasured the memory of the masquerade, taking it out for comfort whenever she was sad or lonely. But now Mr. Darcy's words had tarnished the memory.

Honestly, I should be relieved. The situation between their families was so difficult that even friendship would not be possible. And there was no question of indulging even a shred of any deeper feelings she might harbor. *Why must he be a Darcy?* Elizabeth had never met another man who suited her so well, no other man who tempted her half as much as Mr. Darcy. But he no longer found her tempting—if he ever did.

Driven by the need to escape Mr. Darcy's vicinity, Elizabeth had sought out Charlotte Lucas, and she had not resisted the temptation to repeat the man's words to her friend. Charlotte had listened sympathetically and without complaint as Elizabeth vilified Mr. Darcy's character.

But Elizabeth still found herself wondering how she would survive to the end of the evening. Even a quick glimpse of Mr. Darcy caused nausea to roil her stomach. Naturally, the moment she resolved to avoid him, he suddenly seemed to be everywhere: dancing with Miss

Bingley, talking with Sir William, and laughing with Mr. Bingley. He was clearly enjoying himself.

Mr. Darcy did not stand up with any ladies from Meryton; Elizabeth was not sure whether to be appalled at his pride or relieved that he showed no partiality to another woman. Once or twice she thought she sensed his eyes on her, but when she looked, his head was always turned away.

Most balls finished too quickly, but this one dragged on interminably. When her father announced it was time to depart, she nearly wept with relief. Elizabeth had never before been so happy to leave behind the bright lights of a soiree. With a headache pounding in her forehead, she could not wait to crawl into bed. As their carriage pulled away from the assembly, her heart did lighten a little at the thought that she need never see Mr. Fitzwilliam Darcy again.

Chapter Six

This is a bad idea, Darcy thought for at least the hundredth time. He had departed the assembly with every intention of distancing himself from Elizabeth and the Bennet family. It was the right course of action. It was the prudent course of action. It would be best for Darcy and his family. Best for Elizabeth and her family. Really, there was no earthly reason why he would ever want to be within fifty feet of Elizabeth Bennet. Even to be seen talking with her could rain down all kinds of trouble on both of their heads.

But that night he had lain awake, staring at the moon outside his window and tormented by speculations of what Elizabeth must think about him. She had avoided him for the remainder of the torturous ball. Was she simply obeying her father's edict or had she heard Darcy's cutting remark about her? Was she lying awake cursing his name?

At about three o'clock, he realized he would never rest easy until he had spoken with Elizabeth one last time. He resolved to do so at the first light of day. This decision had permitted him to drift into a brief, uneasy slumber. He had crept out of Netherfield before dawn for a walk to Longbourn.

Now he lurked behind a large bush nestled next to the trunk of an ancient oak and watched Longbourn's back entrance. Already he had hidden from a kitchen maid venturing forth to draw water from the well.

Elizabeth had mentioned her fondness for early morning walks; this would be his best chance of catching her for a private conversation. Already an hour had passed. Doubts continued to plague him. What if she no longer took morning walks? Or she was feeling unwell today? Or she left by the front entrance?

The longer he stood there, the greater the risk of discovery as more and more people made use of the back door. He would have no plausible way to explain his presence, and to be seen lurking outside the Bennets' house would add to Mr. Bennet's suspicions. Yet he could not bring himself to depart.

Dew soaked his boots, and damp cold penetrated his coat. A thump from the direction of the house caused Darcy to huddle further down behind the bush, but it was a false alarm; no one was exiting Longbourn. Curse it, he was as skittish as a cat in a roomful of dogs.

The door opened, and Darcy ducked down again, daring to peek through a gap between two branches. This time the figure that stepped into the sunshine was Elizabeth. His breath caught. In the golden morning light she was particularly lovely. A light breeze ruffled her dark curls, and the cool air turned her skin pink.

At the mere sight of her, something inside Darcy's chest melted and loosened. How could this be their last conversation? It would be too painful. But Darcy's attention was drawn to Elizabeth's face—solemn, dark rings under her eyes. Had he caused her to have a sleepless night? His heart ached at the thought. If only he could enfold her in his arms until that bleak look disappeared.

After ascertaining that she was in fact taking the westward road, Darcy followed behind her, concealed by a series of bushes until he could cut across a field unnoticed and intercept her. He felt vaguely ridiculous; the heir of Pemberley should not be sneaking around country fields like a smuggler or highwayman. But he would endure far more for Elizabeth's sake.

Emerging from a hedgerow, Darcy found himself slightly behind Elizabeth, who was striding down the road with a steady and purposeful gait. He longed to call out to her, to call her "Elizabeth" as she had been so often in his dreams. But doing so would surely offend her further.

"Miss Bennet!" he cried.

She stopped abruptly and whirled around, holding her bonnet in the slight breeze. Her face was a mask of cold civility. "Mr. Darcy." The words barely emerged past gritted teeth.

He gave her a brief bow. "I wanted to explain my behavior last night."

"*Explain?*" Her tone lost some of its hostility.

He took a few steps toward her and counted it as a minor victory that she did not retreat. "I did not know your surname until last night. I did not realize our fathers were at odds. But you did when you learned my full name the night of the masquerade."

It was not quite a question, but Elizabeth nodded anyway. Something inside Darcy loosened. At least now he knew why she had run so precipitously. It was not anything he had done or said; unfortunately, it was also not something he could easily fix.

"I was most shocked by the revelation of your family name. I had despaired of ever finding you again, so I was elated…"

Her brows drew together. "Elated?"

Darcy continued. "But then learning of your family circumstances—"

"So this is the excuse for your uncivil behavior?" Elizabeth's voice was level, but her eyes glittered dangerously.

"No, no." Never had he longed for the greater facility of language enjoyed by the likes of Wickham or Richard. Taking a deep breath, he started again. "You do not know my father. He is a ruthless man who is accustomed to imposing his decisions on others—no matter who he hurts. He cannot know what passed between us at the masquerade ball!"

Elizabeth's eyes narrowed. "Nothing passed between us at the ball. We danced."

Darcy ran his hands through his hair. On the face of it, her assertion was correct, but there was so much more beneath the surface. He sighed. There was nothing for it; he must reveal all. He fixed his eyes on the dirt of the road. "After the masquerade at Tilbury, I spent weeks attempting to ascertain your identity. My father may have heard about it; I believe he has spies among my staff."

He glanced up to see her reaction. Her lips were parted and her eyes wide. "You tried to find me?" Her hand flew to her mouth. "I-I never—I am so sorry."

Darcy shook his head. "I understand now why you left so abruptly." He stopped himself before he reached for her hand. "The important thing now is to prevent my father from connecting that Elizabeth to Elizabeth Bennet."

She took a step toward him. "If he did, he would hurt you?"

"Not me. I am his heir. But he might hurt you. He hates your father with an unholy passion. If he suspected that I harbored any partiality to one of your father's daughters, he would take any measures to separate us."

Elizabeth swallowed visibly.

"I pray you, believe me!" he pleaded.

"I-I—" She blinked. "Yes, yes, of course, I believe you. You would never make up such a story about your own father."

Some of the tension in Darcy's shoulders eased. "For this reason I believe it is best if we conceal our previous meeting."

"But you remarked that I was not handsome enough to tempt—"

The misery in her voice squeezed Darcy's chest. He closed the distance between them until they were almost touching. "Another misdirection on my part. There are those in my party—not Bingley, of course—who would happily report any of my missteps to my father. He will soon learn that I have encountered Thomas Bennet. Most likely he will write to demand that I quit Meryton immediately."

Elizabeth's brilliantly blue eyes were fixed on his face, drawing him in as easily as the night they had danced. *Good Lord, I want to kiss her!* Unbidden, a part of his mind was even now imagining how she would taste and smell. How her lips would feel under his, her waist under his hands. The sounds she might utter as they kissed. And the passion in her eyes when her lips were red and swollen with his kisses.

Control yourself, Darcy! He swallowed and forced himself to hold her eyes. "It is a bald-faced lie that I do not find you handsome enough to tempt me. I find you unbelievably beautiful and all too tempting." Her eyes widened, and she drew back slightly. Did she disbelieve him?

"And after our conversation at the assembly, I thought you had forgotten me…you were indifferent to me," he murmured.

Their gazes locked; he could not have torn his eyes from hers if the woods were on fire. "I am not indifferent to you." Her voice was low and firm, revealing more than she intended, no doubt. It was wonderful and all wrong at the same time.

There was no containing his desire now. His hands ached with the need to touch her; this might be his only opportunity. He reached up and ran his fingers down the side of her face.

Elizabeth closed her eyes and tilted her head toward his hand as if savoring his touch. Growing bolder, Darcy gently palmed her cheek. But she took a step backward, out of his reach. "W-We cannot…"

Darcy's hands clenched into fists. He was well aware he should not touch Thomas Bennet's daughter. This was a fool's errand. But he could not stand this close to her without touching her; every inch of his body cried out for contact with hers.

"We can never be anything to each other. We must pretend we never met and act as common and indifferent strangers," Elizabeth declared, her eyes downcast.

Darcy fell silent. There was no possible retort; she was entirely correct. He focused on a tree behind her as he spoke. "We may be in company again. Bingley and your sister—"

"Jane has been instructed not to speak with you any more than is strictly necessary. My father wanted her to discontinue her association with Mr. Bingley, but my mother convinced him otherwise." There was a small blessing! Life would be unfair indeed if George Darcy's feud interfered with Bingley's happiness.

"Were you instructed not to speak with me?" Concern creased his forehead. Would her father punish her if he found she had disobeyed?

To his surprise she laughed. "Yes, but my father would not be astonished to find I disregarded his instructions. It would not be the first time."

How could she be so cavalier about it? He grabbed her hand. "Your father will not beat you for disobedience?"

"No!" Her expression was horrified. "Would your father—?"

Darcy gave a short, bitter laugh. "Not anymore. I am too big."

Now her hand caressed his cheek. "Oh, William…how horrible. I am so sorry." Ordinarily he would disdain any sympathy, but somehow coming from Elizabeth, it made him feel warm and peaceful. How long had it been since someone cared about him that way? Touched his face in concern? Not since his mother's death.

But he could not indulge this feeling forever. Darcy sighed. "It is for the best if we do not speak. In fact, it is the safest course if our families believe we dislike each other—they will have little cause then to suspect any attraction." He removed her hand from his cheek and clasped it between his.

Elizabeth bit her lip. "I do not wish to speak ill of you to my family and neighbors!"

Her distressed expression made him smile. "I am not demanding that you vilify me, but perhaps you may complain that I am proud and difficult. I have been accused of it before." Elizabeth arched an eyebrow at this, and Darcy was forced to laugh. "I daresay whatever you told your friend in the blue dress last night was probably a good start."

"Oh!" Elizabeth's hand flew to her mouth, and her cheeks reddened.

He chuckled. "I believe you may have betrayed yourself."

"I do not know what you mean, Mr. Darcy," she replied primly. "Charlotte and I only spoke of lace and ruffles."

He laughed heartily this time and pulled her close to him. "You do delight me!"

Their faces were inches from each other. Elizabeth's breath caught.

He must do it. She was too close. Too tempting. And Darcy had passed far too many long carriage rides imagining how it would be to kiss "his Elizabeth" should he ever find her. He bent his head and brushed his lips over hers, feeling her shiver at the contact. When she did not pull back, he pressed their lips together again, this time demanding a response from her, imbuing the kiss with passion pent up through years of restraint. Her lips parted, and his tongue swept in, exploring every part of her mouth in a sensual delight. She tasted of tea and chocolate. A moan escaped him. The reality of kissing Elizabeth far surpassed his most vivid imaginings.

Her scent filled his nose as he pulled her body closer to his. No matter how tightly he held her, it was never enough. He wanted her body pressed up against every inch of his. Then Elizabeth moaned, a primal sound that further enflamed his passion. His tongue probed deeper into her mouth as his hands explored her neck, her waist. He wanted more, damn it! He wanted everything she had to offer.

Finally, a lack of air forced him to release her lips, but his hands remained on her body. Pressed against her, he touched their foreheads together while their heartbeats returned to normal.

"I must see you again!" he gasped. "This cannot be the last time."

He felt rather than saw her shake her head. "No, Will—Mr. Darcy. You were correct before. We must pretend antipathy. There is no other way."

"But—"

She pulled away, out of his arms, and looked up into his face. "I pray you, for my sake? This must be the last—the only—time we indulge this…attraction between us."

Eventually, Darcy gave a slow, reluctant nod. His body suddenly felt heavy and awkward as if someone had attached iron weights to each of his limbs. "Very well. It is for the best."

Elizabeth took another step away from him, but impulsively, he seized her hand. "Please know, however, no matter what I do or say, I remain your…friend. Always."

Elizabeth's eyes shimmered suspiciously. "And I yours. Always."

She turned and walked back the way she had come, back to Longbourn. Darcy stood and watched her figure dwindle until she rounded the bend in the road and was lost to his sight.

Chapter Seven

He should have left Hertfordshire. Darcy had considered it several times since speaking with Elizabeth near Longbourn; he could have invented urgent business in London. Even now he was uncertain why he remained in this accursed place. But Elizabeth was here, and he had passed so many months not knowing where—or who—she was that he could not bear the thought of leaving her so soon after discovering her.

Nevertheless, it was an indisputable fact that he should have left Hertfordshire. He certainly never should have attended this insipid party at Sir William Lucas's house. Now he was standing next to Sir William and pretending attention to the man's inane prattle—all the while attempting, and failing, not to stare at Elizabeth, who graced the other side of the room where she spoke with Charlotte Lucas.

Just as Elizabeth began to drift in their direction, her sister at the pianoforte struck up a lively Scottish tune, and three couples lined up to dance. Darcy ground his teeth together. There was scarcely space in the crowded room for dancing, and the gathering was supposed to be a quiet evening of conversation and cards. Why did people insist on dancing everywhere?

Unfortunately, Sir William was charmed by this development. "Dancing is such a splendid occupation for young people. One of the hallmarks of polished society."

Darcy barely refrained from rolling his eyes. Not only must he watch others enjoy themselves when he could not, but he also must make conversation about it with this ridiculous man. "Hardly that. Any savage can dance." He knew he was scowling but did not care.

Sir William's brows drew together, and he regarded Darcy more closely, as if perplexed that anyone could hold a different view on the subject. Then Elizabeth wandered into the man's view, distracting his attention. "Mr. Darcy, you must allow me to present this young lady to you as a very desirable partner. You cannot refuse to dance, I am sure, when so much beauty is before you." Sir William took Elizabeth's hand and would present it to Darcy.

Elizabeth's lips were set in a tight line and her eyes averted. "I pray you not to suppose that I moved this way in order to beg for a partner."

All prudence fled when faced with the prospect of dancing with Elizabeth. Darcy could stare into her fine eyes, hold her hand, laugh at her witticisms, and pretend for a moment that she could be his. "Miss Elizabeth, I request to be allowed the honor of your hand for the next dance."

Her gaze was sharp and disdainful. "I thank you, sir. But I have not the least intention of dancing."

Her refusal shattered his pleasant fantasy. *She is only playing the role*, he told himself. There was no reason to feel as though she had struck him. *Is this how she felt when she overheard my comment at the assembly?* The gnawing ache in his chest persisted no matter how he reassured himself.

Across the room, Darcy felt eyes upon them. He turned his head to see Mr. Bennet observing their exchange with a solemn expression. Then he saw Hurst nearby, within earshot. Blast! He hated that their every conversation was noted by other, unrelated parties. But he must play to their audience.

"It is just as well." He shrugged and allowed a mask of indifference to settle over his face. "As I remarked to Sir William, any savage can dance."

Elizabeth stilled completely, and her face paled as she perceived the insult. Sir William's gaze switched from one to another, increasingly agitated. "I say—!" he began, indignant on Elizabeth's behalf. But Darcy had no intention of receiving a rebuke for words he loathed uttering. Fixing his eyes on Elizabeth, he bowed curtly and left in search of refreshment.

The ache clawed inside his chest as he walked away, but he kept his face impassive. The words had flown from his mouth with little forethought. Once they had been uttered, however, he could not mitigate the damage since the insult served to conceal his inexorable attraction to Elizabeth. No doubt Sir William would be spreading the story within minutes—and with it the conviction that Mr. Darcy did not care for Miss Elizabeth. Darcy recalled the hurt expression on Elizabeth's face but reminded himself it was for the best.

This reminder did nothing to ease the ache in his chest.

How much longer need they remain? He glanced around at the assembled revelers and thus missed Bingley's sister standing in his path. "I can guess the subject of your reverie," she said, regarding him with a sardonic expression.

Elizabeth's pale, anguished face sprang to mind. "I should imagine not."

"You are considering how insupportable it would be to pass many evenings in such society." Miss Bingley leaned toward him as if they were sharing a secret.

Darcy could not prevent himself from bristling. "I was meditating on the pleasure of a pair of fine eyes in a pretty face." His tone was forbidding, but Miss Bingley entirely mistook his meaning.

She preened. "What lady has inspired such reflections?"

No. It was impossible that he would allow her to believe *she* was the object of his admiration. But he could find no plausible misdirection. "Miss Elizabeth Bennet."

Miss Bingley started. "I am all astonishment."

Damnation! Now he had drawn her attention to Elizabeth. Clearly, proximity to her was detrimental to his clarity of thought. If Miss Bingley should mention Darcy's comment to Hurst, he might write something to Darcy's father.

I must direct Miss Bingley's suspicions away from Elizabeth! He said the first thing that came to mind. "But her teeth are rather unfortunate…so…white."

Miss Bingley's brows drew together. "Her teeth? I had not noticed."

Darcy cast about for other imperfections to name but found few.

"And her hands! Her fingers are so…short."

Miss Bingley stared down at her long fingers. "Indeed? That is unfortunate."

What else could he say? "And her hair…" Miss Bingley looked bewildered, as well she might. Elizabeth's hair was glorious. "It is…extremely…copious."

Miss Bingley could not help touching her own rather sparsely populated coiffeur. "Yes, too much hair. I had noted it before."

"With all of these flaws, one barely notices her eyes. It is a shame."

Miss Bingley gave a condescending smile. "Yes, none of the Bennet girls are likely to attract a husband."

If Darcy continued this conversation he feared he might be sick. "As you say." With a bow, he stalked past Miss Bingley into the card room.

***

Elizabeth had hoped that Mr. Darcy's insulting words to her had been noted only by Sir William, but her hope was in vain. Some unknown neighbor had overheard the confrontation, and within minutes the women of Meryton were whispering and laughing behind their fans while throwing Elizabeth sidelong glances. Her face flamed hot, a sure sign she was blushing—which only made her blush more fiercely. She did not know if she was angrier with Mr. Darcy or herself. He should not have agreed to Sir William's scheme to partner them for the dance, but she should have found a more gracious way to decline his invitation. Naturally, he was piqued at the way she refused him.

Having lost all inclination to dance or even converse, Elizabeth helped herself to a glass of punch and retreated to a corner of the room. She wondered if it would be a faux pas to slip into Sir William's library and help herself to a book. Watching others dance was so dull.

"Oh, Lizzy! Oh, my dear girl!" Elizabeth only had a few seconds of warning before her mother swooped down on her like a hawk—if hawks dressed more like peacocks. "Oh, Lizzy!" Her voice preceding her, Mrs. Bennet pushed through the throng with her husband silently following in her wake.

Elizabeth was immediately clasped to the maternal bosom. Then her mother started her tirade, punctuated by the flapping of her fan. "That horrid man!" Flap. "Lady Lucas told me what he said!" Flap. "It was abominably rude for him not to dance with you and then to compare you to a half-dressed savage! Well—!" To emphasize the point, the fan was now a blur.

"To be fair, Mama, he said nothing about half-dressed savages," Elizabeth countered.

"It was implied, Lizzy. Do not attempt to defend that man to me. He practically announced to the entire party that you wear a skirt made of grass and eat pork sitting on the ground!"

Elizabeth sighed. Upon occasion her mother's penchant for exaggeration was wearying.

Her father narrowed his eyes. "Why were you conversing with Mr. Darcy in the first place?"

"I had no intention of doing so," Elizabeth said. "But Sir William recommended me as a dancing partner." Her father shot a black look at Sir William on the other side of the room. "Sir William knows nothing of the feud between you and Mr. Darcy's father. He thought he was doing a good deed."

Mr. Bennet drew himself to his full height. "The feud is not only between me and George Darcy, make no mistake! He would love to destroy my entire family."

"But it does not follow that his son is likewise bent on our ruin." If only she could show her father Mr. Darcy's true character!

Her father was shaking his head vigorously before she even finished speaking. "That man," he gestured vaguely in the direction of the card room, "was raised by George Darcy—no doubt weaned on lies about us from the cradle. We cannot trust him."

"But—"

"Lizzy, consider what he said following your first encounter!" Her father's face was red, and sweat beaded his forehead. "And now he has insulted you once more."

From that perspective, Elizabeth admitted Mr. Darcy's behavior did not look good.

Her father took several steps toward her. "You have not been taken in by the man, have you?" Her mother's hand flew to her mouth in horror at this suggestion. "He is rich and handsome to be sure, but you must keep your distance. If he senses any softening of our resolve, he could use that." Her father's voice grew low and soft. "He might even *take advantage* of you." Her mother gasped.

Elizabeth opened her mouth to issue a heated denial, but she had agreed to pretend a dislike for Mr. Darcy. He had acted his part admirably; she must do her best to honor their agreement. She widened her eyes in horror. "Do you believe he would stoop so low?" Her father nodded solemnly. Inside she was screaming denials, but she faked a shudder. "How horrible!"

"You must stay away from him." Her father looked her directly in the eye.

She nodded but made no promises. It was a small rebellion but slightly heartening. Of course, she was not likely to have the opportunity to converse with Mr. Darcy again, but holding onto that thin thread of hope helped to stave off despair.

***

Once more Darcy debated the merits of quitting Netherfield as he listened to Miss Bingley's and Mrs. Hurst's chatter, which was inane at its best and vitriolic at its worst. They did not care for the society in Hertfordshire, the countryside, or even the weather, which was vastly inferior to the weather in Town.

Miss Bingley was piqued that Jane Bennet had the gall to actually *accept* their invitation to luncheon at Netherfield; Miss Bennet should have understood they extended the invitation only as a courtesy and did not actually desire the pleasure of her company.

Now, however, Miss Bingley was positively indignant. The young woman had the bad taste to have fallen ill and was required to remain at Netherfield for the night. Mrs. Hurst's head bobbed along with everything her sister said while Mr. Hurst added nothing but an occasional belch. Bingley sometimes made noises of disagreement, but otherwise Miss Bingley's soliloquy continued unchecked.

If Darcy disagreed with her, he might draw unwanted attention to his affection for Elizabeth. However, he could not bring himself to agree, so he remained silent. Finally, he had enough. As Miss Bingley continued her disparaging remarks, Darcy excused himself from the breakfast table and strode toward the door. Perhaps he would take his stallion out for a ride; it would at least allow him to gaze on Longbourn and imagine what Elizabeth might be doing.

However, as he opened the door to the breakfast room, Darcy nearly collided with an equally astonished Elizabeth Bennet, accompanied by one of Bingley's footmen. Her cheeks were reddened by the chill outside, and her eyes were bright. His eyes were drawn down, and he noticed that her shoes, stockings, and the hem of her dress were coated in mud. She must have walked from Longbourn. Good Lord, what was she thinking? She could catch a cold.

"Eliz—Miss Bennet!" Darcy cried in surprise.

Elizabeth took a step backward as if the very air around him was forbidden. "Mr. Darcy. How do you do?" Her tone was icy and formal. Was she playing a role or had he actually offended her? How he hated this deception! Darcy bowed in response. "I have come to visit my sister."

Elizabeth's essence filled his senses —her delicate rosewater scent, her soft, pale complexion, and the husky quality of her voice. Basking in her proximity, Darcy gave no thought to moving or speaking. Elizabeth regarded him with a crease between her brows. Did she not feel it, the electricity between them? "Mr. Darcy?" she prompted.

"Um...er..." What question should he be answering? The footman glanced between Elizabeth and Darcy uncertainly. Apparently "um, er" was not the correct response.

"Miss Elizabeth!" Bingley's voice behind Darcy was his salvation. He stepped out of the doorway, allowing Elizabeth to enter the breakfast room.

She exchanged greetings with the room's inhabitants and received information about the health of the invalid. Darcy took those moment to collect his thoughts and avoid presenting quite such a good imitation of a sleepwalker.

The eyes of everyone in the room were fixed on Elizabeth, but Miss Bingley watched Darcy with narrowed eyes. Hurst glanced up and followed her gaze, staring briefly at Darcy. What did they see on his face? Did he betray himself? He attempted to school his features into his usual impassive expression but did not know if he was successful. Damnation! He must be more cautious.

Finally, Bingley summoned a servant to take Elizabeth to her sister's bedchamber, and Darcy could breathe easily again. Restraining an urge to frown at Miss Bingley and Mr. Hurst, Darcy pivoted on his heel and strode toward his room. His morning plans were decided; he would take a long ride and hope Elizabeth Bennet would be gone upon his return.

**

As Elizabeth sat at her sister's bedside, she considered how events could have unfolded differently. Mr. Bennet had not wanted his daughters to visit Netherfield or associate with any of its inhabitants. Mr. Bingley's friendship with Mr. Darcy had lowered the man in his estimation, but Mrs. Bennet was loath to lose the opportunity for Mr. Bingley's five thousand a year. So when an invitation came for Jane to lunch at Netherfield, her mother—unbeknownst to Mr. Bennet— insisted on sending their daughter on horseback even though rain threatened.

No one was surprised at her father's anger when a letter arrived from Netherfield announcing that Jane was too ill to travel to Longbourn and would remain with the Bingleys overnight. Her mother and father had a terrible row; however, Elizabeth was more concerned with Jane's condition. Jane had not cared for their mother's scheme but would not contradict her. In addition to being ill, Jane would be uneasy being under the same roof with a man her father disliked; Elizabeth knew it.

Thus, the following morning, Elizabeth had resolved to visit Netherfield and ascertain for herself how Jane was faring. Mr. Darcy's presence there naturally played no part in her decision; she was still bent on avoiding him. But as she walked, she found it difficult not to think how his intent gaze caused shivers along her spine.

Once at Netherfield, however, she instantly wished she had not come. At first stunned by her sudden appearance, Mr. Darcy said nothing to her thereafter. Perhaps he was too appalled at the mud on her dress. She had told herself a little dirt did not signify, but the look on his face... *I should have sent Mary or Kitty.*

Elizabeth spent the day by Jane's bedside, concerned about her sister's pallor and frequent coughs. By late afternoon, Jane had fallen into a deep slumber, so Elizabeth had no excuse for avoiding dinner with Netherfield's other inhabitants.

After desultory conversation about the weather, Mr. Bingley asked quite anxiously about Jane's condition—an inquiry that was echoed rather less urgently by Miss Bingley. "Her coughing has improved, but her fever seems to have worsened," Elizabeth replied. Mr. Bingley wondered again if he should send for a doctor and insisted that Elizabeth spend the night at Netherfield before lapsing into an uneasy silence.

Mrs. Hurst shoved a grape in her mouth. "How shocking it is to have a bad cold!"

"Indeed, I am grieved to hear it," agreed Miss Bingley.

"I so dislike being ill," Mrs. Hurst remarked.

Most people do, Elizabeth thought, but she said nothing.

"I do as well, Sister!" cried Miss Bingley. "I dislike it excessively. It is most unpleasant."

Not feeling equal to responding to such remarks, Elizabeth merely nodded.

"Do you recall the dreadful cold I suffered in Bath a year ago?" Mrs. Hurst asked her sister. "I was forced to miss two musicales! Two!"

And now we are finished with discussing Jane's condition, Elizabeth thought to herself.

"Oh yes, most unfortunate," Miss Bingley said, cutting her meat into very small pieces.

Mrs. Hurst described in great detail each of her symptoms and what fine social occasions she had missed. Miss Bingley chimed in upon occasion to clarify when her sister had a detail wrong, but otherwise the rest of the table was silent. Elizabeth carefully focused her eyes on her wineglass so she did not run the risk of staring at Mr. Darcy. But her skin prickled as if her whole body was aware of his proximity. When she heard her name, she realized she had not attended to the conversation.

"And we must allow that you are an excellent walker, Miss Elizabeth." Elizabeth's head jerked abruptly upon being so addressed by Miss Bingley.

By now Elizabeth was accustomed to Miss Bingley's criticisms delivered like compliments. She shrugged. "It is three miles, no great distance."

"Perhaps." Miss Bingley tilted her head slightly as she watched Elizabeth. "But it is not one woman in twenty who could do what you did. Why, even in London nobody walks. Everyone takes a carriage or hackney."

Miss Bingley is very good at this game. "What a shame they do not take the opportunity for fresh air and exercise." Elizabeth drove her spoon into the pudding before her.

Miss Bingley's smile could not have been more condescending. "It does have the virtue of keeping one's clothes clean."

Elizabeth felt herself flush under the weight of Miss Bingley's stare.

"I would imagine Georgiana customarily takes the carriage when she is in Town?" Miss Bingley asked Mr. Darcy.

He rubbed his chin, unhappy at being drawn into this conversation. "Yes, I believe she does."

"When at Pemberley, does she scamper about the countryside alone?" the woman asked.

"Um…well, Georgiana usually rides." Briefly, Mr. Darcy's eyes met Elizabeth's—with a look of wild desperation—and he took a healthy gulp from his wineglass. Did he dislike being used as a weapon against her? He could hardly defend her without arousing suspicion.

Miss Bingley turned a triumphant look on Elizabeth as if she had scored a great victory. "Well, perhaps they do things differently in Hertfordshire, eh, Mr. Darcy?"

He lowered his wineglass, watching Elizabeth. "I believe the difference may lie in Miss Elizabeth."

"Pray, tell me. What is the difference?" Miss Bingley asked archly.

Mr. Darcy slid startled eyes to the other woman as if realizing he was too close to complimenting Elizabeth. "Er…she has a unique concern for her sister and a distinctive disregard for her clothes."

Bingley frowned. "I say, Darcy. Are you not—?"

Miss Bingley cut off her brother without blinking. "Yes, well said." She regarded Elizabeth with a smirk. "Eliza Bennet is in a class by herself."

Surely her face must be turning red. Every eye at the table was upon her. What if Mr. Darcy's words revealed his true sentiments? Surrounded by people closer to his own station in life, it would be all too easy for him to dwell on Elizabeth's shortcomings—particularly with Miss Bingley conveniently available to point them out.

She reached for her wineglass, a studied attempt at casualness that was marred by the shaking of her hand. She wished to give a witty rejoinder to Mr. Darcy's barb, but his words were not untrue. Only these people could make such preferences sound like a vice. "It is true, Mr. Darcy, I do care more about people than clothing. By all means, share the news, shocking though it may be." She gave Mr. Darcy an arch smile. He seemed a little abashed while Miss Bingley smiled triumphantly as if she had forced Elizabeth to reveal a scandalous secret.

Abruptly, Elizabeth was weary of the whole farce. She set her wineglass on the table with an inelegant thump. "I pray you, excuse me. I will attend to Jane."

Without waiting for a response, she stood and walked briskly out of the room.

Chapter Eight

During the night, unease over Mr. Darcy's attitude was eclipsed by Elizabeth's deep concern about Jane's health. By midnight, her sister was feverish and insensible to the world around her. She shifted restlessly, moaning and uttering incoherent words but never recognizing Elizabeth or her surroundings.

Finally, Elizabeth was sufficiently alarmed to take a candle, pull a shawl about her shoulders, and go in search of assistance. As she slipped from Jane's room, Elizabeth was unsure even of which direction to take. Having never received a tour of Netherfield, she did not know where Mr. Bingley's chambers might lie.

She padded softly toward the house's main staircase. Most of the staff would have retired for the night, but perhaps a footman lingered who might awaken Mr. Bingley to send for a doctor. She rounded the corner to the stairs and for the second time that day nearly collided with Mr. Darcy. As she stumbled backward, he grabbed her elbow to prevent her from falling and reached out to steady her candle.

"Elizabeth! What is it? Are you in distress?" He kept his voice low, but it was edged with alarm.

Although his features, half in shadow in the dim light, reflected nothing but concern, she could not help recalling his criticism at the dinner table. She was torn between the need to deny requiring assistance and a sense of relief that she could lay the problem in his capable hands. As she pulled her arm from his grasp, she chided herself that Jane's health was the current urgency, not the state of her own heart.

"I fear Jane's fever has taken a turn for the worse. I was hoping Mr. Bingley could summon a doctor."

Mr. Darcy's eyes widened, and his eyebrows shot up. "Yes, yes, of course. I will locate a footman who can send for Mr. Jones immediately." He pivoted and strode toward the stairs.

Elizabeth returned to Jane's room; at least this interaction had not lasted long. Seating herself by Jane's side, she took her sister's all-too-limp hand in hers. A few minutes later a knock on the door caused her to start. Opening the door revealed Mr. Darcy, a deep frown on his face and a bowl of water in his hands. "I brought you some fresh water. I thought bathing her face and neck might help reduce the fever."

Elizabeth's heart melted. That bowl of water spoke more toward his feelings for her than a diamond necklace would have. "Thank you," she murmured, stepping aside so he could enter. Strict propriety would not allow him entrance into Jane's bedchamber, but a sick room was hardly the place for an assignation—and everyone else was abed.

Mr. Darcy set the bowl carefully on the table beside the bed, and Elizabeth immediately dipped a clean cloth into it so she could cool Jane's face. Her sister had fallen into an uneasy slumber but remained alarmingly pale. When Elizabeth felt she had done all she could, she wrung out the cloth and stood to thank Mr. Darcy.

He had retreated to the doorway. "I will await the doctor and bring him here when he arrives."

"You need not trouble yourself," Elizabeth objected, putting out a hand as if to stop him. "Surely a servant—"

He took a step into the room, his hand catching and holding hers. "I could not sleep in any case. I will be of service to you." He swallowed. "I must."

The fierceness in his voice stole Elizabeth's breath. Earlier in the evening she had feared a waning in his affections, but with one sentence he had proved her wrong.

His hand squeezed hers reassuringly, and a moment later he was gone, leaving Elizabeth to nurse her sister.

***

Darcy paced in the hallway outside Miss Bennet's bedchamber, awaiting Mr. Jones's verdict. For the twentieth time he cursed the rules of propriety that would ban him from the room while Miss Bennet was examined. When he closed his eyes, he saw Elizabeth's face as it had been when he had encountered her in the hallway—white and drawn. He would do anything to prevent that expression from reappearing on her face.

Finally, the door opened, and Mr. Jones hurried out and down the hallway, carrying his black doctor's bag. Darcy desperately wished to question the man but knew he had another urgent patient in Meryton.

The door remained open, tempting Darcy to enter, but after a moment, Elizabeth emerged. If he thought she had seemed anxious before, now she was positively ghastly. Her skin had taken on a grayish tinge, and her hands trembled.

All resolutions to maintain his distance were immediately forgotten as Darcy rushed to her side. Barely restraining himself from embracing her, he touched her shoulder gently. "What news from the doctor?"

Elizabeth dragged a weary hand through hair that was already disheveled and coming loose from its braid. "He gave her some medicine…but he said the fever is dangerously high. He was very concerned but said there was nothing else he could do." Her voice grew more ragged with each word. "He said if the fever does not break tonight…things could go very ill for her." Elizabeth's voice broke, and any semblance of composure vanished. Tears first trickled and then poured down her cheeks.

Darcy could stand it no longer; he reached out and enfolded her in his arms, willing his body to convey all of his concern and affection as he pressed against her. Elizabeth sobbed into his shoulder, holding nothing back. He further tightened his arms, pulling her closer.

As her sobs quieted, he dared to stroke the top of her head, marveling at the silkiness of her hair. Despite the circumstances, he could not deny the pleasure he experienced having her body pressed against his. She was such a warm and welcome weight—the perfect size to fit against him as if they were two puzzle pieces. His hands moved slowly over her back, soothing and caressing. How would it feel to caress her bare skin? Would it feel as soft as it looked?

Without thinking, Darcy bent to kiss the top of Elizabeth's head. She stiffened in his arms and stepped back although she did not pull completely from his embrace. Silently, Darcy cursed himself for the impulsive act. Extracting her handkerchief and wiping her eyes, Elizabeth gave a rueful laugh. "I beg your pardon. I am not usually such a watering pot."

"It is completely understandable given the circumstances."

Elizabeth glanced over her shoulder at the still form lying on the bed. "I love all my sisters, of course, but Jane and I...we are closest in age, and she understands me so well. I do not know what I would do if..."

"She is young and strong, Elizabeth. There is every reason to believe she will throw off this illness." He dared to bring his hands up to her face, using his thumbs to gently wipe away the tears rolling down her cheeks. Her eyes fluttered closed, causing wet, dark lashes to fan out against her cheeks. Darcy's only thoughts revolved around how he could shelter and protect the woman in his arms.

Elizabeth swallowed heavily. "Yes, I remind myself of that hourly, but...the doctor was not optimistic..."

Damn the man! Darcy's eyes stung, and his throat ached as if he shared Elizabeth's distress. In the morning, he would have Bingley send to London for a physician. It was not enough—not nearly enough—but at least he would be taking some action.

Elizabeth's face turned up to him. Somehow the tears had darkened and intensified the blue of her eyes. He drew closer to her.

Without making a conscious decision, Darcy's head bent down, and his lips sought hers. She made a muffled noise of surprise but yielded immediately. Her mouth was... heaven itself. Her lips opened when his tongue sought entrance. What a relief to be kissing her! He had been restraining this impulse for days. At their every encounter, he had fantasized about kissing her, even while he simultaneously attempted to rein in those desires and deny them. Now he released them. His tongue deepened its exploration, wishing to seek out every corner, taste every part of her mouth. Someone moaned, and a distant part of Darcy recognized the voice as his own.

Too soon, Elizabeth backed away, but they stared at each other, both panting as if they had run a race. "Mr. Darcy, we cannot—!" Despite the alarm in her voice, her face still shone with a desire that mirrored his.

He groaned, rubbing his hands over his face. "I cannot be near you and not want you. Everything in me forbids it."

Her hand covered her mouth as if to scrub away the sensation of his kiss. "It does not matter. I cannot—"

A loud moan sounded from the bed, causing Elizabeth to whirl around. With a small cry of concern, she hastened to her sister's bedside. Miss Bennet rolled her head from side to side, muttering incoherently. Her skin was a sickly shade of gray.

How could he have forgotten Elizabeth's sick sister? What kind of man burdened his beloved when she was already under such duress? At that moment, he despised himself.

Elizabeth dipped the cloth, wrung it out, and carefully bathed Jane's neck and face. "I am here, dearest, you will be well again." Elizabeth bit her lip, not appearing to believe her own words.

Darcy stepped further into the room. "Is there anything I can do to help?"

Elizabeth's gaze remained fastened on her sister. "No, thank you, Mr. Darcy. You have been a great help already. It would be best if you retire." Her words were not cold, but they were hard, uncompromising. Darcy could recognize a dismissal. Was she angry about the kiss he had forced on her?

"Very well," he said. "I will remain dressed." He could not sleep in any event. "Please do not hesitate to knock on my door should you require my assistance."

Elizabeth said nothing but gave a curt nod. *This is as it should be*, Darcy reassured himself as he exited the room, closing the door behind him. *She cannot be mine.*

***

Darcy rose at first light to awaken Bingley so he could send for a London physician. All morning he cursed the necessity. Darcy could easily have sent his own servant on such an errand but needed to avoid any appearance of concern for the Bennet sisters' welfare. Really, the situation was quite frustrating and more than a little ridiculous. However, a thoroughly alarmed Bingley was happy to dispatch a footman on the errand.

Darcy then ventured to Miss Bennet's room, but the door was firmly closed, and he did not have the courage to knock. What if a maid was within? How would he explain his intrusion? He lingered in the hallway, hoping Elizabeth would emerge, but the sounds of an awakening household soon drove him back to his bedchamber where he finally fell into a restless sleep.

When he awoke again, it was late morning. He dressed in fresh clothing, hoping to obtain information about Miss Bennet's condition from someone at breakfast. As he descended the stairs, he found the front hall full of Bennets; the entirety of Elizabeth's family witnessed Mr. Bennet's conversation with Bingley. Mrs. Bennet fluttered about in agitation, worrying a handkerchief in her hand, while the two youngest girls whispered and giggled to each other. The third girl stared, awestruck, at the ornate décor of the hall. Caroline Bingley and the Hursts smirked near the entrance to the breakfast room.

"She cannot be removed to Longbourn." Bingley's voice held a pleading tone. "She is far too ill!"

"My daughters have spent enough time under this roof!" Mr. Bennet thundered. As Darcy descended the last step, the man glared at him. Oh yes, his presence was the reason the man wished his daughters removed from Netherfield.

Perhaps here was an opportunity to convince Mr. Bennet that he was not the same as his father. "Mr. Bennet—" he began.

Mr. Bennet turned his back on Darcy. Caroline Bingley gasped, and Hurst uttered an oath. Darcy himself felt a flare of anger. No one had ever given him the cut direct before. And now this country squire presumed? Darcy would happily tell the man off! Then Darcy caught a glimpse of Bingley's unhappy face. His friend really did care for Jane Bennet—perhaps even as much as Darcy cared for Elizabeth. Bingley and Elizabeth both would be hurt if Darcy quarreled with Mr. Bennet.

So Darcy took a deep breath and willed his shoulders to lower, reminding himself that Mr. Bennet's quarrels were with his father. He might know George Darcy, but he knew nothing about Fitzwilliam Darcy.

His face a mask of distress, Bingley took a few steps toward Mr. Bennet. "Miss Bennet is far too ill to be removed. She had a high fever all night. It has eased slightly, but who knows what this evening will bring?"

Mr. Bennet glared at Bingley. "I have no quarrel with you, young man, although I do not commend your taste in friends." Bingley flushed but stood his ground. "I can do nothing about the company you keep, but I must remove my daughters from this poisonous atmosphere at once." Mrs. Bennet uttered a cry of distress and fluttered her hands uselessly, undoubtedly worried about the prospect of losing Bingley's five thousand a year.

Bingley ran his fingers through his hair in an uncharacteristic sign of anxiety. "I have sent for Mr. Foreman, a physician from London. Would it be possible for Miss Bennet to remain here until the man has examined her?"

Mr. Bennet blinked. "A physician from London?" Darcy wanted to explain that sending for the physician was his idea, but such a declaration might turn Mr. Bennet against the doctor.

"Yes." Bingley's voice was a bit more forceful now. "Mr. Foreman is an excellent doctor who has cared for my family for many years. I quite depend on his judgment."

Mrs. Bennet had been bursting with the need to speak for several moments, and finally the words exploded from her. "Oh yes, Mr. Bennet! My precious Jane must be examined by a London physician!" Idly, Darcy wondered if she was truly concerned about her daughter's health or if she was excited about the prestige of a London physician examining her. Then he glimpsed the twisted handkerchief in her hand; perhaps he had been too harsh in his judgment of her. "It was very good of you to send for your family's physician, sir," she said to Mr. Bingley in a somewhat unsteady voice.

Mr. Bennet's lips twisted as if he tasted something unpleasant. "Very well, I will allow Jane to remain until the doctor has examined her and will abide by the man's recommendations about whether she can be removed. However, I demand that you return Elizabeth at once!"

Darcy suppressed an urge to roll his eyes. Mr. Bennet behaved as if they kept Elizabeth at Netherfield against her will.

He heard quick steps on the stairs behind him "Papa, I cannot leave Jane here alone!" Elizabeth said as she descended the last few steps.

Mr. Bennet frowned at his second eldest daughter. "You must return to Longbourn! We will send a maid to care for Jane during her illness."

Elizabeth lifted her chin as she regarded her father. "Jane is comforted by my presence, particularly now that she is more sensible of her surroundings." Mr. Bennet's lips thinned; he had not missed Elizabeth's suggestion about the previous status of her sister's health.

"But these people—!" Bennet gestured to Bingley and his sisters as if Elizabeth were consorting with ragmen and grave robbers. Darcy bit his lip against the impulse to object.

Elizabeth interrupted. "They have been nothing but kind to me since I arrived." Darcy eyed Miss Bingley, thinking this was a bit of an exaggeration. "Although…" She thoughtfully tapped her lip with the tip of a finger. "Perhaps they do not like me well enough to invite me to join in their debauchery."

The younger Miss Bennets giggled. Miss Bingley gasped, highly offended. Mrs. Hurst fanned herself furiously, and Bingley appeared bemused. But Darcy suppressed a chuckle. Only Elizabeth would make such a jest.

"Perhaps if I told them I was *available* for debauchery they would rectify this oversight…" Elizabeth continued in a thoughtful tone.

Mrs. Bennet fluttered her hands in greater agitation. Miss Bingley was growing red in the face. But a corner of Mr. Bennet's mouth twitched; perhaps Elizabeth did know how to disarm her father. Darcy could not prevent a snort of laughter but turned it into a cough when Mr. Bennet's eyes fell on him.

"Very well, you may remain as well." Mr. Bennet glared daggers at her. Darcy fervently hoped the man was not the kind to beat his daughters or wife.

"Thank you, Papa." Elizabeth smiled demurely as if she had never uttered such shocking things.

Mr. Bennet whirled on his heel and stalked toward Darcy until they were almost nose-to-nose. Darcy refused to give any ground. Elizabeth's father pointed with a furious finger. "And *you* will stay far away from my daughters! There is no need for you to *ever* be in company together."

Darcy had no desire to create an enemy—or a greater enemy—but he took orders from nobody. "Your preference is noted."

"Will you abide by my wishes?" Mr. Bennet's eyes pinned Darcy in place.

Darcy straightened his shoulders. "I will go where I wish and associate with whomever I wish."

"I see." Mr. Bennet's voice was so cold that icicles could form on it. Would the man force Elizabeth to leave after all?

"Mr. Darcy has been quite solicitous of Jane's health," Elizabeth put in.

"Has he?" Mr. Bennet narrowed his eyes as he regarded Darcy. Did he suspect Darcy of some scheme involving Jane Bennet? Or that he was meddling in her relationship with Bingley?

Darcy met the other man's glare without blinking. Finally, Elizabeth's father glanced away and turned toward the door. "Lizzy, walk us to our carriage."

It was a command, not a request—and just as clearly a dismissal of everyone else. Elizabeth hastened to accompany her parents to their carriage while the younger girls trailed behind. As she passed him, Darcy attempted to catch her eye, but she carefully did not look in his direction.

Chapter Nine

Mr. Foreman was more optimistic about Jane's condition than Mr. Jones had been and supplied a new medicine that helped Jane rest more easily. By evening, Elizabeth's anxiety had abated considerably. Jane's fever had decreased, and her breathing did not seem so labored.

Nevertheless, Elizabeth elected to have her dinner on a tray in her room. She was not equal to making polite conversation with the other inhabitants of Netherfield— particularly after her family's display in the front hall. Undoubtedly, the dinner-table conversation revolved around her family's vulgar manners; at least in Jane's room, Elizabeth did not need to face the veiled insults.

Thus, she also avoided facing Mr. Darcy, who confused her more with each encounter. He was publicly so disdainful that it seemed believable, but in private he was solicitous. He had promised not to pursue her, but then kissed her so tenderly. Her lips still tingled at the memory of the kiss. On the other hand, Elizabeth had not protested. Perhaps the relevant question was why she allowed him to kiss her. He was the worst possible object of her affections. Why did she find herself wondering when he might kiss her again?

At times she could hardly credit his claim of having harbored affection for her for almost two years despite not knowing her full name. At other times this was all too easy to believe since she had felt the same. Despite the problems he brought, when Mr. Darcy entered the room something inside Elizabeth uncoiled, a tension she did not know she carried within her. When she saw him, it melted away, and inside she practically purred like a contented cat.

No. It was dangerous to think this way about Mr. Darcy. It was dangerous to think of Mr. Darcy *at all*. Dangerous for both of them, if Mr. Darcy was correct. *I must turn my thoughts in other directions*, she resolved. Of course, dozens of similar resolutions had been broken.

No, she would focus her attention on Jane. It was the safest course, and Jane needed her. Sighing, Elizabeth again mopped her sister's brow with a wet cloth and was rewarded with a gentle exhalation. If only Jane would wake! Then Elizabeth might believe she was truly on the road to recovery.

It was now past midnight; sounds of the household's other residents had long since abated. Earlier in the evening Mr. Bingley had sent a maid to inquire about Jane's condition; later a different maid had arrived to ask if Elizabeth needed anything. But she had not seen anyone from the family. Naturally, the men would not intrude into Jane's room, but Bingley's sisters might at least pretend an interest in their guest's welfare.

A gentle knock sounded on the door, and Elizabeth started, realizing she had dozed off sitting next to Jane's bedside. The knock came again. Who could it be this time of night? Elizabeth padded to the door and opened it cautiously. There stood Mr. Darcy, his brow wrinkled with concern.

"May I speak with you, Miss Elizabeth?"

He looked so handsome and kind that Elizabeth longed to admit him, but it would not be proper.

He might be tempted to kiss her again.

She might be tempted to let him.

"My sister is much better, thank you for inquiring." As she closed the door, Mr. Darcy blocked it with his foot.

"I must speak with you."

The corridor outside the room must be empty, for he would not take the risk otherwise. "I do not think that would be wise."

"Please…Elizabeth." The words emerged as a half-strangled groan, and Elizabeth's resolve wavered. Over the past two days her appreciation of Mr. Darcy had increased.

He had been a true friend, quick-thinking and caring. Surely he had thought to summon a doctor from London. But this realization was bittersweet. The obstacles between them had not disappeared, and she only grew more aware of what she was losing.

Suddenly she was very tired, with the weight of two days in a sick room pressed upon her. "I am immensely grateful for your help, Mr. Darcy. But I…cannot…"

He bowed his head, not meeting her eyes. "Very well. I understand."

She closed the door and leaned her weight on it, praying for strength as she listened to Mr. Darcy's retreating footsteps.

***

How many times will I resolve to leave Netherfield before I actually take action? There is nothing for me here. Darcy stared at the book in his hand without actually reading it. Wordsworth's poetry deserved his full attention but could not hold him today. Whenever he thought of poetry, his mind was filled with Elizabeth.

It had been two days since he had spoken with her at the door to her sister's room. As her sister's health had steadily improved, he had seen her in company at meals and after dinner, but she had said little to him. Perhaps she was maintaining the façade of distrust between them, or perhaps she was simply weary from nursing her sister. *Was she unhappy I wished to speak with her that night? We both know we have no future.* Yet not speaking with Elizabeth hurt. Absently, Darcy massaged his chest as if he could rub away the dull ache forming there.

I should leave.

But he would not, because she was here. She was his best reason to depart and best reason to stay. He had the notion that he somehow protected her from the worst of

Bingley's sisters' malice. Although he could not defend her openly, he could redirect the subject of the conversation when they attacked her.

She did not ask for your protection. She does not want it, he reminded himself. But that reasoning made no difference to his heart.

If he were honest with himself, he would admit that he remained because he might never see her again. The thought made him want to punch something.

I should leave. Or at least read some damned poetry!

He refocused his eyes on the print in the book he held but was immediately disturbed by the sound of the library door opening. Elizabeth crept into the room, dark circles under her eyes betraying her fatigue. Her face was carefully blank when she noticed him. He stood and bowed.

"Miss Elizabeth."

"M-Mr. Darcy."

"How fares your sister?"

Elizabeth lingered in the doorway as if unsure whether to bolt from the room. "She is much improved. She ate some breakfast this morning and then walked around the room a little."

"I am pleased to hear it." *I am staring at her. I should stop staring at her.* Yet he could not find the strength to redirect his gaze. Sunlight from the windows caught in her hair, creating golden highlights, and faint lines around her eyes marked where she would smile. If only he could be the reason she smiled.

Her eyes were carefully focused on the shelves to his right. After a long pause, she cleared her throat. "I…um…thought I could find a book to read…to pass the time while Jane is asleep."

Do not think about the softness of her skin.
"Ah…yes…Bingley has a fine collection here…not very large but a good selection."

Her eyes surveyed the room. "Not large?" She laughed. "Your standards are very high, sir!"

He felt his face heating and shrugged. What could he say? *I was comparing Netherfield's library to Pemberley's?*

There was a pause. When Elizabeth realized he would not speak again, she coughed. "I was hoping Mr. Bingley would have Mr. Wordsworth's latest volume. I have not read it."

"I happen to have it here." Darcy removed it from his lap. *How would she respond if I offered to read it to her?* Instead he held it out to her.

She did not move toward him but wrapped her arms about her waist as if hugging herself. "I would not deprive you of the pleasure."

"I insist. I have read it before, and it is well worth reading." His arm remained outstretched.

She hesitated, then took a few quick steps in his direction and plucked it from his hand. Their fingers brushed. It was like touching a lightning bolt. His entire body awoke, alive to her presence and very aware of her body.

Her eyes widened. "Oh!" She felt it as well! Surely that was a sign.

How could they do this? How could they continue to torture themselves?

He surged to his feet, causing her to stumble back a few paces. He advanced, standing far closer to her than was proper. "Elizabeth, you do not know how you haunted my dreams for two years. Not knowing who you were or where." His voice was low and hoarse.

Elizabeth swallowed hard as her eyes looked anywhere except at him. "We must not do this." But she remained frozen in place.

Darcy leaned closer until he could smell her delicate rosewater scent. "I know. Anything further between us is impossible." Of its own volition, his hand reached up to caress the small curls at the back of her neck. She shivered; Darcy was obscurely pleased to have provoked such a response.

"When you sent me away the other night, I did not want to go," he murmured.

"I am sorry. I did not wish to hurt you. It hurt me as well…" Her eyes returned to his face, and her voice trailed off as if she could not recall what she planned to say. Her lips parted slightly, and she licked them. Darcy was undone.

For perhaps the first time in his life, Darcy did not allow himself to think, only to feel. He bent his head and captured her lips with his. She responded to his every move perfectly; they were like dancers in perfect harmony. When he pressed his tongue to the seam of her lips, she opened immediately, and his tongue swept in. With his arm behind her back, he drew her against his body, and she yielded without hesitation, melting against him until they felt like one being.

Darcy had kissed a few other women, but those occasions resembled this experience like a stream resembled the Thames. She overwhelmed his senses until he could think of nothing but her—feel nothing but her body warming his.

Without a conscious decision, he maneuvered her to a nearby sofa. When the backs of her knees met the sofa, she sat with a muffled exclamation of surprise. Darcy sat next to her and immediately pressed her back against the cushions; one hand remained behind her neck and shoulders where he could touch her freely—skin-to-skin. *I*

must stop! Someone could enter the library at any time.
He knew such wildly inappropriate behavior should cease,
but he could not help marveling that she allowed such
liberties.

She moaned deep in her throat, further undermining
Darcy's self-control. *She likes it!* He allowed his fingers to
slip under the edge of her neckline to the soft, forbidden
skin of her back. At first he started when her hands
reached inside his coat and around his waist and back. But
then he relaxed into her touch. The tentative caresses were
a lovely surprise; he pressed closer to her so she could
access more of his back.

One of his hands traveled up to touch the soft curls
at the back of her complicated coiffure. Her hair was as
silken as he had imagined; he relished the slide of the
strands between his fingers

There was a loud ping from the floor. Startled,
Elizabeth pulled away from Darcy, and they both looked
down, seeking the source of the noise. One of her hair pins
lay accusingly on the wood floor next to the sofa.

Elizabeth's hair had fallen from the pins on one
side, and her lips were swollen and red. She looked like a
woman recently ravaged on a sofa. Darcy withdrew his
hands from her as if she had burned him.

*What have I done? How did I allow things to go so
far?*

Elizabeth's hands flew from Darcy's waistcoat, and
he immediately missed the warmth. He slid away from her,
allowing her to sit up and rearrange her hair, tucking and
pinning as necessary. When the repairs were complete,
they regarded each other, both still breathing hard. He
assumed his lips were as red as hers. If anyone noticed his
lips they would assume a dalliance with a maid, but if
someone noticed her lips...? What would they assume?
Was he to be responsible for ruining her reputation?

He could not stop from touching her mouth with the tips of his fingers. "I cannot...apologize enough for my inappropriate behavior."

Her lips quirked in a smile. "Would you have stopped if I had asked it of you?"

"Naturally!"

"Then I believe we are equally culpable since I did not ask you."

Although Darcy did not necessarily agree, he recalled the sensations of her hands on his waist and back. It was a heady feeling, knowing she returned his passion. *How can I do without it for the rest of my life?* "Of all the women in the world, why did you have to be Thomas Bennet's daughter?" he murmured.

Elizabeth frowned. "I have met many ladies in the last few years," he explained. "None have made my heart beat half so rapidly."

She closed her eyes and took a deep breath, sitting up straighter. Finally, she opened her eyes and regarded him seriously as if steeling herself for an unpleasant task. "This is wrong. We must not—someone might enter the library at any moment."

She tried to stand, but he slid toward her and pulled her to him with one arm. He might never hold her again, and he would not relinquish her so easily. Rather than object, she leaned into his embrace.

"There is nothing wrong with this." Darcy used his free hand to gesture to the space between them. "With us." He did not dare give a name to the state of affairs between them. "This feud is not of our making. Why should we abide by it?"

Elizabeth glanced down at her hands. "I love my father. He is a good man." How Darcy wished he could say the same about his father! "He asks little of us, but he wants us to avoid you because he is trying to protect us."

"I would never hurt you," Darcy swore.

Elizabeth's eyes darted up to meet his. "I think you could hurt me more than anyone else." He shook his head in vehement denial, but Elizabeth hushed him with a finger to his lips. "Not deliberately, but I would be destroyed nonetheless."

"But—" Darcy began to formulate a vehement denial, but then he reflected on how easily she could destroy him—and fell silent.

"Are you hoping to convince me to agree to a courtship, Mr. Darcy?" The formality of her words stung after the intimacy they had just shared. "You yourself said we could not associate."

She is correct. In the aftermath of that spectacular kiss he had been consumed by his feelings. Never before had he been led by his heart, and it was the last thing he could allow now. He let out a long breath. "No. No, I am not. I simply wish things could be otherwise."

"As do I." She stood, straightening out the skirt of her dress.

Darcy stood as well but clasped his hands behind his back. "I should quit Netherfield." Her mouth opened to object, but he shook his head. "I cannot see you every day and not want you. It is…obscene…"

"We will return to Longbourn soon," Elizabeth murmured.

"Longbourn is still far too close."

She did not respond immediately but sighed. "I will miss you."

He closed his eyes, attempting to master his ragged breathing. "I pray you, Elizabeth, do not say such things. Those words undo me completely."

"I will not say it again," she whispered.

When he opened his eyes, she was gone.

***

Elizabeth helped Jane out of the carriage. Although she was still pale and had lost weight, her sister had recovered sufficiently that she was out of danger. Their father had been most eager to bring her home to finish her recuperation.

She dispatched Jane into the care of their father, who helped her up the stairs to their bedroom. Elizabeth could hear her mother fussing over Jane and directing the servants to do many (often contradictory) things at once.

Her father descended the stairs slowly, an ironic smile on his face. "So you survived six days at Netherfield, eh? Did Mr. Darcy find you any more tolerable when you left than when you arrived?"

Elizabeth hid her wince. Why had she ever shared Mr. Darcy's words with her family? At the time she had been angry, but her father hardly needed more reasons to hate Mr. Darcy. On the other hand, did it really matter what her father thought of the man? They would most likely never see him again.

"I do not know. He did not see fit to inform me." She attempted a version of her usual pert smile. "I hardly know what they said about me behind closed doors."

"True, true." Her father nodded his head.

"In any case, Mr. Darcy departed for London yesterday and is not likely to return to Netherfield." That, at least, was the complete truth.

"Did you take care not to be alone with him? He might take advantage of a pretty young woman."

"No! He is not like that at all. He has quite proper manners." *Most of the time*, she thought to herself, shivering a little at the memory of his kisses.

"Are you defending him?" Her father seemed not so much angry as hurt.

Elizabeth bit her lip, not wishing to lie to her father. "I am simply saying he does not seem the type to do such things. I daresay he is not like his father." At least this was not an outright lie. "And after all, I am not handsome enough to tempt him."

"Yes. I suppose you are hardly worth his trouble, a fine man like him." Sarcasm laced every word. "That is exactly what I would expect of George Darcy's son. Proud and unpleasant, eh?"

Elizabeth thought a silent prayer of forgiveness, but she did not want her father to believe Mr. Darcy had any interest in her; it would only cause him unwarranted anxiety. "I think many would call him proud and unpleasant."

Her father sighed in satisfaction. "Just as I thought."

Chapter Ten

A few days after her return to Longbourn, Elizabeth joined her sisters—all but Jane, who was still recovering—on a walk to Meryton. Despite the chill in the air, Elizabeth enjoyed the sun and the exercise. She had been confined for too long at Netherfield. And any activity was a welcome distraction from constant thoughts of Mr. Darcy.

In spite of the cold, Meryton's main square bustled with activity: people were strolling or buying food and other necessities. Lydia eagerly surveyed the crowd, no doubt hoping to see an officer or two, a favorite activity since the militia's arrival in the neighborhood. She exclaimed, "Oh, there's Denny!" Elizabeth looked where her sister pointed and saw the man himself and a companion peering into a shop window.

"Who is that with him?" Kitty asked, blinking in the bright sunshine.

"Let us inquire." Lydia darted forward with Kitty only a step behind. Mary and Elizabeth followed at a slower pace. Although Elizabeth was happy to converse with the soldiers, she did not share Lydia's eagerness.

Mr. Denny gave a courtly bow to the ladies, a bright smile on his face. "Well met! May I introduce you to Mr. Wickham? I am happy to say he has accepted a commission in our corps."

At these words, Elizabeth took a closer look at his companion. It was the same man who had attempted to seduce Mr. Darcy's sister! As Mr. Denny introduced the Bennet sisters, Elizabeth schooled her features into a semblance of a smile, reminding herself that Mr. Wickham could not possibly recognize her. She had worn a mask, and the garden had been dimly lit. Mr. Wickham had *not* been disguised; his identity was certain. He had no business conversing with honorable citizens of

Hertfordshire, but she could say nothing. How could she explain her knowledge of his past misdeeds?

At that moment, Mr. Bingley rode by on his horse and nodded a cordial good day to the Bennet sisters. Elizabeth winced when Lydia remarked that at least "that odious Mr. Darcy" was no longer in residence at Netherfield.

"Mr. Darcy? Of Pemberley? I have been acquainted with the family since my childhood," Mr. Wickham remarked.

Elizabeth bristled. She did not know their entire history, but no words from Mr. Wickham could be trusted.

"He is not at all liked in Meryton," Kitty observed. Elizabeth bit her tongue.

"What is the Darcy family like?" Lydia asked, excited for some gossip.

Elizabeth cast about for a way to curtail the conversation, which she was certain would not reflect well on Mr. Darcy, but she could not reveal more than a passing acquaintance with him.

Instead she was forced to listen as Mr. Wickham spun a story about being raised as the son of Pemberley's steward and how Mr. George Darcy had promised him the living at Kympton when it fell vacant. However, when the opportunity presented itself, the younger Mr. Darcy persuaded his father to give the valuable living to someone else, so Mr. Wickham was left to make his way in the world as best he could.

"What a shocking tale!" Kitty exclaimed. "I had not thought Mr. Darcy as bad as all that."

"But at least your past has brought you to Meryton and to meet us!" Lydia was not one to overlook any story's pertinence to herself.

If only Elizabeth could draw attention to the gaps in his narrative and the impropriety of telling such a tale to near strangers. Yet doing so risked creating suspicions that she favored Mr. Darcy.

"You must dine with us and tell your story to Papa!" Lydia declared. "He heartily dislikes the Darcy family and would be very interested. We will laugh at them and have a very merry time!"

It was akin to observing an imminent carriage accident—and being helpless to prevent it. Elizabeth dug her nails into the palm of her hand and said nothing while Mr. Wickham produced a practiced smile. "That would be wonderful. We would love to join your family for dinner."

***

Elizabeth was not anticipating the Netherfield ball with any degree of pleasure. She should be grateful for Mr. Darcy's absence; nonetheless, she found herself wishing she could catch one more glimpse of his face. Instead she was promised for the first dance to her odious cousin, Mr. Collins, who had been smirking and simpering opposite her in the carriage all the way to the ball. He had been visiting Longbourn for several days, and she was heartily sick of his pompous pronouncements and endless chatter about the glories of Rosings Park, the home of his esteemed patroness, the Lady Catherine de Bourgh.

In addition to the joys of dancing with Mr. Collins, Elizabeth could also anticipate a dance with Mr. Wickham. He had hinted at his interest in her when he dined at Longbourn a week ago, and the coolness of her response did not deter him. The thought of standing up with either man made her skin crawl. *At least I may wear gloves when I touch them.*

After Mr. Wickham and Mr. Denny had dined at Longbourn, Elizabeth had attempted to persuade her father to discontinue the acquaintance, noting the numerous inconsistencies in Wickham's stories. But her father had not listened. Mr. Wickham spoke ill of the Darcys, and that was enough recommendation for Mr. Bennet.

Elizabeth had likewise warned her younger sisters about the man's unscrupulous nature, but they dismissed her cautions. Mr. Wickham was charming and well-liked in Meryton; the Bennet daughters were flattered by his attentions. The rest of Meryton reveled in stories about his ill treatment at Mr. Darcy's hands and sighed over his charm and good looks. Elizabeth would have had as much luck holding back the tide.

At least Jane had completely recovered from her illness and was bright-eyed and eager to see Mr. Bingley again. Elizabeth prayed that her family's feud with the Darcys would not interfere with her sister's future happiness. One of them deserved to be lucky in love.

The night began as miserably as she expected, with Mr. Collins making a fool of himself (and Elizabeth) during the very first set. With the innate grace God gave a donkey, he turned the wrong way twice in one dance.

Elizabeth would have liked some time to recover from this disaster, but as Mr. Collins led her from the dance floor, Mr. Wickham appeared to partner her for the next dance. Unable to think of a suitable excuse, she was thus forced to stand up with yet another man she disliked. At least Mr. Wickham was an accomplished dancer and maintained a steady flow of amiable conversation. Without prior knowledge of the deceitful nature concealed beneath the man's good manners, Elizabeth might have believed he was as charming as he appeared.

When the set was finished, Mr. Wickham did not relinquish her hand, but he held it tightly and stood a bit too close to her for propriety's sake. Elizabeth longed to be quit of the scoundrel; however, she had noticed him exchanging flirtatious glances with Lydia. It was better to have the man's attentions focused on her; at least she was safe from his "charms."

As they walked away from the other dancers, she forced herself to laugh in response to one of his witticisms. He invited her to take a drink of lemonade with him, and Elizabeth mustered an outwardly enthusiastic reply. However, the path to the lemonade table was unexpectedly obstructed by a tall figure. Elizabeth was shocked to see Mr. Darcy.

Mr. Wickham was equally surprised. "Darcy!" he spluttered. "I-I did not think you were in attendance."

"My horse threw a shoe on the way from London, or I would have arrived earlier." Mr. Darcy was an imposing sight, looming over the other man by several inches. Elizabeth's heart sank. *Would he be angry I danced with Mr. Wickham? Does he understand I would never trust the man?* All his attention was focused on the other man; he seemed to avoid Elizabeth's gaze.

Mr. Wickham produced a rather mocking smile and pulled her a little closer to him. "How fortunate that you arrived in time to enjoy the festivities." His tone managed to suggest the exact opposite. "I was about to enjoy some lemonade with one of those Bennets your family so loves to hate." Mr. Darcy's breath hissed through his teeth.

Elizabeth's mind was a blank. *Where are my wits when I need them?* She had never been in a more uncomfortable position. She did not wish to accompany Mr. Wickham anywhere, particularly in Mr. Darcy's presence. But how could she politely decline an invitation she had just accepted?

"Even Miss Bennet does not deserve you," Mr. Darcy spat. He turned to Elizabeth, his face a perfectly blank mask that suggested he fought his own distaste. "Would you do the honor of accompanying me for the next set?" He held out his hand.

Elizabeth was a tangle of conflicting impulses. Ever since the night of the masquerade, she had wanted to dance with Mr. Darcy again. But it had felt like a betrayal of her father. On the other hand, Mr. Darcy's well-known dislike of Mr. Wickham would make rivalry appear to be the reason for the request.

Finally, desire won out, and Elizabeth firmly disengaged her hand from Mr. Wickham's to rest it in Mr. Darcy's. "It would be my pleasure." She kept her face blank. If she appeared too delighted, it might raise suspicions.

Mr. Wickham regarded Mr. Darcy with narrowed eyes and a clenched jaw but made no protest. Indeed, there was nothing he *could* say. Mr. Darcy's lips curved into a brief smile, which disappeared immediately. But a slight loosening of his shoulders conveyed his pleasure.

Without another glance at Mr. Wickham, Mr. Darcy led Elizabeth into position for the next set. Elizabeth longed for an opportunity to speak privately with him, but they were surrounded by other dancers. His face could be carved from stone. Was he angry with her?

The music commenced, and they came together as he turned her in a circle. His voice was hard, uncompromising. "It is dangerous to dance with Wickham."

"Not my choice, I assure you. I remember him well from the night of the masquerade." She kept her voice low.

His shoulders lowered a fraction, and the furrow between his brows disappeared. "I am pleased you are one person he cannot fool."

They parted and returned to their respective lines, but he seemed somewhat more relaxed. They came together again. "Everyone here is quite taken with him," she murmured. "I could not refuse him without raising suspicions."

Mr. Darcy said, "Yes, Mr. Wickham is very adept at making friends. Whether he is capable of keeping them is another matter." Elizabeth knew the truth of these words, but she kept her face neutral.

The dance brought them together again, and he stepped very close to her. "Watching you dance with him aroused…unfamiliar emotions in me. I wished to do violence to him." His face remained serene, but the words were uttered with great vehemence. Anyone watching would not guess the passion behind his utterances.

As they parted again, Elizabeth thought of how to respond without provoking others' suspicions. "Violence is entirely unnecessary. I assure you my sentiments in this regard are quite fixed and cannot be altered."

"I am pleased to hear it," he responded without inflection.

As Elizabeth's eyes traveled around the ballroom, she realized their dance had attracted quite a bit of attention. No doubt many in Meryton were now aware of the feud between the Darcys and the Bennets. Their dance would undoubtedly be a subject for gossip for days. Mr. Wickham stood near the doorway, an amiable expression now firmly in place, but his eyes narrowed when they drifted over Mr. Darcy.

Someone must have summoned her father from the card room, for he was watching with a scowl. Beside him, Elizabeth's mother was wringing her hands as if observing a terrible house fire. Charlotte Lucas's hand covered her mouth. Was she worried that Elizabeth had somehow been coerced into dancing with Mr. Darcy? Fortunately, nobody knew how much she was enjoying it! Not for the first time, Elizabeth found herself desperately wishing things could be different. If their families had not shared this painful history perhaps they could have met and formed an attachment with no other obstacles blocking their path.

She gave Mr. Darcy a smile as they once more turned in a circle. "I believed you had quit the neighborhood."

"I had, but then a letter from Bingley happened to mention Wickham's presence." Pulling her a little closer than strict propriety would allow, Mr. Darcy whispered in her ear. "I feared the worst, knowing the blackguard was near you."

Elizabeth warmed at the knowledge that he still cared for her and wished to protect her—no matter how unnecessary the sentiment was. "I do not desire his friendship, and he has bestowed it most unwillingly."

"I trust you, but him not at all."

The dance ended, and Mr. Darcy took her hand to escort her from the dance floor. They were immediately met by her father, who was accompanied by Charlotte's younger brother, while Elizabeth's mother hovered in the background. Mr. Bennet did not spare a glance for Mr. Darcy. "Lizzy, I believe James Lucas would like to dance with you."

Mr. Lucas had the grace to look somewhat embarrassed. No doubt he had been summarily recruited for this task. "Y-Yes, indeed, Miss Elizabeth. I-If you would do me the honor," the young man stammered.

"It would be my pleasure," Elizabeth assured him. Her father's presence made it impossible to continue a conversation with Mr. Darcy, so Charlotte's brother would do as well as anyone.

Darcy took her hand and kissed it gently. "Thank you for a most pleasurable set. I hope we may dance again." His eyes sparkled. He knew he was playing with fire to act thus with her father's eyes on them.

"Thank you, Mr. Darcy," she replied.

Without acknowledging her parents, Darcy disappeared into the crowd.

"What is that man playing at?" Mr. Bennet demanded, a deep scowl etched on his face.

He could not suspect Mr. Darcy's true sentiments. "I believe he asked me to dance merely to pique Mr. Wickham. They do not get on at all."

Her father's face relaxed somewhat. "Ah. So I have heard."

"I hope that man was not too unpleasant to you, Lizzy!" her mother exclaimed rather more loudly than necessary.

"Not at all. He was a perfect gentleman," she responded.

"A Darcy?" Her father's eyebrows lifted. Elizabeth wanted to scream with impatience; her father believed the scoundrel Wickham and granted no credence to an honorable man like Mr. Darcy.

"What did he say to you?" her mother asked breathlessly.

"He warned me not to believe all that Mr. Wickham says."

Her father snorted. "And we should listen to a Darcy? What an amusing idea!"

Elizabeth could find no suitable rejoinder, and soon Mr. Lucas claimed her hand for the next dance.

***

Elizabeth was his lodestone. No matter where Darcy stood in Netherfield's ballroom, he could not prevent his eyes from being drawn to the sight of Elizabeth dancing with Sir William's son. Even during a brief conversation with Bingley, he found his gaze fixing on her. Bingley was soon called away. Darcy should find a partner for the next set, but anyone else would be an inadequate substitute for Elizabeth. The thought of standing up with Miss Bingley made his stomach roil with nausea.

These two weeks without Elizabeth had been quite empty and dull. He had thought it torture before to know she existed but not where to find her. Now he knew her name *and* the impossibility of any courtship. However, being apart from her had not provided any kind of solution.

Only her presence could assuage this new pain—the pain of separation.

He clenched his fists as Elizabeth smiled at her partner. *She does not smile at him the way she smiles at me*, he reassured himself. Lucas did not receive the sly grin that made her eyes sparkle but rather a polite curving of the lips. Although she appeared to find Lucas more pleasing than the buffoonish clergyman she had partnered when Darcy had first arrived.

Returning to Netherfield had been a bad idea. He had planned to attend the ball, reassure himself that Elizabeth was safe from Wickham, and return to London. The trip would give him an opportunity to glimpse her, but the public nature of their meeting would preclude the risks of revealing their feelings. At least that had been the theory.

The minute he saw Wickham dancing with her, Darcy's plans flew out of the window. For the entire set, he had suppressed a desire to interrupt the dance and tear Wickham's hand from hers. The thought that Wickham was filling Elizabeth's head with poison and lies caused his stomach to lurch and twist. What a relief that she disbelieved Wickham's calumny!

Darcy admired the grace in Elizabeth's steps as the Lucas whelp twirled her around. If only he could enjoy another dance with her, but it was impossible. One dance could be explained by a desire to vex Wickham, but a second would betray a true interest. Damnation! Not for the first time he silently cursed a father whose temper and questionable morality had such far-reaching consequences for his only son.

Elizabeth is still smiling at her dance partner. Darcy caught movement from the corner of his eye; Hurst had emerged from the card room. Blast! If the man suspected anything he would write to Darcy's father immediately. On the other side of the room, Mr. Bennet glared at Darcy distrustfully as if he might disrupt Elizabeth's dance with Lucas. His father's legacy followed him everywhere.

Darcy ran his hands through his dark curls, abruptly wearied of the entire farce. If only he could take Elizabeth to some distant land where no one knew the Darcys or Bennets. Finally, he turned his back on the sight of dancing couples and went in search of some brandy.

Chapter Eleven

During the day following the ball, the Bennet household was alive with the sounds of merriment. Kitty and Lydia could talk of nothing else. Kitty had danced with Denny twice and Wickham once. Lydia had danced with each man twice and thought it quite a triumph with which to taunt her sisters. Mary pontificated about how she did not care to dance while Jane drifted through the house on a cloud of happiness about Mr. Bingley's attentions to her. Everyone questioned Elizabeth about Mr. Darcy's surprising invitation to dance, but she merely reiterated that he disliked Mr. Wickham and had been a gentleman while they danced.

In private moments, she could not help recalling the way his body had brushed against hers as they danced or how his fingers had briefly touched her waist. If only she could talk to someone about it! She considered confiding in Jane, who at least would promise her secrecy, but such a confidence would distress her. And Elizabeth would do nothing to dampen Jane's recent high spirits.

Unfortunately, as the day wore on it became apparent that Elizabeth's mother had another purpose entirely: a private conversation between Elizabeth and Mr. Collins. Elizabeth suspected the subject of this putative conversation and desired to avoid it above all else. Such a discourse could not go well for either party. Elizabeth indulged the hope that if she were unavailable indefinitely, Mr. Collins might abandon his plans altogether.

She had passed most of the day in the room she shared with Jane, knowing Mr. Collins would not intrude. But she finally wearied of reading and succumbed to the call of the outdoors. Quickly grabbing her pelisse, she set a brisk pace through the hallway to the front door, hoping no one would note her passage.

As she reached the road and proceeded away from town, she believed she had managed to escape. However, she soon heard footsteps following her. It could be anyone: Kitty or Jane or Charlotte Lucas—or someone wholly unconnected to Elizabeth. Nonetheless, fearing the worst, she elected not to glance back and instead quickened her pace. After a minute, she heard the distinctive sounds of someone panting with excessive exertion, adding fuel to her deepest fears.

Lengthening her stride, she was able to outpace her pursuer when unfortunately her boot lace came undone, and she tripped, almost falling. Elizabeth caught herself but was forced to stop and tie her lace. Never before in her life had she been more tempted to utter an oath. Soon her pursuer pounced, much like a lion attacking its prey.

"Cousin Elizabeth!" Mr. Collins exclaimed in between pants. "I have been seeking an opportunity to speak with you alone."

Elizabeth sighed and turned toward him. "Good day, Mr. Collins, are you out for a stroll as well?" She suppressed a smile, for "stroll" hardly described her mad dash away from Longbourn.

Mr. Collins fanned his red face with his wide-brimmed hat. "Er, yes. But I had something particular I wished to discuss with you."

Elizabeth finished tying her lace and resumed walking. Perhaps Mr. Collins would give up from sheer exhaustion. "Can it not wait until I return to Longbourn?" *Or perhaps when pigs fly?*

"It is of the utmost urgency!" He gasped for breath. "Might you slow your pace a bit, Cousin? I find it difficult to walk and talk at once." Although that was the point, Elizabeth slowed her speed.

Mr. Collins wheezed a couple more breaths. "It is the dearest wish of my patroness, Lady Catherine de

Bourgh, that I take a wife. And I believe matrimony to be an eminently suitable state for a man in my position."

Elizabeth nodded but made no response.

"Lady Catherine herself condescended to give me advice on the matter. 'Let the woman not be brought up too high for my sake, and for yours she should be a practical sort of woman. Bring her back to the parsonage, and I shall visit her!'"

Here he paused, perhaps expecting Elizabeth to express excitement or gratitude at the thought of Lady Catherine gracing her future home.

Elizabeth bit her lip and said nothing.

"Now as to my particular choice. I long ago decided to choose my wife from among your father's most amiable daughters. I am aware that your portion is not large, but rest assured that no censure on that score will pass my lips once we are married."

"That is very good of you, sir," Elizabeth murmured, wondering why he would mention it at all.

"Yes, indeed." Mr. Collins mopped his brow with a handkerchief. "Therefore, nothing remains for me but to assure you of my most violent affections and ask that you make me the happiest of men!"

Elizabeth had not slowed her pace and was taken aback when Mr. Collins abruptly disappeared from her side. She stopped and turned around, noticing him some three feet back where he was bent on one knee at the side of the road. Should she return to where he knelt and thereby draw attention to the fact that she had not noticed his gesture at first? Or should she pretend not to notice that he was fruitlessly kneeling in the dirt?

While she debated this question, Mr. Collins solved the dilemma by standing (a bit stiffly), crossing the distance between them, and then sinking to his knee once again at her feet.

Now I cannot avoid responding to his proposal, Elizabeth thought in dismay. "I thank you for the honor of your address, Mr. Collins, but it is impossible for me to accept your offer."

Mr. Collins smiled at her. Smiled? "I know it is often the way of elegant females that they first refuse a man they secretly plan to accept."

Oh, Good Lord! Now she must convince the man that she was sincere in her refusal. "I assure you, sir, that I have no pretensions that would consist of tormenting a respectable man."

He blinked several times. "But surely you cannot be sincere."

He thinks very highly of himself indeed. "You could not make me happy, and I am the last person in the world who could make you happy."

He gaped at her. "Need I remind you of your position in life? Your family's precarious situation?"

That was enough. Elizabeth resumed stalking down the road. She did not need reminders of the difficulties her family would face upon her father's death, and she had provided Mr. Collins with all the civility he was due. Noises behind her suggested that Mr. Collins was scrambling to his feet and following her. What would it take to make him recognize a lost cause?

She hurried toward a sharp bend in the road, but Mr. Collins's voice followed her. "It is by no means certain that another offer of marriage will ever be made to you!" *Really, was it possible for him to be more insulting?*

Suddenly, she was face-to-face with Mr. Darcy, who had been traveling in the opposite direction. She arrested her progress, stunned to be confronted with this man at the least opportune time. Had he heard Mr. Collins's shout? How mortifying!

His face was red. Was he angry with her for entertaining a marriage proposal? Oh, but Mr. Darcy's glare was aimed over her shoulder.

Mr. Collins swiftly caught up with them. "You must pardon me, Mr. Collins, but would you care to repeat what you just said to Miss Elizabeth? I did not quite catch it." Mr. Darcy's voice was frosty.

"Mr. Darcy! How wonderful to meet you. Our conversation yesterday about Rosings Park was unfortunately cut short." All thoughts of engaging Elizabeth's affections were apparently forgotten in the face of an opportunity to speak with Lady Catherine's nephew.

Mr. Darcy's face was stony. "Would you please repeat what you said to Miss Elizabeth?"

Mr. Collins blinked rapidly. "Merely that she might never receive another proposal of marriage." He seemed completely unaware of having given any offense.

"Why would you say such a thing to a lady of a good family?" Mr. Darcy's voice was calm, but a muscle in his cheek twitched.

Unaware that he was digging a deeper hole for himself, Mr. Collins smiled ingratiatingly. "We were speaking about my marriage proposal to her."

Mr. Darcy regarded the other man as if he were something found on the bottom of his boot. "You were discussing the possibility that she might marry *you*?" He turned an incredulous look on Elizabeth, therefore missing the moment when Mr. Collins's face registered the possibility he might have miscalculated.

She hoped Mr. Darcy did not believe she sought out her cousin's affection. "Mr. Collins will inherit Longbourn upon my father's death. He wishes to choose a wife from among his daughters," she explained.

"And he chose *you*?" His tone was so disbelieving that for a moment Elizabeth wondered if Mr. Darcy thought she was unsuitable to marry even a lowly clergyman. Then she noticed how Mr. Darcy trembled with barely contained emotion. "Do you wish to marry him?" His face was so pale that Elizabeth wished she could give him a reassuring hug.

"No," she said firmly and was pleased to see the tension drain out of Mr. Darcy's body. "But Mr. Collins has been attempting to persuade me otherwise." At these words, Mr. Darcy's mouth set in a grim line.

"Why do you believe you deserve such a prize?" he demanded of the clergyman.

"As you know, my patroness, Lady Catherine de Bourgh—"

Mr. Darcy had no patience for this argument. "Your connection with my aunt is yet another reason Miss Elizabeth should avoid anything resembling a betrothal to you. She would make Elizabeth's life thoroughly unpleasant." Elizabeth hoped Mr. Collins was too befuddled by Mr. Darcy's attack to notice his use of her Christian name.

Mr. Darcy took another step closer to the parson, now looming over the man. "Let me make one thing clear: this match to which you presume cannot happen. This woman will not be your wife. You must turn your marital ambitions elsewhere. Do you understand?"

Mr. Collins swallowed and licked his lips. "Y-Yes, of course." He nodded vigorously.

"You will cease pestering Miss Elizabeth?" Mr. Darcy asked.

Mr. Collins, his head bobbing up and down, took a step backward, away from Mr. Darcy. "Yes, yes, of course!"

Mr. Darcy gave one brisk, satisfied nod. "I am pleased we understand each other. You may go."

Apparently not considering for one second whether Mr. Darcy had the authority to dismiss him, Mr. Collins turned and scurried around the bend in the direction of

Longbourn.

***

Darcy sighed with relief at the sight of Collins's retreating back. Absent any true power over the man, he had hoped that his station in life and connection to Lady Catherine would be sufficient to intimidate Mr. Collins. Apparently he had been correct.

Elizabeth had covered her mouth with her hand, her eyes wide. Had he overstepped? Was she appalled at his treatment of the clergyman? Then a chuckle emerged from behind her hand, and she shook with laughter. "He may not stop until he reaches Kent!" she said, her eyes dancing.

Darcy was pleased to see her so amused by a potentially distressing situation. "Whenever I leave you alone, unwanted men are insistently seeking your company. Perhaps you need a chaperone." This sally made her laugh all the more.

Finally, her laughter died away, and she regarded him seriously. "Will word of your behavior with him somehow reach your father?"

Darcy stroked his chin. "He does not know my father and is unlikely to initiate such a conversation on this topic with my aunt. Lady Catherine wishes me to wed her daughter, my cousin Anne." Elizabeth's face paled at these words. "I will not do so," he rushed to reassure her. "But Mr. Collins no doubt knows of my aunt's ambitions and would not wish to inform her that I might have other interests."

He surveyed the area to ensure they were unobserved, then stepped closer, stroking her cheek with his hand. "Unfortunately, this changes nothing between us." She nodded. "We must still profess indifference to each other."

Elizabeth swallowed. "I know."

"Would that it were different..." He held her eyes, wishing he dared to kiss her again.

She stepped away from him. "You were coming to Longbourn?"

"Yes," he responded. "Of course, I did not intend to call on your family, but I was hoping for a way to get a message to you. The entire party is leaving Netherfield for Town today." Her eyes widened. "Miss Bingley has succeeded in convincing her brother that your sister does not care for him and is only receptive to his advances because of your mother's interest in his fortune."

Elizabeth gaped. "That is not true!"

Darcy nodded sadly. "I know. I questioned the decision, but I cannot take your family's part too overtly. Once we are in London, I will speak with Bingley privately and encourage him to return to Netherfield. But for the moment, his sister's influence is too strong."

Tears formed in Elizabeth's eyes. What a caring creature she was! How could anyone object to his marrying this woman?

"I would like to tell you when—if— I will see you again, but with Bingley gone from Netherfield, I cannot visit Hertfordshire without suspicion."

She nodded, her eyes downcast. "It is for the best, Mr. Darcy." He longed to ask her to address him by his given name just so he could hear it once from her lips. "It would be better if we do not see each other again."

His head told him that she was right, but his heart ached. He could not tear his eyes from her face. "You may be correct. Whenever we are together, I can barely restrain my impulse to do this." He took a bold step toward her and reached out with one hand to tilt her head up so she could receive his kiss. *This is a terrible idea,* he thought even as his lips descended. The more frequently he kissed her, the more he grew addicted to the sensations.

But then their lips met, and any reservations melted away.

***

Elizabeth was drowning, and she loved it. Mr. Darcy's scent, his taste, his touch filled her senses until she could think of nothing but him. The small voice of protest—of reason—was easily quelled by the parts of her that pleaded for more kisses, more touches, more Mr. Darcy.

But after a minute, her reason reasserted itself. They were on a public road; anyone might stumble across them. No, she must end it, for he obviously did not have the self-control.

Finally, she pulled herself from his grasp. "I am honored by your attentions, sir." She hated the necessary formality of her tone. "But anything further between us is impossible."

His brows knit together. "Surely there is something we could—"

She shook her head emphatically. "Our families hate each other—"

"But you know you may trust me," Darcy said.

She glanced down at her hands. "It is not a matter of trust. You could hurt me by simply being seen with me. And you could be accused of compromising my reputation."

"I would not care for such accusations although the compromising might be enjoyable." His eyes twinkled at her.

"Mr. Darcy!" she exclaimed although she was less scandalized by his suggestion than she should be. If his lips could ignite a fire within her, how would it feel to have his *hands* on her body, touching her everywhere…intimately? She stared at her feet, hoping he would not notice her blush.

He moved toward her very deliberately. "I cannot leave you alone, Elizabeth. I have attempted to treat you as a common and indifferent acquaintance, but I cannot." He took another step toward her. She should back away, but her feet were immobilized. "When I am in your presence, my mind is consumed with thoughts of your kisses, the sound of your laughter, the tilt of your chin when you challenge me. When I am away from you, I can only dream about when I will return to your presence."

Elizabeth's breath caught. Was he declaring his love? The thought was thrilling, but it was quickly dashed by reality as cold as a bucket of water. She held up a hand to prevent him from coming closer. "You cannot say such things. We cannot even contemplate a friendship between us. It is utterly impossible."

His voice took on a pleading tone. "The feud is solely between our fathers. It should not—"

She interrupted. "No. There is blind prejudice on both sides. My father will not credit any words about your true character."

Mr. Darcy took both her hands in his. "To hell with our fathers. We can run away to Gretna Green. Once we are married they can do nothing."

Elizabeth gasped. He was truly suggesting eloping! She indulged in a moment of fantasy: rushing to Scotland, saying vows, kissing Mr. Darcy freely, living with him in a fine townhouse in London. But all too quickly she had to dismiss this delightful vision and stiffen her resolve.

She pulled her hands from his grasp. "Do not speak so, I pray you, Mr. Darcy. We cannot even think of such things!"

He was truly at a loss. "But why—?"

"My father has warned us many times about you. He believes you might plan to compromise one of his daughters. Ruin us in the eyes of society to further your father's aims."

Darcy recoiled as if she had struck him. "I would never do such a thing! Do you believe I could—?"

"Of course not." She soothed him with a hand on his arm. "I have put myself in your hands more than once. I would not have trusted you if I thought you might be a threat." Mr. Darcy's shoulders relaxed marginally. "But my father expects deceit and treachery from you. If we eloped, it would only confirm his worst fears."

"But I would offer you marriage, not ruination."

She bit her lip. "My father would consider me ruined."

He gave her an anguished look and then turned his gaze to the fields surrounding the road. "How could he believe I might be capable of such—?" The man's voice was strangled. "Is there nothing I may do to persuade him differently?"

Every part of Elizabeth's body longed to reach out to him, embrace him, and assuage his pain. She wrapped her arms around her waist, preventing herself from moving. "Do you know how the feud between our families began?" she asked.

Only his back was visible, but his head shook. "My father has quarreled with so many people that I no longer wonder at it. I wonder, rather, about those people who actually remain friends with him." His voice was bitter. "Although his hatred of your father is particularly virulent."

It must be horrible to have such a father. Mr. Darcy did not deserve to live in that man's shadow.

Elizabeth knew the story would cause Mr. Darcy pain, but secrecy did not serve him well. "They attended Cambridge together," she said.

"I knew that much." He faced her but did not move closer.

"I do not believe they were ever friends, but one night in the pub, some students were boasting of their academic achievements. The evening ended with a wager between your father and mine about who would take a first in history."

"A wager." Mr. Darcy bit off the word.

"Do you doubt the story?"

"Not at all. My father has made many foolish bets in his life. Nor do I doubt the outcome. We have a handsome library at Pemberley, but my father is hardly a scholar. He lost?"

Elizabeth nodded. "My father was young and admits to having taunted your father with his loss. But the Darcy name was well known at Cambridge, and your father had a group of friends who would do his bidding. They concocted a scheme whereby they made it seem that Papa had cheated in the examination." Darcy winced as if the information pained him. "He lost his award and was sent down from Cambridge in disgrace."

Mr. Darcy's fingers pinched the bridge of his nose. "I am so sorry."

"It did not end there. Papa went to live in his father's London townhouse. A friend introduced him to a young woman he took an interest in, Anna Fitzwilliam."

Mr. Darcy closed his eyes and his mouth tightened. "My mother." No doubt he suspected what happened next.

Elizabeth nodded. "Your father wanted her for himself."

"My father is nothing if not competitive, and my mother was very beautiful." Mr. Darcy was now rubbing his forehead.

"He and his friends would spread rumors about Papa—about all sorts of dissolute behavior: drunken routs, gambling, sleeping with other men's wives. Papa narrowly avoided being challenged to a duel. He protested his innocence to everyone, but the Darcy cabal, as he called them, were well connected and numerous. No one believed Thomas Bennet's word over theirs."

Mr. Darcy shook his head, his eyes fixed, staring at nothing. Elizabeth continued. "Miss Fitzwilliam spurned him, but the worst was that Papa's father believed the rumors. Eventually, he banished Papa to Hertfordshire and disinherited him." Mr. Darcy's head shot up, aghast. "Longbourn is entailed, so my father still inherited it. But his father left everything else, including his fortune and the house in London, to his other son, who gambled it away after their father died. It has ever been a struggle for my father to maintain Longbourn absent the rest of the fortune that was intended to help support it."

Mr. Darcy's face was pale with shock. "My father has reduced your family to their present state," he whispered in horror.

Elizabeth shrugged. "We have a good position in Meryton. No one here believes the old rumors. And my mother supplied a small income when he married her. We have a comfortable home and good neighbors. I would not complain."

Mr. Darcy was wide-eyed. "But it is not what you were entitled to—this is so much worse than I had imagined. I never thought my father capable of...no wonder your father does not trust me." He took a few faltering steps toward her. "I beg you to forgive my family and forgive me."

"*You* have done nothing that requires forgiveness," she insisted.

"Do not be so quick to absolve me. I should have learned the truth before I...I should not have presumed—"

"You did not presume anything," Elizabeth insisted. "I know you are nothing like your father."

"How can you even stand to look at me?" He retreated from her as if he feared he might inadvertently cause her harm. "I should never have imposed myself on you. I pray you, forgive me."

"You did not—!"

He shook his head over and over. "I will not burden you with my presence again. Please accept my best wishes for your future health."

With those words, he turned on his heel and strode away so rapidly that he was soon lost to sight.

Chapter Twelve

"Welcome to Darcy House, Father."

His son's words caused George Darcy's lips to flatten into a thin line. He might have virtually conceded the use of the house in Town to Fitzwilliam, but he was still the owner; he did not need to be welcomed to his own house. Nevertheless, he bit back an angry retort. He and his son were at odds often enough; he needed to pick his battles carefully. And Fitzwilliam did not appear at all happy to see him.

"Thank you," the elder Darcy replied as they shook hands rather like two acquaintances than like father and son. He took the opportunity to inspect the front hallway of his house. It was spotless, not a speck of dirt or flake of paint to be found. Fresh flowers graced the table at the foot of the grand staircase. He was forced to concede that Fitzwilliam did a good job of managing the staff. Still…the décor was a little out of date. Perhaps it was time to redecorate. Although George Darcy personally cared nothing for the house's appearance, Darcy House must continue to set a standard for elegance in London.

"Did you have a pleasant trip?" Fitzwilliam inquired.

"It was adequate. The quality of posting inns has declined since my youth."

His son nodded but did not respond. Fitzwilliam had dark circles under his eyes and appeared to have lost some weight. Was there something wrong with him? George Darcy immediately dismissed the idea; his son was in the prime of life. How could he possibly be ill?

"How did you enjoy your recent travels?" George Darcy asked. "Did you find Hertfordshire pleasant?"

Fitzwilliam stiffened slightly, a reaction that would have gone unnoticed by someone who did not know his son very well. *Interesting. There is something there. What happened in Hertfordshire?*

"It was very pleasant," Fitzwilliam responded, a calm mask now falling over his features. "Bingley has a handsome house."

George Darcy allowed his disdain to show on his face. He did not care for the company his son kept. Bingley's family fortune was from trade, and his lineage boasted no ancestors of distinction.

Fitzwilliam's eyebrow arched, daring his father to object. His son's friends were a frequent subject of disagreement, but not today. George Darcy refused to rise to the bait.

After a long silence, Fitzwilliam cleared his throat as his gaze moved from his father to the stairs. "I am sure you would like a chance to refresh yourself after such a long journey. Dinner is at seven."

"I prefer it to be at six."

Fitzwilliam's head snapped back to his father's, his eyes fixed. "We eat at seven at Pemberley."

"I prefer tonight's dinner to be at six," George Darcy repeated. He did not give a reason. Darcy House was his; Fitzwilliam could not be allowed to forget it.

Fitzwilliam inclined his head very slightly. "Very well, six. I will make sure the cook is informed." He turned smartly and disappeared down the hallway.

Darcy senior smiled. He had won the first round.

He gestured his footman to follow with his valise and ascended the grand, marble-clad staircase. At the top of the stairs, George Darcy turned left for the suite of rooms belonging to the master of the house.

The footman opened the door to the bedchamber for him. He noted with satisfaction that his trunk had already been brought up from the carriage and that Wilkins, his valet when at Darcy House, awaited him. Darcy dismissed the footman and seated himself in a chair by the room's fireplace.

Wilkins bowed. "Would you like to dress for dinner, sir?"

"In a minute. First I would like to hear your report."

Wilkins grimaced. "I don't have much, sir. You know the young sir always keeps his own counsel."

Darcy scowled. "You share the same damned house! Surely you have learned something. Visits to a brothel, gambling, drinking?" Darcy himself had practiced all three in great quantities when he was Fitzwilliam's age. "He is not a monk, God damn it!"

Obviously his son was simply being overly discreet. There was some secret—an indiscretion or misstep. When Darcy discovered what, then he would have more leverage against Fitzwilliam. The younger Darcy was growing too independent. His father needed to clip his wings.

Wilkins scratched his head. "No whoring or gambling. In truth, he is here most nights. He doesn't even go out to balls and soirees much. But he…has been drinking more than usual since returning from Hertfordshire. Brandy and port in his study. The butler needs to keep refilling the decanter."

This was interesting…Fitzwilliam had always been a moderate imbiber. "Does he get foxed?"

Wilkins gave a thin smile. "Two or three nights the footmen have needed to help him to bed, if you know what I mean."

"And it started after his return from Hertfordshire?" Darcy asked.

Wilkins nodded. "Come to think of it, he hasn't been himself since then either. Mrs. Baker noticed it—and Jameson too. He's been all quiet like—well, quieter than usual. All brooding, Mrs. Baker calls it."

"Interesting…" Darcy remembered Fitzwilliam's gaunt appearance. Something had happened in Hertfordshire. Something that might prove to be his long-awaited leverage. "And you are unaware of the source of his malaise?"

Wilkins shrugged. "I took a glance at his correspondence when I had the chance. But he didn't say anything suspicious in his letters."

Hurst's reports from Hertfordshire had not hinted at any untoward incidents. Of course, Fitzwilliam disliked Hurst and would hardly confide in him. There could easily be something that Hurst did not know. An indiscretion with a local lass? Gambling losses? Perhaps he had struck someone in anger.

Hurst *had* written that Fitzwilliam had encountered that fool Thomas Bennet and his daughters but that Fitzwilliam disliked the family and avoided them. "Did Fitzwilliam say or write anything about the Bennet family? There is a father, Thomas, and five daughters."

Wilkins stroked his chin. "No. I don't remember aught about a Bennet family."

"Very well." George Darcy had other sources of information about his son's activities. He would discover what was troubling Fitzwilliam and make use of it.

***

For a few weeks after the Bingley party left Netherfield, Elizabeth held out hope that Mr. Darcy would convince Mr. Bingley to return to Hertfordshire, but hope waned as the house remained closed up. Jane received a letter from Caroline Bingley saying they would pass Christmas in Town. Jane tried valiantly to hide it, but Elizabeth knew how much her sister was hurting on the inside. She focused her efforts on distracting Jane in the hopes that it would help them both forget the absent men. But she had little success.

Mr. Collins did not renew his addresses to Elizabeth; in fact, he paled at the very sight of her. However, two days after his proposal to Elizabeth, it was announced that he had offered for Charlotte Lucas and been accepted. Elizabeth was surprised that her friend would settle for such a man, but when she visited Longbourn, Charlotte assured her that she was quite content with the arrangement and excited to have her own household. She also procured a promise from Elizabeth to visit her in Kent.

Otherwise life at Longbourn was rather dull. Elizabeth tried to keep busy with walks, visits to friends, and reading, but it was not enough to fully occupy her mind. She had resolved to think of Mr. Darcy no more...than once or twice a minute—which was a vast improvement over ten to fifteen times a minute.

Five times a day she wondered if she should have told Mr. Darcy the true story about their fathers, and five times she reassured herself that it had been the right decision. But that did not prevent the doubts from creeping in again. Occasionally, she found herself fantasizing about what would have happened if she had agreed to elope with Mr. Darcy. It was difficult not to imagine what it would be like to be kissed by the man or loved by him every day. What a charmed existence that would be! But she would remind herself that she had made her decision, and it was the correct one. In any case, Elizabeth would need to live with the consequences of that decision—right or wrong— for the rest of her life.

Eventually, Elizabeth was so desperate to escape her own thoughts that she eagerly anticipated her trip to Kent at Easter. Even Mr. Collins would provide a welcome distraction from her endless self-doubts and fantasies about what might have been. Hertfordshire was too full of memories about Mr. Darcy for Elizabeth's true happiness.

At least nothing at Hunsford Parsonage would remind her of him.

***

"Shall we call at the parsonage?" Richard inquired of his cousin.

Darcy patted his mount's neck to quiet the beast. "The parsonage? Whatever for?" He had been pleased to join his cousin for a ride around the grounds of Rosings Park—anything to escape his aunt and her overly baroque house. But the thought of Collins's simpering visage was enough to put Darcy off his dinner. Bad enough that he would encounter the man in his aunt's dining room. Any visit to Collins was likely to remind Darcy of Elizabeth, not that she was ever far from his thoughts. But Collins's face would recall those brief shining moments of happiness Darcy had enjoyed in Hertfordshire—and would emphasize to him how they were never to be repeated.

Of course, Darcy's memories of Collins were not, in the main, positive. What would have happened if he had not rescued Elizabeth from the clergyman's presumptuous proposal? Would he have bullied her into accepting?

"I have no desire to visit Collins!" Richard chuckled. "But he has a new wife. Someone he met during a recent visit to Hertfordshire."

Darcy froze in horror. Was it possible? Oh, Good Lord. He had quit Netherfield confident that he had thwarted Collins's designs on Elizabeth, but what if the man had returned to press his suit? What if her father had insisted on the match? Blast! Darcy should have stayed and protected her.

Darcy's horse danced restlessly, and he patted his neck to quiet him. He forced words out of a suddenly dry throat. "Do you know her name?"

Richard frowned. "No. Why does it matter?"

"She—" The words emerged as a croak. Darcy swallowed and tried again. "She may be an acquaintance—someone I met at Netherfield."

"So we shall pay a call and find out. Aunt Catherine said the wife has a friend visiting as well. An unmarried friend!" Richard gave a playful leer.

Darcy rolled his eyes. His cousin enjoyed playing the rake, but he mostly flirted with the ladies and rarely let anything go further.

A visit to the parsonage was now even less desirable. To visit and see Elizabeth married to that man and forever out of his grasp…it would be torture of the highest order. She might as well draw and quarter his heart.

However, postponing the visit would only allow Darcy more time to fret and worry. At least if they called now the worst would be over. If she was Mrs. Collins, he would need to invent some pressing business in Town—then get foxed as swiftly as possible. And stay foxed for at least a week. Yes, that was a plan. Not a good plan but at least a plan. And it would serve the purpose of leaving Hunsford behind as quickly as possible.

The thought of watching that oaf Collins even smile at Elizabeth made Darcy's stomach turn. If he put his hands on her—Darcy shuddered.

Why had he arisen from bed that morning? That had been his first mistake. But there was nothing for it. Best to get it over with. "Very well." Darcy pulled on the reins to direct his horse to the parsonage.

As they settled into a trot, he said a silent prayer. *Please let this wife be a stranger. Someone I have never met.* But in his heart, Darcy knew fate had been too cruel to him of late to now grant him a reprieve. It would be the crowning blow to see the woman who haunted his every waking dream married to that fool of a cleric.

As they were ushered down the parsonage's hallway, Darcy noticed that the hand holding his riding gloves was trembling. He took a deep breath, steeling himself for the worst. The maid showed them into the modest drawing room. The first sight that greeted him was Elizabeth on the settee. Oh, God! It was true! Darcy's stomach roiled, and he feared he would be sick. He took an involuntary step back as if he could somehow flee from the truth.

He could not drag his eyes from her face—which had gone from surprised to welcoming to perplexed. People spoke, but he could not hear anything over the great roaring in his ears as if he were standing under a waterfall. With great effort, he turned toward his cousin, who regarded him with a furrowed brow.

For some reason, Charlotte Lucas was standing next to Richard. Was she the friend visiting from Hertfordshire? But she was the one who had spoken, had she not? "Sorry?" Darcy inquired in her general direction, hoping this was an appropriate response.

Miss Lucas gave him a rather tentative smile. "Welcome to our home, Mr. Darcy." Darcy's thoughts moved sluggishly through the white-hot horror that clogged his brain. Why was *she* welcoming him? Was that not Elizabeth's place?

Then he noticed Miss Lucas was wearing the white cap of a married woman. Darcy whipped his head around and saw that Elizabeth's head was bare. Miss Lucas was the one who had married Collins! Relief washed over him like a cold bath, and his knees were suddenly too weak to support him. He sat abruptly in the nearest chair, hoping that Mrs. Collins had already invited them to take a seat.

***

What was wrong with Mr. Darcy? When he had first entered the room and seen Elizabeth's face, he had turned so white that she had feared he would lose consciousness. Had he been so shocked to find her at Hunsford? Was he now ashamed of his affection for her in Hertfordshire? Now that he was seated and drinking the tea that Charlotte had poured out, his color had returned, and he seemed more at ease. Yet he seemed incapable of tearing his eyes from her face.

Every time she raised her eyes from her embroidery, Mr. Darcy was observing her. When she noticed him, he always glanced away again, but his attention would drift back to her after a few minutes. Heat crept up her face; others would notice his interest if he was not more discreet! Fortunately, Mr. Collins was from home, and if Charlotte suspected anything, she would not reveal it. But Colonel Fitzwilliam was Mr. Darcy's cousin. Was he among those people who might report Mr. Darcy's actions to his father?

The conversation ebbed and flowed around them. Mr. Darcy said almost nothing, only responding to inquiries from his cousin and Charlotte. Elizabeth was nearly equally tongue tied, mortified, and made anxious by the weight of his regard. The preponderance of the discourse was carried by Colonel Fitzwilliam, who was an open and pleasant conversationalist.

Elizabeth did have occasion to inquire after Mr. Bingley and his sisters.

"They are very well," Mr. Darcy replied. "I had hopes of convincing Charles to visit Netherfield once more, but so far I have not been successful." His eyes held hers, encouraging her to understand what he could not say: he was endeavoring to reunite Mr. Bingley and Jane. Elizabeth gave a slight nod but did not pursue the subject.

More than once, Charlotte followed Mr. Darcy's gaze to Elizabeth. Her friend must notice the man's attention to her. At a break in the conversation, Charlotte suggested, "It is a lovely day. We could stroll in the garden."

Mr. Darcy rushed to his feet. "I thank you, no. I have business with my aunt's steward. We have tarried longer than we should."

The colonel frowned at his cousin but stood as well.

"I hope we will see you again. Perhaps at dinner at Rosings Park on Thursday," Charlotte said.

Mr. Darcy peered through the now open door and made no response. After a pause, the colonel responded in the affirmative and thanked her for her hospitality. Then both men were gone as swiftly as they had arrived, taking Elizabeth's good spirits with them.

Once the door was closed behind them, Elizabeth sank back into her chair, quite shaken by the unexpected visit. Charlotte turned to her friend with raised eyebrows. "I thought Mr. Darcy would take the opportunity to walk in the garden. He seemed so taken with you! But it appears my suggestion had the opposite of the intended effect."

The familiar anxiety seized Elizabeth. "He is not interested in me, Charlotte. He was simply brooding, and I happened to be seated opposite." Elizabeth regretted the necessity of misdirection, but Charlotte must not become caught up in the feud between their families. "If he felt any attraction, surely he would have seized the opportunity to spend more time with me." Elizabeth felt the truth of that statement most forcefully. Why had he not taken the opportunity to walk with her? It was an innocent enough activity. Had he lost interest?

"I suppose." Charlotte picked up her needlework. "He is a most puzzling man."

"I cannot dispute that."

Chapter Thirteen

Darcy strode away from the parsonage with Richard only a few paces behind. If he walked fast enough, perhaps he could mount his horse and be away before his cousin said—

"What was that about?"

Too late.

Darcy used his most forbidding tone. "I do not know what you mean." He carefully did not glance at his cousin as they reached their tethered horses.

Richard made an impatient gesture. "Do not feign ignorance. It does not suit you."

Darcy sighed. He should have known better than to attempt misdirection with his cousin. One hand on the saddle steadied him as he stared at the ground.

"Why on earth did you leave so impolitely?" Richard demanded. "That is not like you."

"It is nothing," Darcy muttered.

Richard snorted. "Is this the 'nothing' that has pushed you to imbibe more and eat less of late—and become short and snappish with those around you?"

Good Lord! Had his low spirits been so noticeable to everyone? "Please dispense with the flattery, Richard, and speak plainly." He quirked his lip at his cousin.

Richard waggled a finger at him. "Nay, you shall not distract me with jokes. What has you so unhappy?"

Darcy rubbed a hand over his face. Richard knew him too well. "I like Miss Bennet." Darcy's voice emerged low and hoarse.

"I like her as well. She is intelligent and a good conversationalist—" Richard stopped and blinked. "Oh! You *like* her." He clapped Darcy on his shoulder. "Well, that is wonderful, old man. It has taken you long enough."

"She is—" Darcy cleared his throat. "Do you recollect the woman I met at the Berwicks' masquerade? The mysterious Elizabeth?"

Richard gave a short laugh. "She is the same woman? What an extraordinary coincidence!"

Darcy did not move, continuing to stare at the ground, but he could feel Richard's eyes on him.

Richard coughed. "I must say you have an interesting wooing technique—rushing out of the room when invited for a stroll in the garden. I must remember it when I am next courting a lady."

Darcy's hands curled into fists. "I *cannot* woo her." Richard continued to stare. "Did you not notice her surname?"

"Bennet? What does it signify if—?"

Darcy slid his eyes sideways to witness the dawning realization on his cousin's face. "Oh! She is part of *that* Bennet family?"

"She is Thomas Bennet's daughter."

Richard whistled. "You never were one to take the easy path. Does your father know?"

"Hurst undoubtedly reported that I encountered the Bennet family in Hertfordshire, but I was very careful not to betray myself." Darcy turned his face toward the saddle, reassured by the smell of the leather. "At least in public. But when we were alone...I kissed her—more than once," he confessed in a murmur.

Richard shook his head as he closed the distance between them. "When you do something, you do not do it by half measures. She returns your feelings?"

Darcy snorted. "I would hardly kiss an unwilling woman!" This provoked a laugh from his cousin. Then Darcy sobered. "She has not said as much, but I believe she does. However, her father hates me—naturally. He has ordered his entire family to avoid my company.

Undoubtedly, he would require her immediate return to Longbourn if he knew of my presence here."

Richard shook his head. "Damnation! That is a tangle, Cuz!"

Darcy shook his head. "No, not a tangle. I must simply stay away from her. Hence, no walks in the garden."

"I see." Richard's voice was soft and sympathetic.

Silence fell. Lost in thought, Darcy gathered his horse's reins and started the walk toward Rosings Park. He could ride, but the distance to Rosings was short, and he was not eager to arrive too quickly. Richard followed suit, falling into step next to Darcy.

After a few minutes of silence, Darcy cleared his throat. "When you confided that Collins had married a woman from Hertfordshire, I feared it was Elizabeth. Collins is her cousin and had proposed to her once."

"Oh!" Richard exclaimed. "No wonder you behaved so oddly. I did not mean to cause you distress."

"You had no way of knowing. And truthfully, I cannot tell you how relieved I was to be wrong. When I saw her in the parlor…" He shuddered at the memory.

"You turned quite pale. I could not imagine what was wrong."

How did he betray himself so easily in Elizabeth's presence? Darcy was grateful that Mr. Collins had not been present; anything he might have noticed would be reported immediately to Aunt Catherine. At least Richard could be trusted, and Mrs. Collins seemed loyal to Elizabeth. But how would Darcy survive a full dinner at Rosings without betraying himself?

"Darcy," Richard's voice pulled Darcy from his musings, "have you considered making an offer for her? If you feel that strongly about her, perhaps it is worth incurring your father's wrath."

His frustration boiled over. "Of course, I have considered it! I lay awake nights staring at the ceiling and dreaming of what it would be like to make her mine!" He closed his eyes briefly and sought to regain control. "I apologize. I should not vent my vexation on you." Richard waved away this apology. "Her father would never allow her to marry me."

"Is she of age?" Richard asked.

"Soon. I know not when her birthday is." He had considered this as well. "But she has no desire to go against her father's wishes; she is particularly close to him. I will not divulge the sordid details, but he has excellent reasons for hating my father."

"Yes, but you are not your father. Perhaps Mr. Bennet's mind might be changed."

Darcy pictured Mr. Bennet's face as he demanded that Darcy stay away from his daughters and rather doubted the possibility.

"And then there is the matter of my father...."

"What do you think your father would do if he suspected your attachment?"

"He would do everything in his power to sabotage our relationship. He might even have her hurt or disgraced," Darcy replied promptly.

Richard gasped. "Truly? Surely he would not be so..." His cousin's voice trailed off.

Darcy ran his free hand through his curls. "Richard, you know he demanded that I take an appropriate wife within three years." His cousin nodded. "He already threatened that if I do not marry, he will cut off my allowance and forbid me the use of Darcy House. I would be a virtual prisoner at Pemberley." Richard stared at Darcy, his jaw slack with horror. "Can you imagine what measures he might take if I even considered marrying the daughter of the man he hates above all others?"

Richard gaped. "Cut you off? But-but, you are his heir!"

Darcy gave his friend a mirthless smile. "But until I inherit, he controls everything with an iron fist. I am completely dependent on him." He did not attempt to conceal the bitterness in his tone. "He gives me an allowance, but he controls it; I might as well be a second son for all the independence he grants me."

"Blast and damnation!" Richard swore. "I knew your father was a tyrant, but I did not realize how much he tries to control you."

Darcy squinted at the road before them. "I believe fate is laughing at me, Richard. Over the past three years, I have found many women whom everyone would deem eminently suitable, but they were not what I wanted. Now I finally meet a woman whom I would joyfully take to the altar, and only I find her suitable."

They were now standing before Rosings, in all of its opulent, baroque splendor. Darcy stared at the house, having no desire enter it. Richard clapped his hand on his cousin's shoulder. "I am so sorry, Cuz! It is indeed a conundrum."

Darcy heaved a sigh and tugged the reins so the horse would follow him. He could not avoid Rosings forever. "Will you join me in some brandy? Today there are things I would like to forget."

Richard agreed, and they walked their horses toward the stable. But Darcy knew there was not enough brandy in the world to make him forget Elizabeth.

***

Elizabeth laughed at some bon mot of Richard's, and Darcy ground his teeth together—again. Following dinner, the party had inhabited the Rosings drawing room for nearly an hour. His aunt had insisted Darcy sit near

Anne while Richard had been free to seat himself next to Elizabeth. That unfortunate development was compounded by Richard's complete inability *not* to amuse Elizabeth. Pleasant conversation and jokes seemed to fall from his cousin's lips with no effort. How did he come by such a felicity with words when Darcy seemed perpetually tongue-tied?

As Elizabeth laughed again, Darcy reminded himself forcefully that she would hardly transfer her affections on the basis of a few jokes. Nor would Richard attempt to engage her affections when he knew of Darcy's feelings. But his cousin was free to act when Darcy was not. Hence the grinding of his teeth.

Deliberately, Darcy returned his attention to his aunt and noticed her eyes on him. He met her gaze with a bland expression; she must not suspect his attachment to Elizabeth.

"Miss Elizabeth!" Aunt Catherine addressed her in imperious tones, interrupting the conversation.

Elizabeth slowly turned her countenance to the lady, which undoubtedly irritated his aunt. "Lady Catherine?"

"Do you play and sing?"

"A little."

Elizabeth was being exceedingly modest. Darcy had greatly enjoyed her performances, but he restrained the impulse to blurt this out.

"Then some time or other we shall be happy to hear you." The wave of Aunt Catherine's hand made this statement practically a royal command. "Our instrument is a capital one, probably superior to any you have played." Elizabeth pursed her lips, no doubt biting back some pert remark. "Do your sisters play and sing?"

"One of them does."

Aunt Catherine feigned great shock. "Why did not you all learn? You ought to all have learned. The Miss Webbs all play, and their father has not so good an income as yours." *Good heavens, does my aunt have no sense of propriety?* Darcy grabbed the arms of his chair, restraining the impulse to intervene. "Do you draw?" she asked Elizabeth.

"No, not at all." Elizabeth's frank responses did not suit the tone most would use when replying to Lady Catherine de Bourgh. Sitting opposite Darcy, Collins wiped sweat from his forehead, observing the exchange with growing horror.

"What, none of you?"

"Not one."

Elizabeth's unrepentant attitude provoked a nervous tic in Aunt Catherine's right cheek. "That is very strange. But I suppose you had not the opportunity. Your mother should have taken you to Town every spring for the benefit of masters." Aunt Catherine leaned forward in her chair. "Do you not agree, Fitzwilliam?"

Caught up in his admiration of how Elizabeth defied his aunt, Darcy had not expected to be drawn into the conversation. He opened his mouth to deliver a forceful defense of Elizabeth's upraising but remembered at the last minute that he could not appear partial to her.

"Indeed, London masters would have been instructive." Would Elizabeth forgive him for taking his aunt's part in this ridiculous argument?

"Indeed!" Lady Catherine crowed triumphantly.

Elizabeth's face was blank; had he angered her? His stomach clenched at the thought. *I cannot leave it like that!* "Of course, your playing could hardly be improved," he added hastily. From the corner of his eye, Darcy saw his aunt's head turn sharply in his direction. Silently, Darcy cursed himself. He had done it again! The impulse to compliment Elizabeth was difficult to restrain. He scrambled to think of something appropriately condescending to disguise his faux pas. "However, Miss

Mary Bennet's playing could have benefited from hours with the right instructor."

Pursing her lips, Elizabeth did not glance his way. Had he gone too far? Mary Bennet's playing was execrable, but it was hardly polite to mention it. Finally, Elizabeth responded with a falsely lighthearted note in her voice. "My mother would have had no objection to such a trip, but my father hates London."

Darcy cringed inwardly. Had his father ruined Mr. Bennet's enjoyment of the city?

His aunt opened her mouth for another pronouncement, but Richard was quicker. "Since you play and sing, would you favor us with a piece or two?" he asked Elizabeth. Elizabeth smiled and nodded as Aunt Catherine scowled.

Darcy watched enviously as Richard led Elizabeth to the pianoforte and helped to select some pieces of music. As his aunt droned on about how she would have been a great player if she had ever bothered to learn, every bit of Darcy's attention was consumed by the activity at the pianoforte. He took a swig from his after-dinner brandy, but it tasted bitter. Why must he be constrained to this sofa when his soul longed to accompany Elizabeth?

It was ridiculous! Someday he would be one of the wealthiest men in England, the envy of many. Yet he had no control over his life—or at least the part that mattered most to him.

Finally, when he could no longer tolerate the separation, Darcy levered himself from his chair and stalked over to the pianoforte. Hopefully his aunt would believe he was taking further opportunities to belittle Elizabeth's family. Richard greeted Darcy with a smile, but the laughter in Elizabeth's eyes died. Was she angry with him?

Richard turned to Elizabeth. "And what say you about my cousin, Miss Bennet? How did he acquit himself in Hertfordshire? I should like to know how he behaves among strangers."

Elizabeth met Darcy's gaze, blushed, and glanced away. She opened her mouth to respond, closed it, and then opened it again. Finally, she directed her eyes to the instrument's keys. "I do not know, sir. We were not often in company together. Would you like me to play the Mozart?"

Darcy knew why Elizabeth dissembled, but hearing her deny the many pleasurable hours they had spent together still felt like a knife in his heart. *I should have stayed with my aunt*, he berated himself. But now he must stand with Richard and listen to Elizabeth play.

Was it his imagination or was her playing more stilted than usual? He felt it lacked the vivacity he remembered, and she made a number of small errors. Did his presence disturb her? Darcy only seemed capable of causing trouble for everyone. This was likely the only trip Elizabeth would enjoy all year, and he was ruining it.

Perhaps I should quit Rosings altogether. No. Now that he was with her, he wanted to drink in every second of her company. Their time was all too brief.

***

Elizabeth reflected that she was not sure how she had survived the previous evening at Rosings with her composure intact. Between Lady Catherine's insults and Mr. Darcy's coldness, it had been an unpleasant experience. As soon as was polite, she escaped the breakfast table at Hunsford for some solitary rambles on the grounds of Rosings Park. The trees were just coming alive with the fresh green of new leaves along the branches, and early flowers peeked out of the ground at the base of some of the trees. The sun was bright, but the air was still cool: the perfect spring day.

Yet Elizabeth found it difficult to focus on the nature around her. Instead she shivered at the memory of Mr. Darcy's dark gaze upon her. Although he had been cold to her, his eyes had followed her everywhere as though she were the only light he could see. His gaze was so intent that he seemed to bury himself under her skin and grab onto her heart. When she was honest with herself, Elizabeth admitted she did not wish him to relinquish it. She should avoid him, but her heart craved *more* time in his company, not less.

"Oh!" Elizabeth stopped and slapped herself on the forehead. The exercise of a walk was intended to clear away obsessive thoughts of Mr. Darcy, but instead it merely provided more time to ruminate about him.

As she sped up her pace, she resolved to push such thoughts from her mind and instead focus on the beauty around her. Following a narrow, irregular dirt path, Elizabeth soon found herself in a little glade so perfectly beautiful that it looked like faeries should inhabit it.

An open, grassy area was ringed with smaller trees that boasted yellowish-green leaves unfurling on their branches. Tall, majestic pines stood behind the smaller trees, shielding the glade from the rest of the woods and creating a sense of privacy. Several of the trees and shrubs were in bloom. The tree immediately before Elizabeth had magnificent white flowers with velvety petals. Reaching out her hand, she stroked one petal with her fingertip.

"Elizabeth."

The voice was low and sure, compelling. Not a shout or a summons. Nevertheless, she started and nearly stumbled, grabbing a tree branch to prevent a fall. Finally, she raised her eyes to the source of the voice. There he was, standing on a little rise, the morning sun behind him casting him in silhouette.

I should be frustrated that he is here when I am attempting to forget him. Instead she felt a sense of inevitability. She was fated to be here. Meeting Mr. Darcy here was her destiny.

She used a hand to hold her bonnet in place as she beheld him. "How did you know I would be here?"

He shook his head as he descended from the small hill. "I did not. I have been wandering the woods near Hunsford with this outrageous idea that I might see you. I recalled your love of walking."

How could I have ever doubted his devotion?

Mr. Darcy now stood opposite her, such a welcome sight that she fought back tears. But were they alone? She peered through the trunks and branches surrounding them.

"There is no one else about. We would hear them," he assured her. He took a step forward but then hesitated. "Are you angry with me?"

"Angry?" she echoed in bewilderment. "No. Why should I be?"

His shoulders relaxed, and he blew out a breath. "I took my aunt's part in criticizing your family last night."

"Oh!" She barely recalled his words. Had it been weighing on him all night? "I know you cannot defend me openly. You were perhaps a trifle cold, but I understand."

"Thank God," he said fervently. Then he swallowed, gazing down at the toes of his boots. "Can you forgive my blood as well?" Elizabeth blinked in confusion. "I am the son of the man who has treated your family so abominably."

The story about their fathers had really disturbed him. "There is nothing to forgive, Mr. Darcy. I do not hold you responsible for your father's actions. Nor do I believe you should avoid my society because of that history."

The naked hope when his eyes met hers was almost unbearable. "You do not long for my absence?"

She smiled. "Indeed not. Quite…the opposite." Elizabeth's conscience warned her not to reveal so much when there could be nothing between them. However, she could not bring herself to regret the spark of happiness in Mr. Darcy's eyes.

He took another step forward but did not touch her. Intention burned in his eyes. *I should retreat or warn him to keep his distance.* But every part of her body remembered his touch. She wanted his hands in her hair, his body pressed against hers, his lips entangled with hers. A small voice warned against the horrible impropriety of these desires. But the rest of her recollected the moment when he had first touched her.

His hands touched her waist, and any doubts dissolved. She was his, completely and totally. He pulled her toward him and lowered his head to hers, moving slowly and granting her plenty of opportunities to object. She did not. First he brushed his lips gently over hers and then plunged his tongue into her mouth, taking possession. Elizabeth moaned, returning his passion. The rest of the world faded away as they poured their thwarted desires into the kiss.

One of Mr. Darcy's hands untied her ribbons, and her bonnet fell away. The other hand crept up her back and into her hair, where it played merry havoc with her hair pins, sending them flying all over the forest floor. As her hair fell to her shoulders, he drew his fingers through it, murmuring appreciatively. The sensation of his hand caressing her hair was so sensual that Elizabeth closed her eyes and allowed her head to fall back.

This was the sort of liberty she should only allow a husband, but she was long past caring. His hands in her hair felt so…right. Their bodies pressed together from knee to shoulder, molding together as if made for each other. Mr. Darcy moaned deep in his throat, and the hand around her waist pulled her closer still as if they could never be close enough. Elizabeth understood. Even their clothing seemed a barrier to true intimacy. If only they could remove it so every inch of their bodies could enjoy the tactile sensations of being skin to skin.

Oh, Good Lord! What am I thinking?

Shocked back to reality, Elizabeth finally pulled away, panting for breath. She made a halfhearted effort at retreat, but Mr. Darcy held her firmly, so she settled her head on his chest.

"What if someone sees us like this?" she asked.

"Then I have compromised your reputation and would be forced to marry you. How wonderful that would be!" She felt the deep sigh rushing through his chest.

She pushed away from him. "Do be serious!" Yet even as she said it, she feared he was.

He still clasped her waist loosely. "Elizabeth, you have no idea how difficult it is to sit with you hour after hour wishing to hold you, kiss you, even smile upon you— all the while required to pretend my disdain. Medieval torturers could not have devised a better punishment for me."

"I feel the same."

"Ah, this is wrong!" He released her and turned away, facing the ring of trees. "I do not mind shouldering this burden, but it is wrong for you to suffer as well. I would not have you—"

She scrambled in front of him and laid a finger on his lips. "This situation is not of your making. I am responsible for my feelings; do not feel guilt over them."

He nodded in reluctant agreement.

She managed a pert smile. "In the meantime, we find ourselves in the same place. We have these few days. Let us make the most of them."

His eyes lit with hope. "What do you suggest?"

"I am accustomed to taking a walk after breakfast. No one will think it odd if I continue this habit at Rosings Park. And...I might choose to return to this pleasant glade that I enjoyed on my previous walk."

"Hmm. I am fond of morning rides. I am very fond of the glade as well, if you will share it." He regarded her solemnly, and she nodded eagerly. "But there is no need to mention it to others."

"No, indeed." She could not stop herself from smiling at him. "I find I am praying it does not rain tomorrow."

He grinned. "As am I."

"Unfortunately, I must return to the parsonage now—before I am missed." Reluctantly, she stooped to gather hair pins from the grass, and Mr. Darcy bent to help her.

After Elizabeth had pinned up her hair once more, Mr. Darcy took her hand and kissed it slowly, lingeringly. Elizabeth swallowed, suddenly feeling quite hot. "Until tomorrow then," he murmured.

"Yes, until tomorrow."

***

So passed a week of sheer bliss. Darcy had not known such happiness was possible in this lifetime. He and Elizabeth met every morning in the glade, to kiss but also to talk and laugh and hold hands. Even in a light rain, she insisted that they not forsake a ramble together.

The remainder of each day—eating and conversing with his aunt and cousins, riding, attending to correspondence—passed in a blur of gray and brown, colorless by comparison. He lived for those moments when he would see Elizabeth. Twice the party from the parsonage was invited for dinner, and he had the pleasure of regarding Elizabeth, but he seldom allowed himself to address her. Instead he required himself to agree with his aunt's veiled—or not-so-veiled—criticisms about her family despite Richard's appalled expressions. Elizabeth, however, would give him discreet sidelong glances, and her eyes would dance with merriment. Such moments sustained him through the long dreary times until he would see her again.

The only thing that marred the perfection of these days was the looming shadow of time. Their days together were limited, and the number decreased with every sunset. Elizabeth must return to Longbourn soon, and Darcy could not remain at Rosings indefinitely. Darcy tried to prevent the intrusion of such thoughts, but he could not conquer them altogether.

On the eighth day, he arrived for their regular assignation and discovered Elizabeth was not alone. Hearing a male voice before he reached the glade, Darcy lengthened his stride. Had Collins accompanied her? Despite Collins's marriage, Darcy did not quite trust the man.

As Darcy paused at the edge of the glade, he saw Richard sitting beside Elizabeth on the fallen tree they often used as an improvised bench. Damnation! Darcy's hand tightened on the trunk of a nearby sapling. Now their interlude was ruined for the day.

Richard must have happened upon her, for Darcy had not confided anything about the secret meetings. Nevertheless, here they were, side-by-side, laughing at some shared joke. *Does she ever laugh like that with me?* Perhaps she would prefer to marry Richard. She should. His father was not at war with the Bennets, and there would be few objections.

The thought cut through him like a knife. *No, Elizabeth and Richard would never betray me.* But relief from that realization was brief. Elizabeth must marry *someone.* There were five sisters living on an estate that would be entailed away upon their father's death. They must marry or their situation would indeed be dire.

So she might not walk down the aisle with Richard, but seeing her with him forcefully reminded Darcy that one day she *would* wed. She would wed a man who was not

Darcy. He would open a paper, and there would be an announcement. Or a letter from a mutual acquaintance would casually mention it. He could practically picture the words on the paper. *Do you remember Elizabeth Bennet? I attended her wedding…*

Crack! A thin branch from the sapling had broken off in Darcy's hand. He cursed silently; he had not meant to do that.

Of course, Darcy must marry someone as well—not only to satisfy his father's demands but also to provide an heir for Pemberley. The thought made his stomach churn, and he swallowed lest he be sick.

He could not survive her marriage to another man. Nor could he pretend to love another woman. How could he live with a lifetime of sorrow and regret? How could he live without Elizabeth?

In retrospect, the answer was inevitable: he could not.

Surely he could survive the loss of his allowance. Many of his friends, such as Richard, managed to live well on very little. The thought of leaving behind the life of the *ton* was actually something of a relief. He might be banished from Pemberley, and that thought cut more deeply. His father was hale and hearty, but he would not live forever. Eventually, Darcy would return to Pemberley and the tenants he knew so well. However, he could not imagine becoming master of Pemberley without Elizabeth by his side. His life would feel hollow, lacking purpose.

His fingers worried the stick, peeling the bark from the wood. *Perhaps Father would come to appreciate Elizabeth eventually.* Then he snorted; he could not fool himself. His father would fly into a towering rage and do everything in his power to destroy their lives. But if Darcy was with Elizabeth, he could shield her from the worst of his father's vindictiveness. No one could shield Darcy, but he had resources. He would survive.

Sitting on the log, Elizabeth laughed again, reminding him of the other obstacle. Would she agree to marry him? It would require defying her father's wishes and perhaps losing her family forever. *Was it even fair to ask such a thing of her?*

He would have nothing to offer in return. Darcy rubbed the back of his neck as he considered this. It was an unaccustomed weight on his mind—the thought of having nothing. He could go into a profession, perhaps as a barrister. However, Darcy and his new wife would struggle for a few years while he established himself in a position. Would she be willing to accept him under those circumstances? He did not believe her feelings depended on the carriages and gowns that he could provide for her, but her affection might wane in the face of deprivation and uncertainty. Perhaps she did not require a lifestyle equal to Pemberley or Rosings, but what would she think of a husband who could not even provide the equivalent of Longbourn?

Glancing down at his hands, Darcy realized he had broken the stick into myriad smaller pieces.

Indecision was an unaccustomed state for Darcy, and it made him want to punch something. He envisioned a life with her and a life without her. *Honestly,* he realized, *there was no comparison. I must ask her at least. Even if she refuses me, I will be free of this horrible indeterminate state and can begin the impossible process of attempting to forget her.*

His decision was made. He would propose at the first opportunity.

He had spied on Richard and Elizabeth long enough. Darcy raked his fingers through his unruly hair, hoping he looked presentable. Stepping into the glade, he was rewarded by the way Elizabeth's eyes lit at the sight of him.

Chapter Fourteen

It had been an awkward day, Elizabeth reflected. Rather than encountering Mr. Darcy in the glade, she had found Colonel Fitzwilliam at first. Although she always enjoyed his company, she could not deny her complete joy when Mr. Darcy finally appeared. But he had been rather more stiff and taciturn than usual.

The colonel was aware of Mr. Darcy's interest in her, so he could not have been unhappy at that revelation. Was he anxious that his cousin would guess about their regular meetings in the glade? Or was Mr. Darcy reserved simply because of the colonel's unexpected presence? Perhaps he was having second thoughts about the propriety of their meetings.

Colonel Fitzwilliam had sent frequent puzzled looks to his cousin, but Mr. Darcy had given no indication about the source of his discomfort. When the two men had mentioned their desire to return to Rosings, it had been a relief.

However, the incident reminded Elizabeth that her arrangement with Mr. Darcy could not last. Eventually, they would both depart from Kent. The thought created a hollow ache in her chest, for she could not imagine ever feeling this way about another man.

An afternoon of fretting brought about a headache, rendering Elizabeth unequal to the planned visit for tea at Rosings. Charlotte bustled about, attending to Elizabeth's comfort with pillows and a cool, damp cloth, but eventually, the Collinses departed amidst a great concern over their punctuality at Rosings. Hoping the headache would pass with some quiet and rest, Elizabeth settled into a chair in the parlor.

After only half an hour, the maid entered. "If you please, miss, Mr. Darcy is here—" Before the poor woman could finish, Mr. Darcy entered the room hard on her heels.

"Very well. Thank you, Evie," Elizabeth said, and the maid departed, closing the door behind her.

"Miss Bennet." Mr. Darcy bowed very correctly, but he was visibly agitated; his color was high, and his movements were rough and jerky. Had something occurred to upset him?

"Please be seated," she invited him.

He took one of the green upholstered chairs in the corner but almost immediately stood and moved restlessly about the room, finally settling by the fireplace mantle. After a long pause, he spoke, staring into the flames.

"In vain I have struggled. It will not do. My feelings will not be repressed. You must allow me to tell you how ardently I admire and love you." Finally, he turned his head to regard her with those piercingly blue eyes.

Elizabeth felt faint. Had she ceased breathing? This should not—could not—happen. Yet she could not help but notice how her heart surged with excitement at these words.

"I know the circumstances are undesirable and that these actions will have consequences, but I cannot do otherwise. I cannot contemplate my life without you standing by my side. Please, Elizabeth, will you do me the honor of being my wife?"

She saw stars at the edges of her vision. Lungs starved for air took a huge breath, sounding like a gasp in the quiet of the parlor. This declaration was so much more than she had expected. Indeed, she had expected to never hear those words, but now that they had been uttered, they carried with them a sense of inevitability.

"I…" She started speaking and then stopped; words failed her. But she was driven to stand and see Mr. Darcy eye-to-eye.

He held her gaze but lifted one hand in a warning gesture. "Before you decide, I must disclose all. If I marry you, I expect that my father would discontinue my allowance and ban me from Pemberley. He would do everything in his power to bend me to his will."

Elizabeth gasped. No! Surely this man could not contemplate surrendering his fortune and his beloved family home for her!

"I would need to take up a profession." His eyes remained fixed on the window, his lips a tight line. "The first years of our married life would be difficult."

His eyes returned to her face, watching her with a furrowed brow.

"No!" she cried out.

Mr. Darcy's shoulders slumped, and he lowered his eyes. "Very well. I—"

She darted forward and placed her hand on his forearm. "That is not my answer." Renewed hope crept back into his eyes. "However, I do not wish you to sacrifice your world for me. That is too high a price."

His eyes narrowed. "Is that not for me to decide?"

"I would not be the instrument of separating you from your family."

"There is precious little connection to sever. I will miss Georgiana, but she can visit us when she comes of age. As for my father…even before I first met you, he had granted me three years to find a wife or he would discontinue my allowance. That was two years and seven months ago. He wishes me to marry Anne but would be amenable to an acceptable substitute. However—"

"He would never consider me an acceptable substitute," Elizabeth finished for him.

Darcy lowered his gaze as his hands tugged on the cuffs of his coat. "I am sorry, Elizabeth. It is not a judgment on your character—or even your father. My father values rank and social position above all else, even moral character." Darcy's voice was laced with bitterness.

"And as his feud with your father illustrates, he makes judgments about people and holds grudges forever."

"But to lose everything—"

Darcy regarded her gravely. "I have already resolved that I will not marry Anne or any other woman he would find acceptable. So the allowance is already lost to me." Elizabeth felt the weight of the awesome responsibility he laid upon her shoulders.

"Are you sure he will not relent? Perhaps it was just a threat."

He shook his head. "That is not my father's way. He never changes his mind."

She held his hands in hers. "I am so sorry. You deserve better."

He shrugged. "After all these years, I am accustomed to his manipulative ways. But you must know you would be marrying a veritable pauper. I will understand if you would not want me under such circumstances."

This noble self-abnegation prompted a realization in Elizabeth: there was no decision to be made. If Mr. Darcy was willing to surrender everything to be with her, she could do no less. She would run the risk of separating herself from her family, although she still held out hope that her father might be persuaded to reconsider. Nonetheless, that outcome did not affect her decision.

She put a finger to his lips. "That does not matter to me one bit. Put it out of your mind."

"But if I cannot provide a secure home—"

She stepped closer to him, almost within the circle of his arms. "I love you. That would not matter."

"You love me?" She had not known his face was capable of such a smile.

"Yes."

"Will you marry me?"

"Yes."

"Even though I will be a pauper, and my father will do his utmost to ruin our lives?"

"Yes."

"Even though it would defy your father's express wishes?"

"Yes. Do you have any *other* objections to the match, Mr. Darcy?"

He laughed at her aggrieved expression. Then he laughed some more, picking her up and twirling her in a circle. "I pray you, say it once more!"

"Yes, I will marry you, Mr. Darcy."

He swung her around once more until she was a little dizzy. "William," he insisted.

"William," she agreed, provoking another marvelous laugh from him.

These are not the actions of a man about to become a pauper, Elizabeth thought.

He set her feet on the floor and then commenced kissing her—not only her lips but also her neck, brow, and even, daringly, the soft swell of skin visible above the neckline of her dress. One hand in her hair dislodged some of her carefully arranged curls. Elizabeth was dimly aware that she should be shocked at such forward behavior, but the rest of her consciousness was too overwhelmed by Mr. Dar—William's touches and kisses to care.

Finally, he detached himself enough to drink in the sight of her undoubtedly disheveled state. "You have made me the happiest man on earth!" She laughed with him; his joy was infectious.

Nothing would do but to kiss her again.

Then he sobered enough that Elizabeth could raise practicalities. "I have one condition."

"Yes, my love?"

"May we keep the engagement a secret for a while?"

He frowned. "Why?"

"I would like to give my father an opportunity to reconsider his opinion about you. When I return to Hertfordshire, I will attempt to change his mind. Otherwise a wedding must wait until I come of age."

"When is that?" William appeared to be holding his breath.

"In about three months. July sixteenth."

William smiled like she had given him a gift. "That is not long although I would be happier if it was tomorrow. I will procure a special license so that we need not travel to Gretna Green. Our wedding might seem irregular but not scandalous."

She nodded, happy at the thought that she would not be the occasion for scandal to her family. "So maintaining secrecy will not bother you?"

He sighed. "I would like to announce to the world that you will be mine."

"And that means more to me than I can express." He was not embarrassed by her or her family!

"I would be happy to keep it a secret for three months if," with both hands on her waist, he pulled her toward him, "at the end of that time, I may visit Hertfordshire and claim you."

Elizabeth bit her lip. "You do not mind?"

"I do not mind anything as long as you do not have second thoughts."

She laughed. "I will not. I cannot imagine marrying anyone else."

"I do like the way you think." His lips met hers for a passionate kiss. The moment seemed drawn out, timeless. Nothing existed except William and the lips that were creating such wonderful sensations throughout her body. Families, feuds, and fathers were forgotten. It was a moment apart.

They were startled from their reverie by the sound of thumps and voices. The Collinses had returned from Rosings!

Elizabeth and William sprang apart, and she raced back to her chair, grabbing her needlework from a nearby table. As the door opened, she was still patting a few last strands of hair back into place. William leaned on the fireplace mantle, attempting to look casual, but his color was high, and every line of his body was stiff with tension. Would the others notice?

Mr. Collins entered first. "Mr. Darcy! We did not expect you, sir. Not that you are unwelcome. Quite the contrary. We are pleased you have graced our home with your presence." Behind him, Charlotte's face was carefully blank. Was she trying not to roll her eyes?

Mr. Collins surveyed the room as if he only now noticed that Elizabeth and Mr. Darcy had been alone. "Yes, um, Mr. Darcy. What brings you here? We took tea at Rosings Park."

William's eyes narrowed. "I had heard Miss Bennet was not feeling well. I thought to inquire after her health."

"That is very good of you, sir," Charlotte said. "How is your headache, Lizzy?" Her voice was full of concern for her friend.

"Actually, Charlotte, it has quite disappeared!" Elizabeth could not help a small grin in William's direction.

But Mr. Collins frowned as his eyes traveled from her to William. Could he somehow guess what had taken place? Too late, Elizabeth realized an incriminating strand of hair was tickling the side of her neck. She could not pin it up again without drawing more attention to it. The room was overly warm; no doubt her cheeks were flushed. Surreptitiously, she smoothed her skirts, wondering how she could account for her disheveled state but could think of nothing.

Mr. Darcy cleared his throat. "I am sorry to have missed tea with you at Rosings Park. The conversation is always so delightful." He met her eyes with quirk of his lips. His cravat was askew and definitely rumpled. On another man the flaw might have been dismissed as carelessness, but because Mr. Darcy's appearance was always immaculate, it was all the more noticeable.

Mr. Collins beamed at the compliment while Charlotte appeared puzzled as if she now had cause to question Mr. Darcy's good judgment.

"Yes, well, Her Ladyship—as I have often told her—has the finest cook outside of London." Mr. Collins preened as if hiring such a cook was his own accomplishment. "Indeed, her lemon biscuits are—" Elizabeth witnessed the precise moment when Mr. Collins noticed the other man's cravat. His eyes widened with horror as if he had found Elizabeth and William sacrificing small children in the parlor.

Oh, heavens, Elizabeth thought. *What could Mr. Darcy possibly say if he asks about it?*

Charlotte must have followed her husband's gaze but was eager to avoid any awkwardness. "Indeed, the lemon biscuits are not to be rivaled anywhere." Her overly loud voice attracted her husband's attention.

Mr. Collins averted his gaze from the cravat as if the garment disgusted him but then cast a suspicious look at Elizabeth.

She cleared her throat. "Yes, Lady Catherine's cook is indeed very good."

Mr. Darcy retrieved his walking stick and hat from a chair near the door. "Well, my aunt will be expecting me for dinner, so I must bid you good day." He nodded to Elizabeth, catching her eye. His face was heavy with anxiety, and she did not doubt her expression was similar.

Would Mr. Collins act on any suspicions? On the one hand, he was intimidated by Mr. Darcy and always sought to ingratiate himself. On the other, the parson's primary allegiance was to Lady Catherine, whose daughter Mr. Darcy was supposed to wed. Elizabeth suddenly felt a bit faint. What would they do if her cousin revealed everything?

***

The next morning, Darcy could not sit still as he awaited Elizabeth in their usual rendezvous location. He paced rapidly back and forth, his long coat whipping around his legs. He had come to a resolution during a long and sleepless night, but he was not happy about it.

Finally, Elizabeth hurried into the clearing. Darcy could almost feel his heart expand at the sight of her charming smile. Surely nothing too awful had occurred with Collins or she would not be so happy!

Without a word, he opened his arms, and she melted into his body as if she belonged there. After a long, lingering kiss, Darcy felt compelled to ask, "Did Collins mention any suspicions to you last night?"

"No." Elizabeth gave a shaky laugh. "However, if we are to give the appearance of two people who dislike one another, we will need to give a more convincing performance."

"Yes, indeed." Darcy pulled her more tightly against his body as if Collins might appear at any minute to tear her from his arms. "If he has any suspicions, will he reveal them?"

"I cannot be sure," Elizabeth admitted. "What will Lady Catherine do if he does tell her?"

Darcy frowned. "There is little love lost between my aunt and my father—they are too much alike. But our betrothal would also thwart her plans for my marriage to

Anne. Undoubtedly, she would try to threaten you." His entire body tensed at this thought. "Perhaps she would tell my father if she thought he would force me to marry Anne." He stared at the horizon as he contemplated the situation.

He felt Elizabeth stiffen in his arms at these words. He kissed the top of her head. "Nothing will force me to surrender you, my love. Nothing!"

She sighed. "I just wish you did not have to sacrifice so much simply to love me."

Darcy shook his head. "That is not your doing; it is my father's." He gave her a brief squeeze and then released her so he could look into her eyes. "However, I have determined I must depart."

Elizabeth froze, her eyes wide.

"Collins is less likely to mention anything to my aunt if I am not present." Darcy sighed. "And it appears we cannot be in the same room without betraying our sentiments."

"Surely those were unusual circumstances, sir!" Elizabeth retorted. "We had just agreed on a betrothal. It will not always be so."

Darcy watched her for a moment, feeling as if he could devour her with his eyes. She did not turn her gaze away, but her lips parted slightly, and her breathing became more rapid. He could feel his entire body responding as if waking a sleeping giant. He tilted down his head to kiss her, and she lifted hers.

Before they kissed, a smile quirked the side of Darcy's mouth. "Not always?" He challenged her.

Elizabeth averted her eyes. "P-Perhaps you are correct. It might be best if we separate." She was quite flushed.

Darcy nodded. Although he knew it was for the best, his heart twisted in his chest. Here at Rosings, it had been difficult to remain separate from her for most of the day, but once he left…

He tried to banish the thoughts from his mind. "I will invent urgent business in Town and leave today." Elizabeth nodded jerkily, tears collecting in the corners of her eyes. "If you need assistance, Richard will be able to help you. He is in my confidence. Or you may write to Georgiana; she would be pleased to hear from you and can relay a message to me." She nodded once more, blinking rapidly.

"When will I see you again?" Her voice quavered slightly.

"I will try to convince Bingley to return to Netherfield, but I do not know if he still remains in London. Failing that, I will be at Longbourn to claim you in three months' time. July sixteenth." The thought made his whole body feel alive.

Elizabeth smiled despite her tears. No doubt she still hoped for a resolution with Bingley and her sister. "Please hurry."

The simplicity of this plea made Darcy's eyes sting. It was in small moments such as these that the warmth of her love shone through.

He pulled her against him once more. "I will. And I love you."

"I love you as well."

***

"What do you mean, you are leaving?" Richard glared at Darcy, a bewildered expression on his face. But Darcy watched the footmen load his trunk onto the back of his carriage.

"I will send my carriage back to retrieve you when you are ready to leave. I told Aunt Catherine I have urgent business in Town. "

"Do you?"

"Not at all."

"Then why…?" Richard's gestured encompassed the carriage and all the ongoing activity.

"I proposed to Elizabeth last night, and she accepted." Darcy finally gave Richard his full attention, allowing a smile to creep onto his face.

"That is wonderful, Darcy!" Richard smiled broadly.

"I am very happy."

"So, naturally, you are abandoning her the next day. Now everything makes sense." Richard's smile was sardonic.

Even Richard's sarcasm could not darken Darcy's good mood. "We found that when Elizabeth and I are in the same room, we betray ourselves. If this is to remain a secret, we must maintain a façade of indifference. Her cousin may already suspect."

Richard frowned. "Do you think Aunt Catherine will believe your 'sudden business'?"

Darcy raised a brow. "Yes. I told her I prefer to stay at Rosings when there are fewer people about."

Richard chuckled. "You are a clever devil! She will think you do not care for the company at the parsonage."

"Yes. At least it will put her off the scent." Darcy rested his hand on his cousin's shoulder. "I do have one favor to ask, Richard."

"Anything."

"Please write to me at once if Collins or Aunt Catherine seem suspicious. I would not leave her to face their wrath alone."

Richard grinned. "You really have lost your heart." Darcy could only nod in agreement. "But, yes, I will write to you immediately."

"Thank you." Darcy's heart was lighter already. "It is easier to depart knowing you will watch over her."

Richard shrugged. "Easy enough to promise. I would look after her anyway. She is worth protecting."

Darcy nodded as he climbed into the carriage. "Yes, she is."

Chapter Fifteen

"Sir." The maid handed George Darcy a cup of tea with a curtsey. He took it and sipped.

"What a shame you could not visit when Fitzwilliam and Richard were here," Lady Catherine intoned.

The elder Darcy nibbled on a biscuit. Catherine did have the best cook. "Yes, that was—what? A fortnight ago? It would have been good to see them."

Catherine gave a most unladylike snort. They had been united by thirty years of antipathy ever since he had married her sister, and she well knew the nature of his relationship with his son.

"You and William could have exchanged thinly veiled insults," Catherine remarked dryly. Darcy laughed. Catherine was an old crone, but sometimes she could tell a good joke.

As he sat next to Her Ladyship, her parson—Darcy had forgotten his name—appeared shocked at their bad manners. Good. Darcy was tempted to continue shocking the man further.

Perhaps Catherine guessed that the timing of Darcy's visit was not coincidental. Wilkins's report of Fitzwilliam's strange, brooding behavior had been corroborated by other servants and by Hurst when Darcy had dined with him. However, no one knew the source of his distress. Darcy had even sent a man to investigate Fitzwilliam's actions in Hertfordshire, but the fellow had found nothing of concern. Visits to Catherine always brought out the worst in Fitzwilliam; perhaps he had inadvertently revealed something to her.

"So why have you bothered to grace us with your presence now?" she asked sharply.

Darcy set his teacup on the table beside him. He had no intention of revealing his main purpose to

Catherine, but his secondary purpose would serve as a shield. "Nearly three years ago, I told Fitzwilliam he must marry within three years."

Catherine turned red. "How dare you! He is to marry Anne; you know that."

Darcy shrugged. "He was not so inclined, so I gave him the opportunity to find another bride. I was not in a hurry to inflict you upon him as a mother-in-law; I am not that cruel." He watched as the maid poured him another cup of tea.

Catherine merely sneered at Darcy, refusing to react to his barb.

"However, he has not found a bride to his liking. So I believe it is time for him to marry Anne." If Fitzwilliam had found a suitable alternative, Darcy would not be compelled to deal with Catherine, a particularly loathsome prospect. But joining Pemberley to Rosings Park would add immensely to Darcy's wealth, so there was compensation for the inconvenience. Since Catherine wanted Anne to be mistress of Pemberley as well as Rosings, she would agree to almost anything. It might render her marginally less disagreeable for a time.

"Very good," Catherine intoned. "I do believe his affection for Anne is increasing."

Darcy smiled at Catherine's delusion. Fitzwilliam might visit out of obligation, but he had no attachment to his cousin. Then Darcy noticed the parson shifting uncomfortably in his chair. Interesting…

Catherine continued on, ignoring the others. "Why, when I compared Anne's accomplishments to Miss Bennet's—"

Darcy nearly spilled his tea. "Whose?"

Catherine's smile was subtly triumphant. "Miss Elizabeth Bennet, who was a guest of Mr. Collins's wife at Hunsford." She indicated the parson, whose name, apparently, was Collins. "Her stay coincided with

Fitzwilliam and Richard's; she returned to Hertfordshire about a week ago. Fitzwilliam did not write to you about it?"

No, he did not. But then Fitzwilliam's letters to his father were few and mostly about estate business.

"You received that creature at Rosings?" Darcy was too shocked to dissemble. "Do you know who her father is?"

Catherine waved away the objection. "Yes, I know you had a bit of a contretemps with Mr. Bennet, but *I* have no quarrel with the family."

"The man is despicable, not to be trusted!" Darcy restrained an impulse to raise his voice. No doubt Catherine had been hospitable to the chit simply to vex him. "No one in my family should ever associate with a Bennet," he spat.

Catherine shrugged. "I have reason to believe Fitzwilliam did not care for her company."

Darcy felt his shoulders relax. At least his son was not so disloyal as to *enjoy* the spawn of Thomas Bennet. "Of course, he did not care for her. I am sure the whole family is coarse and ill-mannered." Then Darcy noticed the parson, who had a hand over his mouth and a look of sheer horror on his face. "You! Er...Collins! What is your problem?"

"Oh!" Collins quailed at being the object of Darcy's attentions. "Oh, dear!" His eyes darted about the room as if seeking an escape. "Perhaps it is nothing. I am sure it is nothing."

Darcy narrowed his eyes at the fool. "Out with it, man."

"Before I married my lovely wife, Charlotte, from Sir William Lucas's family, I...sought out Miss Elizabeth Bennet's...er...opinion on a marriage between us. I am to inherit Longbourn after her father passes away and thought it desirable to select a bride from among his daughters."

Darcy rolled his eyes. Would the man never get to the point? "This is fascinating, but…?"

Mr. Collins's hands shook so much that he dropped his biscuit and was forced to peer around the floor to discover it. Finally, he gave up and straightened in his chair. "Mr. Darcy, your son, happened upon us when I was…discussing this possibility with Miss Elizabeth."

Darcy could easily see through the parson's hedging. Collins had proposed and been turned down; apparently Thomas Bennet's daughter had at least a little sense. But where had the fool made this proposal that Fitzwilliam would have come upon them?

"Where were you?" he asked.

"Er…" Mr. Collins coughed. "A country road, not far from Longbourn."

A delightful setting for a proposal. No wonder the chit had rejected him.

"I was discussing the advantages of such a match with my cousin." Darcy translated this: *I was making a pest of myself after she turned me down.* "But Mr. Darcy—that is, your son, not you, of course—" Darcy rolled his eyes. "—requested rather forcefully that I leave her alone."

Annoyance at Collins melted away in the face of this new information. *What?* Darcy leaned forward in his chair. "Did he wish you to avoid all of Thomas Bennet's daughters or just Miss Elizabeth in particular?"

Collins squirmed in his seat. "Er…he did not specify, but I thought it safest to avoid all the Bennet daughters just in case. And then I met my Charlotte!" Collins's eyes went soft. "And I knew we were formed for each other."

Darcy fought the temptation to gag.

"That means nothing!" Catherine cried, gesturing dismissively. "Fitzwilliam was simply being chivalrous to a woman in need. You were disturbing Miss Bennet's walk. He displayed no partiality to Miss Bennet here at Rosings."

Collins nodded enthusiastically. If Catherine labeled him a pest, he would apparently agree wholeheartedly. Then his face fell, and he cleared his throat. "So I thought, but the day before Mr. Darcy—that is Mr. Fitzwilliam Darcy—departed from Rosings, he visited Miss Elizabeth at the parsonage."

"What? Alone?" Darcy cried.

Collins cowered like a rat caught in a trap. "Well, yes. Lady Catherine had graciously condescended to invite us for tea at Rosings Park, but Miss Elizabeth had a headache. I am certain nothing untoward happened," he added hastily. "Mr. Darcy merely stopped to inquire after her health, and she did seem very flushed when we returned home. Perhaps she had a fever."

Or there was a completely different explanation for the flush. Darcy wanted to slap the parson for being so obtuse. Fitzwilliam had warned Collins away from this Elizabeth Bennet; he had called on her alone. His behavior was not that of a man who disliked the Bennets. What if—? Was it possible his son would betray him so? Form an attachment with the daughter of his enemy? It was almost too horrible to contemplate, yet...

No. Fitzwilliam was simply being polite when politeness was not necessary.

"I am certain it is nothing," Catherine intoned. "I saw no signs of particular attachment when they were at Rosings, and he implied that her company was one of the reasons for his departure."

"Implied but did not explicitly state?" Darcy asked.

"No. He is too polite." Catherine uttered the observation with great finality, but Darcy could not shake the sense of foreboding. Fitzwilliam was never so unpolished as to discuss his dislike of an acquaintance— and he was even less likely to share such sentiments with someone like Catherine. Why would he imply his dislike of Elizabeth Bennet…unless he feared Catherine would come to the opposite conclusion?

Now quite frustrated, Catherine glared at a maid standing near the door with a plate of biscuits in her hand. "What is the matter, girl? Are you coming or going?"

The maid's eyes grew even wider, and her whole body trembled as if she fought the effort to flee the room. "Begging your pardon, ma'am. Not that I was eavesdropping or anything, but I couldn't help overhearing—"

Catherine opened her mouth to chastise the girl, but Darcy forestalled the reprimand. "Did you have something to add?"

The girl swallowed, giving Darcy a deep curtsey. "My brother, Jack, works the grounds here at Rosings. And he saw Mr. Darcy meeting with Miss Bennet in the woods, more than once."

Darcy's vision went white for a moment. Rage boiled through his veins. "You stupid girl!" Catherine yelled at the maid. "Why did you not report this before?"

The girl cringed, edging closer to the door. "I didn't know it were important, ma'am. Please forgive me."

There was a strange rattling sound. Darcy looked down and realized it was coming from him; he shook with a rage that rattled the cup and saucer in his hands. Damnation! How could his son be so disloyal? In one motion, Darcy stood and threw the offending china to the floor where it broke into myriad pieces. Mr. Collins gasped.

"George!" Catherine exclaimed. "Control yourself! Do you know what that china is worth?"

Darcy ignored her. "I will stop him! Willful, ignorant fool!" He stalked toward the doorway. "I will stop him—and destroy her!"

"George!" Catherine looked truly alarmed.

He pointed a finger at his sister-in-law. "Fitzwilliam and Anne will wed by the end of the year. Make the preparations." Without waiting for a response, he stalked out of the room.

**

The pub was disgusting. The table was worn with grooves and indentations from years of use. The corners of the room were dim and collecting dust, no doubt. And the windows were grimy, barely allowing any light to shine through.

George Darcy wore his gloves but still could barely stand to touch anything, even the mug of beer before him. If only there were another place for this meeting! He wished there had been time to summon the man he was meeting to Pemberley, but Darcy had to settle for a location where he was unlikely to encounter anyone he knew.

Finally, the door opened, golden sunlight briefly flooding the dark, dusty interior of the pub. Darcy smiled grimly when he saw who it was. At least he would be able to quickly conclude his business and quit this place.

George Wickham slid into the seat opposite Darcy's at the scarred table. He inclined his head, a wary look in his eye. No doubt he wondered what the master of Pemberley wanted with him after all this time. "Mr. Darcy."

"Wickham." Darcy did not bother with any social niceties. "I am pleased you answered my summons. It will be worth your while."

Wickham's eyes narrowed; he was intrigued.

"I have a particular problem with Fitzwilliam that I believe you can help me with."

"Oh?" The other man raised an eyebrow. Wickham had always hated Darcy's son—a weakness Darcy intended to exploit now.

"It appears he has formed an inconvenient attachment to a girl here in Hertfordshire—from a most objectionable family." It pained Darcy to make the necessary admission.

Wickham frowned. "I have heard nothing of that."

"They have hidden it well, but I have it on the best authority."

Wickham shrugged and slouched in his chair. "What is it to me?"

"I must ensure the girl is too *unsuitable* for Fitzwilliam to wed."

"But you just said her family—"

Darcy cut him off. "She must be *more* unsuitable. She must experience a complete loss of reputation. She must be thoroughly *ruined*."

A corner of Wickham's mouth quirked up. "Ruined, eh?"

"I thought you were the man for the job."

"Oh, I can manage it." Wickham gave Darcy a lazy smile. "What is the chit's name?"

"Elizabeth Bennet." Wickham's eyes opened wide. "Will that be a problem?"

"Not at all. I am already acquainted with the family."

"On good terms?" Wickham nodded. "Good, that will make it easier."

"But they hate the Darcys." Wickham surveyed the pub to see if they were observed, but it was nearly empty. "That is why they prefer my company. Why would Elizabeth be angling for your son?"

Darcy's gloved hand formed a fist. "What better way to exact revenge on me? I am certain Thomas Bennet is chuckling at the idea of his grandchild inheriting Pemberley."

"That's despicable," Wickham said with no emotion in his voice.

"Indeed." Darcy attempted to keep his voice level. It would not do to lose control in front of Wickham.

Wickham licked his lips. "How much?"

Darcy slid a small bag across the table. The coins within clinked as Wickham peered inside. "This is for your services as well as your discretion—the other half when you finish. If word gets out, I will know who was responsible."

"Oh, I shan't tell anyone. This is too delicious an opportunity to pass up." Wickham grinned like a fox viewing a henhouse.

He started to stand, but Darcy grabbed his arm and held him to the table. "I know what you attempted to do with Georgiana," he muttered.

Wickham turned white. "It was—I was—"

"You will stay away from my daughter." Darcy's voice was a low, menacing growl.

"Of-of course!" Wickham stammered.

"Because if you attempt anything with her—say, a flight to Gretna Green— you will not live long enough to consummate the marriage." Darcy's fingers dug into Wickham's wrist hard enough to leave a bruise. "That is a guarantee."

"I will leave her alone!" Sweat trickled down from Wickham's brow. "I promise!"

"Good." Darcy released Wickham's hand and patted it in a fatherly manner. "I had a great deal of affection for your father. I would hate for us to be at odds."

Wickham pulled his arm away and rubbed the bruises. "Y-Yes."

"Write to me when the deed is done, and I will send the rest of your payment."

"I will." A moment later, Wickham was gone.

Darcy stood. At least he could now leave this disgusting hole.

Chapter Sixteen

"Mr. Wickham, miss."

Elizabeth sighed and rolled her eyes at Jane, who gave her a sympathetic smile. Lydia and Kitty, however, bounced and squealed at the news.

"Show him in, Hill," Jane said.

A few weeks after Elizabeth had returned from Kent, Mr. Wickham had suddenly become a frequent caller to Longbourn, which amused the younger Bennet daughters and frustrated Elizabeth—especially since the man paid her particular attention.

Elizabeth would have been pleased to do without her share of this attention. She had pleaded with her father to banish the man from Longbourn, but unaware of what Elizabeth had witnessed at the masquerade, Mr. Bennet did not see the need. Instead he reveled in the man's tales of woe at the hands of the Darcys, making it nearly impossible for Elizabeth to change her father's perspective about William. Her mother was worse, insisting that Elizabeth should do everything she could to encourage the attentions of such a "handsome young officer."

When Wickham entered the drawing room, he bowed, and the ladies curtsied. Jane offered him a seat, but he said, "Why do we not venture outside and enjoy the beauties of your garden?"

Elizabeth assented while the younger girls tittered. Mary, however, elected to remain inside, studying scriptures. It was late May, and many flowers were in full blossom; their scent perfumed the air. Soon everyone strolled along the lush green lawn. As the conversation remained sedate, Kitty and Lydia soon grew bored and wandered off in search of wildflowers. After a few minutes, Hill arrived, summoning Jane to their mother.

It was not until Mr. Wickham suggested they retire to a garden bench that Elizabeth realized she was alone with him. *I must find an excuse to leave immediately!* But her mind was a blank. She was forced to attend when the man began to speak.

"You cannot have failed to notice my attentions to you these last weeks, Miss Elizabeth," he said. The words engendered a deep welling panic in Elizabeth's stomach. No, he could not possibly mean to—

He took one of her hands in both of his, grasping it so tightly that she could not easily extricate it.

"I must confess my most violent love for you, and I humbly ask that you would accept my hand in marriage." His expression was open and eager. *He is quite good at this.*

This is my third marriage proposal this year. Elizabeth had to quell a completely inappropriate impulse to laugh. *And I believed no one could be less appealing than Mr. Collins!*

Her thoughts soon leapt to questions of motivation. She had no fortune to tempt him, and despite his declaration, she did not believe he harbored any deep affection for her.

"Will you make me the happiest of men?" he prompted with a large smile.

He pretends sincerity very well. If her experience at the masquerade had not demonstrated his true nature, she might have been deceived.

Elizabeth glanced down at their clasped hands, wishing she could pull hers back. But she could give him no reason to suspect she had met him before his arrival in Hertfordshire.

"I am honored by your attentions," she lied. "But I do not believe I am capable of returning your affection. I must decline."

Mr. Wickham said nothing for a moment, blinking rapidly. *Oh, he is surprised. He did not consider the possibility I might refuse him.* "P-Perhaps your affection might grow over time!" he objected.

"I do not believe so. I do not think we are well-suited, Mr. Wickham. I am sorry to cause you any pain."

"B-But—" He freed a hand to gesture wildly. "I love you—madly, ardently, passionately!" Elizabeth suppressed a smile. This had to be the most dispassionate declaration of passion she had ever witnessed.

"I am sorry—"

"You do not know how you tempt me...your scent, the way you walk, and your fine eyes..." His hand reached out to caress her cheek. She tried to move away from him on the small bench, but he still held her hand in a tight grip.

She tugged gently at her hand. "I apologize that I—"

"It is impossible in every way, Elizabeth! I must have you!"

"It is impossible." She yanked harder to free her hand. Suddenly, his lips were on top of hers, and he kissed her ferociously. His kiss was nothing like Mr. Darcy's. Despite his declaration, his lips did not taste of affection or passion. He was simply frantic to capture and claim her mouth.

As his lips engaged hers, his hands took even greater liberties. One hand curved around her back and caressed the skin where it met her dress. The other...oh, merciful heavens! The other was touching her breast!

This unexpected assault gave her the extra strength she needed to wedge both her hands between them and push at his body with all her might. Mr. Wickham fell away from her but not off the bench as she had hoped.

She stood with the intention of rushing to the house only to find her father standing a few feet away. The expression on his countenance suggested he had seen what had just occurred.

"Papa! I did not—he just—I wanted to—" The words emerged in a jumble.

"Shh, my dear." He opened his arms and enfolded her in his embrace. "I saw what happened, and you are not to blame."

When her father released her, they both confronted Mr. Wickham, who had finally staggered off of the bench. "She is compromised now! No one will take her!" he declared.

Elizabeth's mouth fell open. Had this been his intention all along—a wicked plot to destroy her reputation? Had he never intended to marry her? She shivered in horror at the thought of what might have happened had she accepted his proposal.

"Nonsense," her father declared stoutly. "Nothing untoward occurred."

"But she and I—"

"I was present the whole time; she was adequately chaperoned." Mr. Bennet raised an eyebrow as he glared at Mr. Wickham, daring him to disagree.

Mr. Wickham seemed dumbfounded for a moment, but then a calculating look stole over his features. "I think it is my duty to inform my fellow soldiers of her compromised state—"

Mr. Bennet's fist came out of nowhere and connected with the other man's jaw. The militia officer fell like a sack of potatoes. Her father loomed over him. "Listen to me! I am aware of your numerous debts with the tradespeople of Meryton. What do you think would happen if they all called your debts at once?"

Mr. Wickham's face drained of all color as he scrambled to his feet. "You cannot do that!"

Her father chuckled. "I am a well-known landowner. I think many merchants would be pleased to do me a favor, particularly one that would put money in their pockets."

The other man brushed dirt from his uniform with frantic movements. "I would go to debtor's gaol!"

"Now that would be a shame—for such a nice man, so pleasant to the ladies." Mr. Bennet's voice dripped sarcasm. "Of course, if you do not spread lies about my daughter, I would not be inclined to ask the merchants for such a favor."

Mr. Wickham scowled at Elizabeth's father for a moment. "Very well," he muttered.

"I have your word?" Mr. Wickham nodded. "Good. However, if I hear the least word of scandal concerning my daughter, I will see you carted off to gaol immediately. Do you understand me?"

Mr. Wickham nodded reluctantly.

How did her father manage to loom over Mr. Wickham when he was several inches shorter? "Then leave Longbourn now, and do not return!" Mr. Bennet lifted his arm and pointed.

Mr. Wickham sprinted down the garden path and was gone from sight within a minute.

Her father placed his arm around Elizabeth's waist and pulled her toward him in a comforting gesture.

"But, Papa, I *have* been compromised!" she objected. *What would William think? Would he believe me to be wanton?*

"Nonsense, my dear," her father responded, squeezing her against his side. "A little groping hardly constitutes a compromising situation. You are no less worthy of marriage than you were yesterday." Elizabeth was warmed inside at these words.

Her father's expression darkened. "But I am very sorry it happened to you. I should have done a better job of protecting you girls, and I will do so in the future. We must warn our neighbors about that scoundrel as well."

Elizabeth pressed her palms to her eyes as if she could block out the memory. "It was horrible. He would not release me!"

"I should have struck him twice," Mr. Bennet said grimly.

"No, he is gone, and it is for the best," Elizabeth said. It occurred to her that this was an opportunity to plead William's case. "Mr. Darcy does not care for Mr. Wickham; perhaps he was right to be suspicious."

Her father's face went stony. "Even a broken clock is right twice a day. Seeing the truth behind Mr. Wickham's lies does not mean the man is any better than his father."

Elizabeth opened her mouth to offer a different opinion, but her father was already striding toward the house.

***

George Darcy had hoped to never see the inside of this pub again. If possible, the place was even drearier and dirtier than the last time. The late June heat made the air particularly thick and oppressive. The only improvement was that this time Wickham was waiting for him. Good! At least he would soon be able to leave. It was early afternoon, and the place was deserted. Even the proprietor seemed to be elsewhere; perhaps Wickham had paid him off. Just as well.

Darcy seated himself at the table and waited for the other man to speak, but he said nothing. "So, is it done?" he asked finally.

"It?"

"Have you ruined the chit who is after Fitzwilliam's fortune?"

"Ah…no. Unfortunately, Miss Bennet's father proved a mite too protective. He threw me out of their house. When I attempted to return, he threatened me with a shotgun! I tried to approach her in town, but she would not even listen to me." Wickham sneered as if a refusal to be debauched was a serious character flaw.

Darcy surged to his feet, both his hands flat on the table. "So you have failed?"

Wickham cowered back in his chair. "Well, I would not say that exactly…I have not found a way to succeed yet."

"Unacceptable!" Darcy thundered, pounding his fist on the table. "Need I remind you that you have more than enough debts to land you in prison? I would have no hesitation in sending you there!"

Wickham blanched and sat up in his chair. "Nobody has seen Fitzwilliam in Hertfordshire, and no one speaks of him. Perhaps the Bennet girl has given up her designs on him." Wickham moved his hands restlessly over the tabletop. "Perhaps you do not need my services after all—but I will not return the money!" he said quickly.

Darcy had wondered the same thing. Why had Fitzwilliam not arrived in Hertfordshire to claim his bride? He was not likely to be easily deterred once he had made a decision.

"Her father hates the Darcys. I cannot see how he would approve—"

Darcy had a sudden moment of clarity. "How old is this Elizabeth Bennet?"

Wickham thought for a moment. "Twenty. Her sister related that Elizabeth would have her birthday on July sixteenth, just before she is due to take a trip with her aunt and uncle."

"So then she will be one and twenty," Darcy mused aloud. "Old enough to marry without her father's consent. That is why Fitzwilliam is waiting."

"I do not know if I can ruin her before then! Such things are difficult to schedule. And the garrison will soon depart for Brighton." Wickham's voice had taken on an unpleasant whiny quality.

Darcy rolled his eyes. "There is more than one way to ruin a woman. She does not need to *agree* to Gretna Green."

Wickham's eyes went wide. "Are you suggesting abducting her? I cannot do that! I'd be hanged for sure if they caught me."

Darcy leaned back into his chair. Wickham was sadly lacking in imagination. "Then find another way! I have already paid you half—I must have results!"

Wickham spread his hands wide. "But how?"

Darcy searched his memory for everything he knew about Elizabeth Bennet. "What about her sisters?"

Wickham stared at him blankly. "Sir?"

Darcy rolled his eyes. "If she will not allow you to seduce her, then seduce one of her sisters! Just make sure it is a public enough scandal."

Wickham rubbed his chin thoughtfully. "Her youngest sister, a friend of the colonel's wife, is accompanying us to Brighton when the garrison leaves in a week."

"Will she be alone?"

"Aside from the colonel and his wife, but they won't keep a very close eye on her."

Darcy realized he was smiling. "That would do very nicely. A fitting disgrace for the family. Fitzwilliam would never consider Elizabeth Bennet then! Yes, the youngest girl is the one you must elope with."

Wickham's brows knit together. "But, Mr. Darcy, need I actually elope with her? She chatters without ceasing—and she has the most annoying laugh!"

"I do not care if she is missing most of her teeth and is covered with boils!" Darcy cried. "You do not need to wed her, just run off with her. If she is all that foolish, it will not be that difficult to lure her into your bed."

Wickham smirked. "Not in the least." Then he frowned. "But need I do so before July sixteenth? I am not certain Lydia will arrive in Brighton by then."

Darcy was tempted to tell Wickham that was his problem, but then a solution occurred to him. "We need only keep Fitzwilliam from Elizabeth Bennet until the scandal strikes. I shall send him away on business until it is too late."

"A brilliant plan, sir!"

Darcy narrowed his eyes at Wickham; he hated sycophants. "Just make sure the youngest sister is publicly disgraced, and then you can go about your business."

"And you will give me the money?" Wickham's eyes glowed with avarice.

"Yes. But do not seek me out again until the deed is done."

"I will not," Wickham promised as he stood.

Darcy watched Wickham leave the pub. Now he must visit London again to execute his part of the plan. How could he separate Darcy from his lady love? The possibilities were endless. He could contemplate them on the carriage ride to Town.

Chapter Seventeen

"Happy birthday, Lizzy," Jane murmured as she blew out the candle in their room. Elizabeth was already tucked underneath the coverlet, and Jane quickly joined her. In the darkness, Jane said, "You were very quiet this evening. Did you have a pleasant day? Are you well?"

"Oh yes, very well, Jane," Elizabeth responded at once. "The cake was delicious, and I love the handkerchiefs you embroidered for me."

"But you seemed so…solemn. Is something amiss?"

Of course, something is wrong! Elizabeth wanted to shout. *He did not come. He swore he would be here on my birthday, and he did not come.* How lovely it would be to unburden herself to her sister, but she could reveal nothing.

"I suppose I am simply tired. I did not sleep well last night." That at least was true. Anticipation of Mr. Darcy's arrival had deprived her of sleep, and his absence would likely disrupt her slumber tonight. "I will probably drop right off now."

"Good. I am glad all is right with you…" Jane's voice was already slurred by sleep, and a loud yawn punctuated her sentence. Within a minute, Elizabeth heard the regular breathing that indicated her sister was asleep.

Despite her brave words, Elizabeth knew sleep was far away. She had been so certain William would arrive on her birthday that his absence caused an ache in her chest. *Perhaps he meant the day* after *my birthday*, she thought. But deep in her heart, she knew that was not what he had said. Rationally, she knew she had no cause to repine. He might be a day or two late; it would make no difference in their plans. Still, she had expected him today.

She wished there were some way she could contact him, but writing to him would constitute a grave

impropriety. Netherfield remained shut up, so there was no
one to give her news of Mr. Darcy. *I should not despair; it
is only one day.* But anxiety preyed on her mind. What if he had changed his mind? What if he had realized he did
not want to be saddled with a country miss? What if he did
not come at all? It would be simple for him to deny their
betrothal; no one else knew of it. He would not need to
endure the shame brought on by formally breaking the
engagement. He could simply never return to
Hertfordshire, and Elizabeth would never know what had
happened.

Elizabeth was supposed to accompany her aunt and
uncle Gardiner on a trip to the Lakes. In a week, she would
not be at Longbourn even if Mr. Darcy came looking. And
there was no way to get a message to him.

Surely he will come before then, she reassured
herself as she dropped off to sleep. *He promised. He loves
me. He will come.*

A week later, Elizabeth had stopped saying those
words to herself. Her uncle handed her into his carriage,
and she settled next to her aunt Gardiner. She would be
traveling with the Gardiners and not at Longbourn. But it
did not signify because Mr. Darcy was never coming for
her.

***

Aunt Gardiner tied the ribbons of her bonnet. "Are
you certain you do not wish to join us for our trip to
Pemberley, my dear? The staff here assured us the family
is from home."

"Yes." Elizabeth was quite certain, but she
restrained the urge to shout at her aunt.

Her aunt peered more closely at Elizabeth. "I wish
you would accompany us. You have been so tired and
quiet on this trip." Elizabeth recognized the unasked

question in the other woman's voice but did not respond to it.

Instead she repeated her reply from an hour ago. "Papa would not wish me to have any association with the Darcy family—even their house." That was the most innocuous of her many reasons for avoiding Pemberley, but it would serve the purpose. Once again, she cursed the evil fate that had prevented them from visiting the Lakes and instead had given her aunt the idea to explore Derbyshire. With all of England to choose from, why did they need to travel to the one place that reminded Elizabeth of all her dashed hopes? She was counting the hours until they departed the accursed place. At least she could avoid Pemberley even if she could not avoid Derbyshire.

Her aunt's brow furrowed. "Your mother wrote that you did not get along well with the younger Mr. Darcy when he visited Meryton."

If only it were so! Elizabeth considered her response to her aunt. Even now her first impulse was to defend him, but that would betray too much. "He did make some disparaging remarks about me," she conceded.

Her aunt patted her cheek. "I am so sorry, my dear. I have always heard that the elder Mr. Darcy is a difficult man, but people here speak well of the younger."

My trust was misplaced. Eyes stinging, Elizabeth fixed her gaze on her feet lest her face betray her. *Perhaps father and son are not so dissimilar after all.*

"I am sure it is not you, Lizzy." Aunt Gardiner gave her a reassuring smile. "You could not have done anything to make him dislike you." *But what if I did? What if he decided he could not face the prospect of being shackled to me?*

Concern flooded her aunt's eyes. "Perhaps we should not go; I do not like leaving you alone at the inn."

"No!" Elizabeth cried. It was bad enough she was deceiving her aunt and uncle; she did not wish to interfere with their enjoyment of the trip as well. "You said Uncle has not seen Pemberley. He should not miss it. His family has no quarrel with the Darcys."

"Very well." Aunt Gardiner clasped Elizabeth's hand briefly and then quit the room.

From the window in their second-floor room, Elizabeth watched her aunt and uncle climb into their carriage and depart. Truly she burned with curiosity to view Pemberley but knew it would be too bittersweet to actually visit the house. The sight might bring her to tears.

Elizabeth wiped moisture from her eyes with the back of her hand. *This is for the better*, she told herself. If he no longer loved her, their betrothal should be ended. She would not want him to wed her from a sense of obligation. He had done nothing wrong save failing to inform her of his change of heart.

But it was past time for Elizabeth to cease wallowing in her sorrow. *I must look to the future, a future that does not include Fitzwilliam Darcy.* This thought caused new tears to trickle down her cheeks.

After several minutes, Elizabeth was left with a sodden handkerchief and swollen, achy eyes. *This will not do. I must stop weeping.* If she remained in the room with nothing but her thoughts for company, misery would overtake her, so she determined to take a walk.

She did not know the countryside around Lambton and did not feel safe walking it alone, but she could explore the village. After splashing some water on her face, she took her bonnet, descended the stairs, and began to stroll along the bustling street.

Lambton was not a large village, but it was a little larger than Meryton and boasted a number of fine shops. Elizabeth lingered along the main market street, enjoying the sights in the milliner's window and the dressmaker's shop. But it was not until she reached the bookseller's that she found a shop she wished to enter. Here at least was a place that might divert her from her gloomy thoughts.

***

  Darcy's head was full of the preparations he would need to review with his housekeeper in anticipation of the arrival of his houseguests the following day. He would need to ensure that Miss Bingley's room was as far from the family wing as possible. Hurst would complain if the food was not fine enough; he must review the menus.

  Again he cursed the fate that had brought Bingley and his family to Pemberley at such an inopportune time, but Darcy would arrange everything so that Georgiana would find it easy to play hostess; then he would be called away on urgent business. Already he longed to be on the road but knew he must attend to these matters or arouse his father's suspicions. Thankfully, George Darcy was not at Pemberley; the last letter Darcy had received from his father had been from Bath.

  He guided his horse through the busy streets of Lambton. Despite his agitation, he was pleased that he would soon be at Pemberley; home always acted as a balm for his agitated thoughts. As he passed the bookseller's shop, a woman emerged who reminded him of Elizabeth— which was hardly surprising. He had caught glimpses of "Elizabeth" everywhere over the past months. Deprived of her company, he would see a woman with dark curls or hear a laugh like hers, and his heart would stop for a moment. Of course, it was never her. It was always someone who was plainer, duller, and less lively than his Elizabeth.

  These encounters always left him feeling melancholy. What must she think of his failure to arrive at Longbourn on her birthday? Without his presence or even a letter, had she lost faith in him? He would hardly blame her. Would her father's distrust of the Darcy family begin to color her perceptions of him? In the darkest nights, he imagined arriving at Longbourn and having her refuse to speak with him. Or worse, he envisioned her accepting a proposal from a nearby country landowner, so that when he did arrive it would be too late. Such nightmares made him want to direct his horse to the southern road and keep riding until he reached Hertfordshire.

I must forget these gloomy thoughts. They serve no purpose.

As a distraction, he allowed his eyes to again linger on the woman from the bookseller's, who clutched a paper-wrapped book against her chest, and entertained a fantasy of Elizabeth. The woman turned her head so her bonnet would block the bright sunlight, and he glimpsed more of her face. The resemblance was remarkable, but much of her face was shaded by the bonnet. If only she was Elizabeth! He allowed his imagination free rein, envisioning how he would greet her.

Enough. It had been a pleasant interlude; still, he should be on his way to Pemberley.

Yet he could not tear his eyes from the woman. Her dress was somehow familiar. Did not Elizabeth possess such a light yellow, muslin dress?

No, his imagination was running wild. Elizabeth was in Hertfordshire, not Derbyshire. What cause would she have to be visiting Lambton of all places? *Enough of this foolishness.*

Then the woman reached up her hand to push her curls out of her eyes, and he *knew*. Elizabeth moved her hand just so. *His Elizabeth.*

Chapter Eighteen

Darcy's first impulse was to leap from his horse and run to her. His second was to call to her. But he stifled both. Already he attracted many eyes. The Darcy family was well known in Lambton, and anything he did would be noted and gossiped about for days. Elizabeth might not receive him well; they should not meet in a public place.

Instead he brought his horse to standstill and watched Elizabeth slip among the people admiring the shop windows. She moved with her characteristic grace and barely contained energy. Finally, when he observed her enter the Lambton Inn, Darcy dismounted and tied up his horse.

How he could possibly pay a call on an unmarried woman—who was undoubtedly accompanied by (potentially hostile) family members—at an inn? What if she was here with her father? As he contemplated this conundrum, Elizabeth emerged again from the inn, without the book, and turned right. This part of the road led out of town and was far less populated. Perfect!

Darcy followed her at a discreet distance, attempting to look as if he was on a casual stroll but feeling a bit like a footpad stalking an intended victim. His height and dress attracted a few glances, but no one inquired about his purpose.

He caught up with Elizabeth at the bridge over the brook. They were now a mile out of town, and the road was utterly deserted. She stood in the middle of the bridge, leaning against the wooden railing and watching the water tumble over the rocks. The burble of water covered the sounds of his approach.

"Elizabeth," he said softly when he was a few feet from her.

She started and turned toward him, her mouth falling open in surprise. For a moment, he glimpsed a glorious smile on her face, but it was immediately replaced by sad wariness. "Mr. Darcy." It was heartbreaking to watch. *You did this to her*, he reminded himself. He only hoped he could somehow repair the damage.

"Perhaps we might have a word over there?" He gestured to a copse of trees growing on the bank next to the bridge. She winced at his words, which sounded cold and formal even to his ears. But she made no objection when he took her elbow and guided her to the place where they were sheltered from the eyes of anyone using the road.

However, once he had her there—so close to him— he could not speak; he could only marvel at her presence. It had been so long since he had seen her; he had forgotten the clarity of her blue eyes, the promise in her smile, the lushness of her hair.

Elizabeth was not similarly tongue-tied. She took a deep breath and drew herself up to her full height. "Mr. Darcy, if you wish to break off our…understanding—" her voice broke a little at that word, "I will not contest it. There is no formal agreement between us, and I will not hold you to it. No one need ever know."

If Darcy had believed for one moment that she meant these words, he would have been devastated, but he could see the pain in her eyes—what the words cost her. He wanted nothing more than to wrap her in his arms and reassure her. But she would not welcome his touch.

"Elizabeth, I apologize that I was not in Hertfordshire for your birthday as I promised. I am loath to break any promise to you, let alone one that was so important. But my father insisted I visit one of his properties in Scotland—why, I do not know, for it was operating quite efficiently without my interference. I tried to defer the trip, but my father was very insistent, and I could not decline without arousing his suspicions. I departed from Scotland as soon as I could."

Elizabeth's shoulders dropped. "Oh."

"I wrote to Georgiana and asked her to send you a letter explaining the circumstances. Only yesterday, I discovered my sister never received my missive. I do not know where it went astray." He reached out to touch her and then stopped himself. "Please believe me, I would never intentionally cause you any distress."

A crease lined Elizabeth's forehead. "We were told the family was not at home."

Darcy understood this apparent non sequitur. "Bingley and his party are expected tomorrow. I came today to arrange matters so that Georgiana could be the hostess while I rode my fastest to Hertfordshire. You have very obligingly saved me a trip."

She did not smile at his small jest. "You were coming to Hertfordshire for me?" she echoed in a small voice.

He took her hands in his. "Always, my darling, always. Unless you do not want me."

He held his breath. But she graced him with her first smile of the day. "That will not happen."

Darcy gave a relieved sigh. "How did you come to be in Lambton?"

"I am traveling with my aunt and uncle Gardiner. We were planning a trip to the Lakes, but our plans changed, and they decided on Derbyshire."

He frowned. "They left you alone this afternoon?"

She gave a little laugh. "They are touring Pemberley. But I thought—" Her voice faltered.

Darcy finished for her. "Such a tour would be too painful for you because you feared I had abandoned you." Elizabeth nodded. "Oh, my darling. I am so sorry." He pulled her into his arms and crushed her against his chest, wishing he could unmake all the days of worry and stress. "I am here now, and I will not let you go again."

After a few minutes, Darcy busied himself untying the ribbons of her bonnet. "I will give you a *private* tour of

Pemberley," he promised as he removed the bonnet to reveal the decadent abundance of her curls. "Very private."

"But your father—"

"My father is in Bath; we need not worry about him. And Bingley's party is arriving tomorrow. It would be the most natural thing in the world for you and your relatives to join us. I know Bingley would like to hear about your sister."

"But the staff, Mr. Hurst—they will report that you have been seen with me!"

He kissed the top of her head, inhaling her delicate scent. "Circumstances have reunited us. We should not waste this opportunity. I am no longer hiding. I would declare to the whole world what you mean to me."

"B-But then they will try to stop us!"

Darcy gave a bold laugh. "Let them try! I have the special license." He heard Elizabeth's breath catch. "We could be married tomorrow."

Elizabeth bit her lip. "But my aunt and uncle...if we...they will feel they have failed my father..."

"It need not be tomorrow." Although Darcy was not sure how much longer he could wait.

"They are supposed to be chaperoning me."

Darcy ran a free hand through his hair. "Perhaps if they are my guests at Pemberley, I can convince them of my true affection for you."

She tilted up her head to gaze at him. "I would like you to meet my aunt and uncle. They are well spoken and of good understanding. I think you would enjoy their company. Their presence at our marriage ceremony would be quite welcome. They may help alter Papa's opinions about you."

When he could restrain himself no more, he again enclosed her in his arms, relishing the simple joys of touching another person and being touched in return. His mother and nanny had hugged him as a child, but he had almost forgotten the sensation, the thrill a simple touch conveyed.

She rested her head against his chest, and he felt a warm pride that she trusted him enough to do so. "I should allow you to return to Pemberley since you have important business, but I am loath to let you go," she murmured.

"I am not ready to depart either," he confessed. He took her hand. "Here. We cannot walk along the road without giving rise to rumors, but we could follow the path of the brook for a while."

"I would love to!" Her voice held unfeigned eagerness.

With her hand in his, he carefully led the way down to the brook. The weather had been dry, and the water was low. They could walk along the grassy banks without fear of wet feet.

Before they embarked on their walk, Darcy pulled Elizabeth toward him and whispered in her ear. "I cannot wait until I may call you Mrs. Darcy!"

Elizabeth rewarded him with a broad grin. "I cannot wait either!"

***

Elizabeth did not know when she had spent a more pleasant afternoon. Truth be told, she was a bit giddy from the relief of discovering that William had not abandoned her. They did not speak much but simply walked, holding hands and admiring the babbling brook and lush greenery of the surrounding world. They both grew rather warm in the bright sunshine. When William removed his coat to cool off underneath a tree, she was very far from objecting to the impropriety. The lines of his form presented quite an elegant picture, which she found (a bit to her embarrassment) drew her eyes again and again.

Finally, reluctantly, they were forced to concede that the sun was lower in the sky, indicating that they must return to town. Once they regained the road, they disengaged their hands, and Elizabeth immediately felt the loss of his warm grasp. As they strolled into town, William clasped his hands behind his back as if he feared they might misbehave if he did not restrain them.

Elizabeth had not required him to walk her to the inn, but he had insisted he must see her safe and promised to leave immediately.

However, fate had other plans. The Gardiners' carriage pulled up just as they arrived at the inn. It took all of Elizabeth's self-control not to allow her dismay to show upon her face. This was happening far more quickly than she had planned, and she was not prepared.

"Elizabeth!" Her aunt waved gaily as they disembarked from the carriage. "Who did you meet?"

Elizabeth's whole body was instantly hot, and she was certain her cheeks were bright red. There was no escaping the introduction now. She took a deep breath and prayed that this would not be a disaster. "Aunt and Uncle, I would like you to meet Mr. Fitzwilliam Darcy. Mr. Darcy, this is Robert and Madeline Gardiner."

Aunt Gardiner's eyes went wide as she gave William a curtsey, which he returned with a bow. He offered her uncle a handshake, which was eagerly returned. "I happened upon Miss Bennet as I was riding through town. I could scarcely believe my eyes or my good fortune!"

"Indeed?" Uncle Gardiner's eyebrows were raised as he looked from William to Elizabeth.

"Yes, it has been many months since we saw each other in Kent."

"Kent?" Her aunt shot a perplexed look at Elizabeth, who knew William was using these disclosures to pave the way for more startling revelations later. When the time was right, he truly intended to tell her aunt and uncle of their betrothal. The thought simultaneously warmed and alarmed her.

William gave Elizabeth a sidelong glance and a little smile as if the visit to Kent were their shared joke. "Yes." He smiled at the Gardiners. "She was visiting her friend at the parsonage while I was staying with my aunt at Rosings Park."

Aunt Gardiner regarded Elizabeth in bemusement. "Oh, I did not know."

"I wished Eliz—Miss Bennet—" William winced at the slip before continuing. "—to convey an invitation. I was hoping you could join us tomorrow for dinner at Pemberley. Others of my party will have arrived by then."

Aunt Gardiner's eyes traveled from her husband to Elizabeth. Whatever she saw in her niece's face gave her confidence that a visit to Pemberley would be to her liking. "We would be pleased to accept your invitation. Thank you."

"I am pleased you may join us." His response encompassed them all, but his eyes lingered on Elizabeth. There was a brief, awkward pause, then he gave them a smart bow. "Until then." Before she knew it, he was striding away.

Aunt Gardiner gave Elizabeth a sidelong glance. "Lizzy, what have you been hiding?" Her expression was stern, but there was a twinkle of mischief in her eye.

Elizabeth ducked her head, uncomfortable with the scrutiny. "I did indeed see Mr. Darcy in Kent when I visited Mr. Collins and Charlotte."

Her aunt gave her a level look. "And?" she prompted finally.

Elizabeth shrugged, attempting a nonchalance she did not feel. "I discovered he was more amiable than I had previously believed. We became friends."

"Friends?" Her aunt snorted. "Lizzy, that man is in love with you!"

Uncle Gardiner gaped at his wife. Elizabeth was hardly less shocked. How had her aunt drawn that conclusion from such a brief conversation?

"Madeline, he was friendly enough, but I believe you are jumping to conclusions," her uncle protested. "Why, his father hates the Bennets! Their feud is well known." Aunt Gardiner simply smiled at her husband. "I cannot believe—well, Lizzy, you do not believe Mr. Darcy is in love with you, do you?"

Elizabeth froze, caught between two impossible alternatives. She did not wish to lie to her aunt and uncle. Mr. Darcy had declared his love for her without any doubt, but they had agreed on secrecy. What could she possibly say?

Aunt Gardiner took one look at her niece's stricken face, and her features softened. She pulled Elizabeth into a warm embrace. "Oh, Lizzy! My dear...you are in a difficult position..."

Uncle Gardiner regarded his wife with a furrowed brow. "She did not answer my question."

"She did not need to," her aunt responded, releasing Elizabeth. "Do you really wish to be privy to such information, Robert?"

Her husband cleared his throat. "I see your point, love." His expression of concern had grown into one resembling panic. "Lizzy, Mr. Darcy's father will not look kindly on any kind of attachment, even a simple friendship. Nor will yours. The safest course would be to cut ties with Mr. Darcy."

Elizabeth could not meet her uncle's eyes. "I believe it is too late for that."

Her uncle gasped. "If he has done something to compromise your—"

"No!" Elizabeth interrupted. "No. I only meant my heart is fully engaged. I cannot disentangle it now." Her aunt's face was full of compassion, but her uncle appeared no less panicky.

"We could leave in the morning—claim an urgent matter of business in Town. It is what your father would want," her uncle said.

Elizabeth made a frustrated noise. "If my father were to meet Mr. Darcy and converse with him, free of prejudice, he would understand what a great man he is. They would like each other." This conversation was tying her stomach into knots. Concealing the betrothal from her aunt and uncle felt like a betrayal, but if they knew, they would feel obligated to inform her father. She did not want to put them in that position—at least not until they were safely wed.

Uncle Gardiner exchanged glances with his wife. "Very well. We shall reserve judgment until after the trip to Pemberley tomorrow. But I will take you back to Hertfordshire if I feel it is necessary."

Elizabeth nodded. "Agreed." She fervently hoped William made a good impression because she shuddered to think what he would do if the Gardiners attempted to remove her from Derbyshire now!

***

Darcy stared into the empty fireplace; now that Elizabeth and the Gardiners had departed, he was replaying the evening in his mind. It had gone well. Georgiana had been delighted to renew her acquaintance with Elizabeth— her savior at the masquerade ball so long ago. The Gardiners were, as promised, amiable and well spoken, and Darcy had enjoyed his conversations with them. Bingley seemed happier than he had in months at the news that Jane Bennet still lived at home, unmarried. Perhaps now he could be persuaded to return to Netherfield and recommence his pursuit of her.

Only the Hursts and Miss Bingley had darkened the mood with their asides and sardonic looks. They had been shocked that Darcy had opened his house to a Bennet, and no doubt Hurst was mentally composing an agitated letter to George Darcy at this very moment. But a letter could not possibly reach his father in time to prevent the wedding. For the first time in weeks, the turmoil in Darcy's stomach had eased.

What a delight to see Elizabeth at Pemberley, just as he had always imagined her! At least he had given her a tour while Pemberley was still his home. He massaged his chest absently as if he could rub away the ache this thought provoked.

Abruptly, he realized Miss Bingley had been speaking for a few moments, and he had not been attending her. "—her complexion was so altered I would not have recognized her! Do you not find her so, Mr. Darcy?"

With no doubt about the subject of the discussion, Darcy reined in the impulse toward a savage rebuke and responded in a more moderate tone. "I do not find her so. She is perhaps a little tanned. No miraculous consequence of traveling during the summer."

Miss Bingley's eyes narrowed; she had expected him to join in her criticism, but he was finished with such dissembling. His stomach for deceit had never been strong, and he had exhausted it.

"I was surprised you invited them to Pemberley. We were acquaintances in Hertfordshire but not so intimate that a visit could not be avoided." Miss Bingley flipped open a fan and began fanning herself.

If only the woman would stop chattering so he could enjoy his thoughts of Elizabeth in peace! "I invited her here because I enjoy her company." How he wished he could say more, but he had promised Elizabeth not to reveal their engagement.

"I thought she was very good company." Georgiana's voice was tremulous; she almost never spoke in company, let alone contradicted Miss Bingley. She must like Elizabeth exceedingly.

"Yes, I find the entire family delightful!" Bingley added, no doubt envisioning Miss Jane Bennet's serene blue eyes.

Miss Bingley's face was pinched with disapproval. "But what would your father say?" She glared at Darcy. "He would not wish you to be entertaining Thomas Bennet's relations at Pemberley."

Darcy gave her a cool look. "Perhaps, but their quarrel is not of my making. I am my own man, and I form my own attachments as I see fit."

Miss Bingley gave a little gasp, and Hurst shifted in his seat. Had he gone too far? Darcy found himself calculating how quickly a letter might reach Bath and then how much longer before his father's carriage arrived at Pemberley. He found the prospect was no longer quite so horrifying. He would marry Elizabeth, his father would yell, Darcy would endure whatever consequences ensued, and then he would enjoy the rest of his life. In fact, now that he thought about it, Darcy was practically eager to take the next step. Perhaps he was being unaccountably reckless, but he did not much care. As long as he had Elizabeth, the rest was unimportant.

He swept his gaze around the room, noting the shocked expressions on the faces of the Hursts, Miss Bingley, and even Bingley himself. Suddenly, he was weary of the entire farce: pretending to dislike her, concealing their betrothal, and faking amiability to people who did not deserve his friendship.

"I fear the day's events have left me rather fatigued," he said. "I shall retire for the night."

Miss Bingley's eyebrows rose even higher. No doubt she had expected him to remain and play at cards for a little while. It *was* rather rude to leave one's guests so abruptly, but Darcy did not care. He could lie in bed and dream about sharing it with Elizabeth. Once they were married, he could run his fingers through her hair and kiss her as often as he liked. By comparison, the present company had nothing to offer.

He stood and strode toward the door. "I bid you good night."

Chapter Nineteen

Elizabeth watched out of the carriage window as Pemberley grew closer and closer. Oh, how different were her feelings from when she had arrived at Derbyshire a few days ago!

"I do not believe you can make the carriage go any faster, Lizzy." Her aunt laughed. Looking down, Elizabeth realized to her embarrassment that her feet had been bouncing eagerly like a child anticipating a treat.

"I am merely excited, Aunt," she replied, mustering what dignity she could. "Pemberley is a very beautiful place."

"It is indeed," her uncle responded, exchanging a knowing look with his wife.

They were to spend the whole day at Pemberley. William had promised to take her uncle fishing, an activity that Elizabeth hoped would solidify their mutual admiration. Georgiana had invited Elizabeth to the music room so they could practice a duet on the pianoforte. And William had whispered something to her about a stroll through Pemberley's gardens at sunset. As long as she could avoid too much of Miss Bingley's company, Elizabeth thought it promised to be a wonderful day.

The entire party awaited them outside of Pemberley's grand main entrance, but as soon as Elizabeth saw William's face, she knew something was wrong. He shifted restlessly and clutched a paper in one hand—agitation written on his features. After her uncle handed Elizabeth out of the carriage, William approached, ignoring the many eyes on them.

"Elizabeth, my father is on his way to Pemberley. Somehow he learned that I departed from Scotland early. He could be arriving tomorrow or the day after!"

Uncle Gardiner was appalled by William's informality. "Now, see here! You should not be addressing her as—"

William ignored him and focused on Elizabeth. "We cannot wait any longer. If you are agreeable, it must happen at once!"

Uncle Gardiner looked from one to another. "What must happen?"

Elizabeth blinked rapidly as she assimilated all of this information. Clearly, William feared that his father might discover a way to prevent the marriage. She bit her lip. These were not the ideal circumstances for a wedding. But then she recalled her reaction to him from the very first glimpse at the masquerade ball. She had been in love with Fitzwilliam Darcy for a very long time. She could not imagine marrying anyone else.

"Yes," she responded.

"Yes?" He seemed to almost disbelieve her answer.

"Yes, I agree, William. Let us do it at once."

Darcy's face broke into a huge grin.

"Mr. Darcy, surely she cannot address you so informally!" Miss Bingley's words were shrill.

"Do what?" Hurst's voice grumbled from behind William.

"Will someone please explain what is happening?" her uncle bellowed.

William slipped his arm around Elizabeth's waist and turned toward the onlookers. Miss Bingley gave a gasp of astonishment, and even Bingley stared at them with an open mouth. Uncle Gardiner was red in the face. Only Georgiana and Aunt Gardiner smiled as if William's actions confirmed what they already suspected.

William cleared his throat. "Elizabeth and I have been betrothed for three months." Miss Bingley made a noise very akin to a squawk. William continued without a glance in her direction. "Since we knew her father would not approve of the match, we waited until Elizabeth came of age. And now we will marry," he finished simply.

"But you hate her!" Miss Bingley cried. William ignored her.

"B-But," her uncle stammered, regarding William like an upstart youth. "You cannot up and marry! The banns must be read. There are dresses to purchase—"

William regarded him calmly. "I have procured a special license."

"I thought your families hated each other," Mr. Bingley said in a bewildered tone.

"I will explain it all to you later, Charles," William said to his friend.

"Oh! Oh!" Miss Bingley was weaving on her feet, her hand up to her forehead in a dramatic gesture. Mr. Bingley was obligated to put an arm around her to hold her up.

William glanced at his pocket watch and tucked it away again. "It is too late to be married today, so I will visit the vicar at Kympton and make arrangements for a ceremony tomorrow. If that is agreeable to you, my dear?"

He smiled down at Elizabeth, who felt quite dizzy at being thus addressed in public. "Yes. That is fine."

"Excellent!" He smiled again. "Then I hope you will all join us tomorrow morning for our wedding ceremony. After a pause, Georgiana tiptoed up to her brother and his fiancée and wished them well. The rest of the party broke into smaller conversations.

"Did you know about this, Madeline?" Elizabeth heard her uncle ask his wife.

"I did not know anything," she replied. "But I suspected."

"I am certain he will regain his senses by tomorrow morning," Miss Bingley said to the Hursts.

Mr. Bingley stood alone with a large smile wreathing his face. "How marvelous!" he said to no one in particular.

William put his arms around Elizabeth and pulled her up against him, ignoring the scandalized looks all about them. "One more day and you will be mine."

**

Today is my wedding day, Elizabeth thought again as she looked in the mirror. She adjusted a piece of wayward lace that would not lie flat; it promptly stuck out again. Oh, well. She examined her hair. A maid at the inn proved to be a genius with hair and had given Elizabeth a very elegant coiffure.

Naturally, there had not been enough time to purchase a new dress, so Elizabeth had to manage with the nicest gown she had packed in her trunk. But Aunt Gardiner had insisted on purchasing a new hat, which blended well with the pale blue silk of her gown. Her aunt had also required the beautiful bouquet of flowers that now rested on the dressing table.

Today is my wedding day. I am to be married today. If she repeated it often enough, perhaps it would seem real.

The previous day, she and her aunt had devoted more than an hour to calming down her uncle. He was unsure the wedding was wise. He feared he had not properly chaperoned her. And he fretted about breaking the news to Elizabeth's father.

Finally, Elizabeth had tactfully pointed out that she was of age, so her uncle could do nothing to prevent the wedding. Perversely, this realization of powerlessness helped calm her uncle. Elizabeth intended to shoulder all of the blame herself and hoped she could convince her father not to blame Uncle Gardiner. Eventually, her father and William might grow to know and respect each other, but it saddened her to think that it might take some time.

But those were worries for another day. Today was her wedding day. In the other room, she heard her aunt and uncle's voices as they readied themselves for the day's event. Her uncle fussed as Aunt Gardiner tied his cravat once more.

Elizabeth rose to answer a knock at the door. Had their carriage arrived already? A rosy cheeked, round-faced maid stood in the doorway. "If you please, ma'am, the post arrived." She handed two letters to Elizabeth with a curtsey and left, closing the door behind her.

Elizabeth gazed on the letters with curiosity, noting that they were both from Jane, but one had been misdirected since her sister had written the directions extremely ill. She glanced at the clock on the mantel. *There is sufficient time. I shall read them quickly now and then peruse them at a more leisurely pace later.*

Elizabeth sank back into the chair as she opened the first letter. Minutes later, she gasped in horror, and her hand flew to her mouth. "No! It could not be!" Jane had written that Lydia had eloped from Brighton with Mr. Wickham! In a great hurry, Elizabeth opened the next letter only to find it contained worse news. Lydia and Wickham had gone to London but were not married!

Tears streamed down her cheeks. "Poor Lydia! Poor, stupid girl!"

At these sounds, her aunt and uncle burst into the room. "What is it, Lizzy?" Aunt Gardiner asked, rushing to Elizabeth's side. Elizabeth acquainted them with the contents of the letter. Soon her uncle paced the room, muttering oaths under his breath as her aunt offered Elizabeth water and a clean handkerchief.

"There is nothing to be done!" Elizabeth moaned. "How is such a man to be worked on?"

Elizabeth attempted to control her wayward emotions while the Gardiners discussed possible plans. Her father had requested Uncle Gardiner's assistance, so he at least would need to depart for London immediately.

Elizabeth was honest enough to admit that some of the tears were for herself. There was no question of holding a wedding today. But when William heard about Lydia's scandalous behavior...would he wish to break off the betrothal entirely? He would be quite right to do so.

Elizabeth considered whether she should insist on it. It was bad enough for William to marry a woman of no family and no fortune whom his father would hate, but to marry into a family in disgrace... Even if he were somehow still willing, Elizabeth could not allow him to further ruin his life for her sake. Yes, even if he wished to continue the betrothal, she must break it off. Her tears fell even more freely.

She remained paralyzed in the chair, staring at Jane's letter—amazed at how one scrap of paper had the power to destroy her future.

***

Darcy quickly tethered his horse and hurried up the steps of the Lambton Inn. Mr. Gardiner's note had not provided any specifics; it had only urged him to come at once. The ride from Pemberley had been sufficiently long for Darcy to imagine all manner of terrible news. Her uncle was forbidding the wedding. Her father had somehow learned of their plans and had arrived to stop her. Elizabeth had run away. Elizabeth was sick. Someone in her family had died. His worst fear was that Elizabeth had changed her mind and no longer wished to marry him. The possibilities were so numerous that Darcy had no difficult imagining new horrors with each passing mile.

When the chambermaid opened the door to the Gardiners' room, Darcy was greatly relieved to see Elizabeth, apparently hale and healthy, sitting at the room's small table. A second glance, however, told him all was not well with his beloved. Her eyes were red-rimmed, and her hand shook violently as she scrutinized a piece of paper in her hand.

Darcy rushed to her side, kneeling next to her chair. "What has happened, my dearest?"

Elizabeth spared him one tear-soaked glance. "Lydia has departed from Brighton, left all her friends, and has thrown herself into the power of Mr. Wickham!"

Darcy could not prevent the oath that emerged, but Elizabeth appeared not to notice, having buried her face in her handkerchief once more.

"How?" His voice sounded choked even to his own ears.

"She fled with him in the middle of the night, leaving a note for her friend, the colonel's wife, saying she would soon be Mrs. Wickham. Jane wrote to say they have been traced only as far as London. Mr. Wickham appears to have no intention of marrying her!" Elizabeth used an already sodden handkerchief to dab her eyes. "My father has gone to London but has had no luck in locating them."

Darcy took the table's other chair, only then spying the Gardiners through the open door to the other room. They were speaking urgently in low tones.

Elizabeth regarded him with steadfast determination despite the watery sheen in her eyes. "Of course, under these circumstances, our marriage cannot happen, and a betrothal between us is impossible. I release you from your promise and any obligations toward me."

If she had plunged a knife into his heart, she could not have hurt him more effectively. He grabbed her hand like a drowning man grabs a rope. "Do not say so! I beg you!"

"I cannot allow my family's disgrace to further damage your reputation, William. Not when you already face scandal and much sacrifice just to marry me."

"It matters not." Darcy could hear the shaking in his voice. "Another scandal will not—"

"Another scandal!" Elizabeth exclaimed. "This is precisely my point. I cannot bear to bring down more grief upon your head."

He shook his head. "No. My father will—" A sudden thought struck Darcy.

"William?"

"Damnation!" Darcy shot to his feet, immediately pacing the confines of the small room. "This must be my father's doing!"

"I beg your pardon?" Elizabeth's expression combined astonishment and bewilderment.

"Wickham has long been my father's protégé. I would wager any amount that he paid Wickham to disgrace your family."

Darcy watched as Elizabeth's face further drained of color. "Why would your father do such a horrible thing?"

He ran both hands through his hair as he paced. "Perhaps he has somehow learned of my interest in you. I thought we were so careful, but…he believed scandal would prevent me from making you an offer."

Darcy had expected Elizabeth to utter another denial. The idea of a plot did seem implausible—if one did not know his father. But when he turned his eyes on her, her face was frozen into a dumbstruck expression. "Elizabeth?"

She closed her mouth as she aroused herself from her contemplations. "Before the garrison left for Brighton, Mr. Wickham—" She stopped, and a delicate pink blush spread over her cheeks.

"What did he do, Elizabeth?" Darcy knelt once more at the side of her chair. If Wickham had harmed her...

Her tongue darted out to wet her lips. "Nothing, except he tried to kiss me in the garden—at Longbourn. I pushed him away, and then my father stopped him."

Suppressing another oath took great effort.

"Then he claimed I was compromised and would have to marry him. At the time, I could not understand why he would want a wife of no fortune—"

"My father hired him to seduce you! He wanted Wickham to render you 'unsuitable' to be my bride." Elizabeth looked slightly green now, and Darcy's stomach felt like lead. His father had stooped to many underhanded tactics in his life, but to scheme to take the virtue of an innocent woman... At that moment, he would have cheerfully punched his father in the mouth. "That blackguard!" Elizabeth's eyes widened to hear Darcy use such a word to describe his own father.

Elizabeth covered her mouth with her hand. "Do you think he knows about us?"

Darcy gave a slow shake of his head. "I do not see how he could have guessed. It is more likely my father ordered him to compromise whichever Bennet daughter was available."

"That is-is despicable!"

Darcy dared to cover Elizabeth's hand with his own where it rested on the arm of the chair. "Now do you see, dearest, why we cannot break off the betrothal? That is exactly what he wants."

"B-But there will still be scandal—"

Darcy stood again but did not resume pacing. "Perhaps the scandal may be minimized. I will travel to London and see if I may locate Lydia and Wickham. Then I will ensure that Wickham weds your sister—if they are not already married."

Elizabeth stood as well. "No, you should not grow further entangled in my family's scandal!"

"This is the least I must do. My family has *created* this scandal. Please allow me to do what I can to prevent your family from suffering too much."

Elizabeth hesitated for a moment, but finally she nodded. "Very well, I will be happy for your help—particularly if you can bring about a marriage—for my family's sake." Darcy released the breath he had been holding. "But," Elizabeth continued, "if there is a scandal, we should discuss the possibility of dissolving our betrothal."

Darcy nodded; he would agree to anything at this point but had no intention of releasing her, no matter what occurred.

"I will prepare for a trip to London." Nothing, he vowed silently, would stand in the way of his marriage to Elizabeth.

Chapter Twenty

George Darcy strode into the front hallway of Pemberley, feeling tired, travel-stained, and rumpled. Thank God, he was home; he was done with traveling for now. The footman took his hat, and the butler greeted him with a bow. Darcy wanted a long, hot bath, but business came first. Wickham had written about the success of his ploy. Darcy was sure it would make Elizabeth Bennet unpalatable to his son, but just in case, he needed to make sure Fitzwilliam understood all of the consequences should he follow through with this lunatic scheme.

"Graves, I need to speak with Fitzwilliam immediately. Send him to my study," he ordered the butler as he continued through the marble-clad hallway. When Graves did not respond, Darcy glanced back over his shoulder. The man's mouth was slightly open, but he had said nothing.

"What is the matter?" Darcy barked.

Graves swallowed. "Mr. Fitzwilliam is not here. He departed for London yesterday."

"What?" Darcy roared throwing his walking stick across the hallway where it clattered on the marble tiles. "I wrote of my impending arrival—told him there were important matters to discuss. He knew I wished to speak with him!"

Graves winced. "I am very sorry, sir."

Darcy pointed his finger in the man's face. "Why did he leave so suddenly? Did he receive some kind of urgent news?"

Graves shrugged helplessly. "I do not know, sir. No messages arrived for him. He merely gave orders that his horse was to be saddled and bags packed for his immediate departure."

Darcy wanted to shout some more, but it was useless to rail at the butler. The man could not have prevented Fitzwilliam's departure under any circumstances. "Who is here?" he demanded from the man. "Georgiana? Hurst? This Bingley fellow?"

"They are all here, sir. Mr. and Mrs. Hurst and Mr. and Miss Bingley. Mr. Fitzwilliam gave instructions that their visit should continue despite his absence. Miss Darcy has been the hostess."

Darcy yanked at the knot of his cravat. The damn thing was choking him. What was Fitzwilliam thinking leaving behind a household of guests that Darcy would now need to feed and entertain? Hurst was of a good family at least, but the rest of them...whelps of a simple tradesman! Darcy did not care if they had money now; they had no breeding, no lineage of distinction. Now Darcy must sit at the dinner table and speak with them as if they were his equals. All because of Fitzwilliam—who was not even here to be yelled at!

Darcy rubbed his neck where the cravat had chafed. He would encourage the interlopers to depart immediately, but first he needed to address the situation with Fitzwilliam. "Where is Hurst now? I must speak with him." Darcy still had not forgiven Hurst for marrying into that family; no matter how much debt the man had incurred it was not worth it.

"I believe the guests are still in the breakfast room," Graves replied.

For a moment, Darcy was tempted to have Graves send Hurst to his study for a private conversation, but he was too impatient. He wanted information now.

Without another word to the butler, Darcy strode down the hall to the breakfast room. He could smell the ham and eggs and hear the low murmur of conversation before he reached the room. Darcy pushed open the doors and strode past the others as he made his way toward Hurst.

"Mr. Darcy! This is a pleasure—" Darcy ignored Miss Bingley's obsequious comments.

"Thank you for your hospitality—" Mr. Bingley stood and extended his hand, but Darcy strode right past him.

"Father, you have returned!" Georgiana cried from her place at the head of the table.

Darcy gave his daughter a curt nod but did not slow his pace until he reached Hurst's seat. He pulled the stout man to his feet by his cravat. "Tell me, Hurst. Why did Fitzwilliam leave so abruptly yesterday?"

Hurst's face turned red. "I do not know, honestly! He merely said urgent business in Town and would not explain any further. I believe he was traveling with Miss Bennet and the Gardiners."

Horror ran down Darcy's spine. "Who?" His voice was a low, menacing growl.

"Miss Elizabeth Bennet was here with her aunt and uncle," Hurst clarified. "I wrote to you, but the letter obviously did not reach you in time."

"Miss Bennet was here?"

Hurst nodded and shook his head at the same time. "Yes...I mean, no! She was staying in Lambton, but Mr. Darcy invited her and her relatives to dinner two nights ago."

"She was *here*?" Darcy could feel his lip curl in disgust. When Hurst nodded, Darcy considered whether he should have everything the woman had touched thoroughly cleaned—or burned.

"He had Elizabeth Bennet to dinner in *this* house?" The thought was so horrifying that Darcy needed to check and make sure it was, in fact, real.

"Yes, sir." Hurst tried to pry Darcy's fingers from his cravat, but he did not release his hold.

"And he says they are betrothed!" These words burst from Miss Bingley, who had clearly been awaiting the opportunity to draw attention back to herself. Darcy turned his head sharply in her direction. "He planned the wedding for yesterday morning, but something happened, and they all disappeared. He even had a special license."

Darcy caught his breath. "They did not wed?"

Miss Bingley shook her head. "I do not believe so."

Darcy felt ill when he thought of how close he had come to having a Bennet for a daughter-in-law. It was a scene from his worst nightmare.

"We—well, *I* tried to convince him not to go through with it." Miss Bingley's superiority had completely returned now. "I told him you would not like it, but he was determined to—"

Darcy had obtained all the information from Miss Bingley he needed. "Will you be quiet?" Miss Bingley's jaw closed with an audible snap.

Darcy released his hold on Hurst's cravat, ignoring the man's great heaving gasps, and thought about this news. Fitzwilliam and the others must have departed because of Wickham's plot with the youngest Bennet daughter; they must have been under the mistaken delusion they could somehow stop the scandal.

But what if the scandal was not enough to dissuade Fitzwilliam from the alliance? Darcy had not taken that possibility seriously before. However, if his son wished to distance himself from the Bennets, Fitzwilliam would have remained at Pemberley. Had Fitzwilliam guessed at his father's role in the scandal? If he was not so angry with his son, Darcy would admire how well he had been out-maneuvered by him. Fitzwilliam had learned to play this game very well, but he would not win.

Darcy brought his fist down on the breakfast table with a loud thump. Everyone in the room started.

Was Fitzwilliam foolish enough to wed into a family mired in scandal? If so, Darcy knew he could still prevent it. He had conceived a foolproof plan as a last resort; there was no chance it would fail. Darcy sighed. There was no avoiding it. He must travel to London in person to explain to Fitzwilliam *all* of the consequences of his action. Damnation! He had no desire to travel again so soon, and he did not like London, particularly at this time of year. Well, there was nothing for it.

Darcy bellowed for Graves. If he packed quickly enough, they could be on the road in two hours.

***

"…If any man knows of a reason why these two should not be joined in holy matrimony, let him speak now or forever hold his peace," the priest solemnly intoned, taking a brief pause after his words.

Darcy shot a glance at Elizabeth, and she smiled wryly. He returned the grin; no doubt they were thinking the same thing.

"And now to the vows." The sour-faced priest turned his attention to the couple in front of him. Lydia was the only truly happy person in the entire church. The Gardiners' faces held weary resignation, and Wickham's smile was more of a grimace.

The new white silk dress Lydia had demanded stood out vibrantly against the church's gloomy interior. The smile she turned on her fiancé was genuine; she was pleased with him and with the wedding in general. However, Darcy knew Wickham well enough to see the anger and frustration seething under his amiable surface. Wickham had expected to play his part in George Darcy's schemes and then be well quit of Lydia Bennet. He was not best pleased to be shackled to her for life.

"I, George Wickham, take thee, Lydia Bennet, to be…"

As Wickham dutifully recited his wedding vows, Darcy breathed a sigh of relief. Finding Wickham had been the easy part of the endeavor. Darcy had spent the better part of a day threatening, cajoling, and bribing

Wickham into marrying Lydia. Wickham had finally admitted to George Darcy's role in the scheme, news which Darcy used to alleviate some of Elizabeth's guilt over the scandal. Truthfully, these events had not reflected well on either family.

Darcy had been a regular visitor to Gracechurch Street as he and Mr. Gardiner worked out the details of settling Wickham's debts and arranging a hasty marriage. By the time Darcy had arrived in London to lend assistance, Mr. Bennet had departed for Hertfordshire. Which was probably just as well, Darcy reflected.

Impressed with Darcy's handling of Wickham, Mr. Gardiner had promised to put in a good word with Mr. Bennet. Darcy did not know whether Elizabeth's uncle might make much progress, but he was grateful for anything that might soften Mr. Bennet's views.

Across the aisle, Elizabeth's smile faltered, and she shifted her weight uneasily. It was difficult to be happy at a wedding when the couple so clearly should not be marrying at all. Elizabeth stood up with Lydia while Darcy performed the same service for Wickham—although his role was primarily to prevent the groom from bolting at the last minute.

Elizabeth shot him a sidelong glance and a sweet smile, which helped lift some of Darcy's darker thoughts. Was she thinking about their upcoming nuptials? About the day when they would be standing before a priest? He certainly was, and he was impatient for that day to arrive. They had agreed to postpone their wedding, at the very least until it would not take place in the shadow of scandal, but she also hoped her father would relent enough that her parents might attend.

Finally, the farce of a ceremony was finished, and the bride and groom paraded down the aisle of the mostly empty church. There only remained the agony of the wedding breakfast Lydia had demanded, and then Darcy could be quit of Wickham—hopefully forever.

***

However, a surprise met the "celebrants" when they arrived at Gracechurch Street. Mr. Bennet was seated in the Gardiners' parlor.

Lydia issued a squeal that that was more reminiscent of a rodent than a girl. "Papa! Why on earth are you here? What a shame you missed the ceremony!"

Mr. Bennet stood and embraced his youngest daughter with a cool smile. "Yes, what a shame." His tone of voice told Darcy the omission was deliberate, but Lydia missed the implications. She chattered about her dress, the flowers, and the weather while Mr. Bennet embraced Elizabeth and Mrs. Gardiner.

But when Mr. Bennet turned to shake Mr. Gardiner's hand, he noticed Darcy standing behind him. His eyes grew wide and then narrowed dangerously. "What the devil is *he* doing here?" he bellowed.

After a brief pause in which even Lydia was silent, Wickham exclaimed, "God knows, *I* don't want him here."

Then everyone spoke at once. Mr. Bennet shouted at Mr. Gardiner. Elizabeth tried to get her father's attention, and Lydia whined that no one was paying her any mind on her wedding day. The Gardiners' children darted around the room, adding to the confusion, while their mother tried to bring them to order.

The noise battered at Darcy's nerves for several minutes. Finally, he shouted, "Quiet!" To his surprise, all the noise ceased, and all eyes turned to him. Mrs. Gardiner took advantage of the silence to usher her children from the room.

Mr. Bennet, nostrils flaring, pointed imperiously at Darcy. "That man must be removed from this house immediately!"

Mr. Gardiner rubbed his eyes wearily. "Bennet, this is my house. I will say who stays and who goes. And Mr. Darcy is my guest."

Mr. Bennet stared at his brother-in-law. "Have you turned against me as well?"

"Papa!" Elizabeth rebuked.

"Somebody got mud on my slippers!" Lydia wailed.

Darcy could see the situation was in danger of devolving into chaos once more. "Mr. Bennet, could we perhaps speak in Mr. Gardiner's study?"

Mr. Bennet's eyes narrowed as he regarded Darcy and then darted to Wickham, who was doing his best to blend in with the wallpaper. No doubt he suspected Mr. Bennet had a few choice words for him as well.

"A capital idea!" Mr. Gardiner exclaimed. He turned to his wife, who had just returned to the room. "Could you have some tea sent in?" Mrs. Gardiner nodded.

"But what about my wedding breakfast?" Lydia protested peevishly.

"You shall still have it. This will only delay it a little bit." Mrs. Gardiner put her arm around her youngest niece. "Come, we will remove the mud from your lovely slippers." Lydia allowed herself to be led from the room.

Mr. Gardiner left the parlor with Mr. Bennet on his heels. Darcy followed, and Elizabeth joined him. He raised an eyebrow, but she gave him a defiant expression, which demonstrated that she fully intended to be part of this conversation. As Darcy quit the parlor, he glimpsed Wickham helping himself to a generous portion of the brandy on the Gardiners' sideboard.

The little party arrived at Mr. Gardiner's study and waited while the servants brought in extra chairs. When Elizabeth seated herself between Mr. Bennet and Darcy, her father looked at her askance. "Elizabeth? Why are you here? This does not concern you!"

She raised her chin. "I beg your pardon, it does concern me, Papa."

Mr. Bennet's brow furrowed further. "*How* does it concern you?"

Mr. Gardiner interrupted. "We will discuss that later. Thomas, the material fact is that Mr. Darcy has every right to be here. He was instrumental in bringing about Lydia and Wickham's marriage."

Mr. Bennet's gaze slid to Darcy. "In what way? I would expect him to be encouraging Wickham's despicable behavior. That would be just like a Darcy."

This was too much! "Now see here, Bennet—!" Darcy growled.

"Silence!" Mr. Gardiner shouted. When everyone quieted, he focused on his brother-in-law. "Mr. Darcy found Wickham and persuaded him to marry Lydia even though Wickham was not so inclined initially."

"Of course, he found Wickham. The gutter is the proper place for a Darcy!" Mr. Bennet sneered.

He would not tolerate this! Darcy shot to his feet— as did Mr. Bennet. But Elizabeth quickly stood as well, placing herself between them and putting a soothing hand on Darcy's arm. At her touch, the anger drained out of him. Begrudgingly, he seated himself once more.

Mr. Gardiner continued as if the interruption had never occurred. "Mr. Darcy paid Wickham's debts in London and Brighton and purchased his commission in the regulars—as well as settling an amount on Wickham directly—a sum I am not privy to. I would have been happy to be of service to my niece, but Mr. Darcy insisted."

Mr. Bennet gaped at his brother-in-law. "No, you told me you had—"

"I wrote that the business was concluded," Mr. Gardiner replied stiffly. "I did not reveal who had concluded it. Mr. Darcy was reluctant to reveal his generosity, but I believe it is imperative that you understand."

"You paid everything? You forced him to marry Lydia?" Mr. Bennet turned wide eyes on Darcy. "Why?"

"I do not wish you to feel beholden to me. You owe me nothing," Darcy said.

"I am...very grateful for your generosity." The words seem to stick in Mr. Bennet's throat. "But why did you incur these costs in the first place?"

Only Elizabeth knew of George Darcy's role in Wickham's schemes; Darcy hoped that Mr. Bennet would never learn of it. However, that was only one of his motivations. "He was raised at Pemberley, and I believe some faults in his character are due to excessive indulgence in his childhood. Furthermore, I should have done more in the autumn to warn the population of Meryton about Wickham's character."

"I did warn Lydia," Mr. Bennet said bitterly. "But apparently it did little good."

Darcy nodded. "Nonetheless, I knew what he was capable of but did not wish to lay bare his association with my family; had I done so, these events might not have occurred."

Bennet's eyebrows climbed into his forehead. "You took this responsibility on yourself?" he echoed incredulously.

Mr. Gardiner nodded. "If not for Mr. Darcy's knowledge of Wickham's associates, we might not have found them until much later—when the scandal had taken root."

Mr. Bennet looked dazed as if someone had just informed him that the sky was purple and geese flew under the water. "But why?" His tone was now more bewildered than belligerent.

"As I said," Darcy repeated, "my family—"

"Yes, yes." Mr. Bennet waved his hand impatiently. "I am sure all of that is true, but is it the whole truth?" His bewildered expression had given way to a shrewd glance between Darcy and Elizabeth. "Why is my *daughter* in this conference?"

Darcy should have known the man who raised Elizabeth would be quick to discern what remained unsaid. Darcy shot her a quick glance, and she gave an almost imperceptible nod.

Darcy straightened his shoulders. He had thought to postpone this conversation for another day—a far future day after they had traveled to Longbourn—but there was nothing for it now. "I would like your consent to marry your daughter, Elizabeth. She has already given hers."

"What?" Mr. Bennet leapt to his feet. "Are you a lunatic?" He glared at his daughter. "What are you thinking, accepting this man? He wishes to ruin our family!"

Elizabeth's eyes blazed as she stood. "I believe he has just proved the opposite! If Mr. Darcy wished to ruin our family, he would have only needed to sit by and do nothing while Lydia's actions did it for him. Instead he has proved himself a great friend to the Bennet family and has protected our name!"

"How do we know that he did not engineer this whole fiasco to act as our rescuer? Wickham is an intimate of the Darcys; he could have been paid to seduce Lydia."

Darcy winced at an accusation that came a little too close to the truth. Fortunately, Mr. Bennet was glaring at his daughter and did not notice.

"And how would marrying *me* serve to ruin our family, Papa?" Elizabeth asked. "Do you think he is greedy for my impressive dowry?" Now Mr. Bennet winced. "Is he planning to ruin me with his money? The benefit is all on my side."

Fortunately, Mr. Bennet does not know how poverty does threaten me.

"Perhaps he intends to leave you waiting at the altar—"

Now Darcy shot to his feet. How dare he suggest that? "I would never—!"

Mr. Bennet ignored him. "Or he will take advantage of you and—" He stopped suddenly, his face draining of color. "Is that it?" He regarded Elizabeth with stricken eyes. "Did he impose himself on your innocence? Are you with—?"

"No and no!" Elizabeth stamped her foot. "William would never do such a thing! He is an honorable man. I wish to marry him because he is a good man, and I love him." Mr. Bennet's rigid posture relaxed a little. *At least he believes her.*

Despite the tension in the room, Darcy was warmed by Elizabeth's vehement defense. He need not defend himself against Mr. Bennet's accusations. Elizabeth was doing a fine job for him.

"Y-You love him?" Mr. Bennet's voice faltered. "No...you cannot...you cannot put your heart in his hands, Lizzy. You cannot trust a Darcy."

"He is not his father."

"George Darcy raised him. The apple does not fall far from the tree."

Mr. Gardiner cleared his throat. "If I may interrupt, Thomas, I have observed Mr. Darcy interact with Lizzy for a number of days now, and I have no doubt of his sincere affection for her." Darcy shot the man a grateful smile.

"I am sure Lydia believes Wickham holds sincere affection for her as well," sneered Mr. Bennet.

"Do not compare me to that—!" Darcy started.

Mr. Gardiner interrupted again. "Mr. Darcy has been open and generous in all of his dealings with us. He is well liked by many in Derbyshire. The same cannot be said of his father."

Darcy stared at Mr. Gardiner. When had the man canvassed the inhabitants of Derbyshire?

His words appeared to affect Mr. Bennet quite forcefully. He stared at Mr. Gardiner, his mouth slightly open.

"You know that the best judge of a man's character is how he treats those beneath him. Fitzwilliam Darcy has an excellent reputation among his tenants, townspeople, and household staff," Elizabeth's uncle continued.

"It does not necessarily follow that he would make a good husband." Mr. Bennet's tone of voice had grown far less forceful.

"Mr. Darcy is eight and twenty." Mr. Gardiner cleared his throat. "He has had many years to marry the cream of the *ton*. There are few women who would turn him down. But he has chosen your daughter despite the disadvantages of the match and the inevitable disapproval of his father. Does that not speak to a sincere affection?"

Mr. Bennet was not the only one struck dumb by these words. Darcy had not been aware of making such a favorable impression on the reserved Mr. Gardiner.

Mr. Bennet sank into his chair as if he could no longer support himself. "She is not yet one and twenty," he observed to no one in particular.

"I am, Papa. My birthday was a few weeks ago," Elizabeth reminded him. "But we would prefer to wed with your blessing." She sat again, taking her father's hand and patting it reassuringly.

As Darcy sat, Mr. Bennet turned to him. "Do you love her?"

"With all my heart," he breathed.

Mr. Bennet closed his eyes, shook his head once, and then opened them. He stared searchingly at Mr. Gardiner, then Darcy, and then Elizabeth. Then he sighed.

"Very well, I give my consent." Elizabeth laughed. "But you must prove yourself worthy of her." Bennet's glare pinned Darcy in place.

"I will strive to do so every day," Darcy promised.

Mr. Bennet removed his eyeglasses and rubbed his eyes. "Five daughters," he muttered. "They will be the death of me."

"Would you care for some brandy, Thomas?" Mr. Gardiner asked, reaching for a decanter on a shelf behind him.

"Good Lord, yes!" Mr. Bennet sighed.

Darcy dared to glance at Elizabeth and saw that her eyes shone with happiness—and perhaps some tears. He stood and reached for her hand, which he now had official permission to hold. "We shall leave you gentlemen to it then."

***

Elizabeth closed the door to her uncle's study behind her. "We should return to the parlor."

"In a minute." William's voice was low and husky. The late morning sun filtered slantwise into the hallway, casting long shadows. He put a hand up to caress one side of her neck; the touch felt wonderful. "We have your father's consent," he marveled in that same hushed voice.

"Yes."

"You have consented, your father has consented, and Wickham no longer threatens scandal. Nothing more stands in our way. I am blessed indeed." Without looking away from her eyes, William drew her back away from the doorway into an alcove next to the window, sufficiently shadowed so that no one would immediately notice them.

"I am the fortunate one," Elizabeth breathed.

His lips were inches from hers. "We must disagree on that point." His voice was still low; the deep notes vibrated throughout her whole body.

He clasped both sides of her face with his hands and kissed her. It was a gentle, sweet kiss, but it was also a claim: he was the only one allowed to kiss her thus.

Elizabeth sighed in contentment and opened her lips for his exploring tongue. She inhaled his purely masculine smell, accented by brandy and leather.

As he continued to explore her mouth, one of his hands traced its way down her neck and the bare skin of her upper back. She shuddered at the light touch. Through her dress, his fingers followed the curve of her spine and all the way to her bottom where he gave a gentle squeeze. Elizabeth shivered with pleasure. Who knew a simple touch could create such sensations? If he could do that to her through her clothing, how would it feel on their wedding night without such barriers....?

With one hand on her lower back and the other at the back of her neck, William pulled her against his body as he placed a series of kisses along the side of her neck. "Elizabeth!" he moaned. "Oh, how I long to take you to Darcy House...to my bedroom." This idea enchanted Elizabeth as well. The feelings he evoked were so exquisite.... Fortunately for her virtue, they were surrounded by people who would insist on a proper wedding first.

"Once we are married..." she breathed into his ear.

"Please let that be soon!" He pulled away so he could peer into her eyes. "My father would have arrived at Pemberley to find me gone, but he now knows I intend to marry you. Even now he is surely en route to London. I know it is irrational, but I fear he will find a way to prevent the wedding."

The tension in his voice caused anxiety to curl in her stomach. "What could he do?" Elizabeth asked.

"I do not know. He is ever scheming, always planning to bend others to his will. I have thwarted his plan with Wickham to disgrace your family, but my father does not concede defeat readily. He will not sit idly by and let our wedding occur if he can stop it."

The wedding ceremony was not important to Elizabeth. The prospect of the marriage was so much more glorious. "We have the special license. We could marry tomorrow if you wish. I see no reason for delay."

"Not tomorrow. It is Sunday, but the day after, if you wish."

"Yes, I wish."

"Such an eager bride!" Darcy exclaimed. "I love that. And I love you."

"I love you, too," she responded, and sealed it with another kiss.

Chapter Twenty One

Darcy scanned the dining room with some satisfaction. The table was elegant, the food was exquisite, and Elizabeth was with him. The room was rather large for such a small party—originally, it had only been Mr. Gardiner, Mr. Bennet, and Elizabeth, but Richard had contrived to obtain an evening free from his duties. Darcy was well pleased with the company.

Darcy caught Elizabeth's eye, and she bestowed upon him the most heart-stopping smile he had ever seen. His only frustration was that they remained unwed. Their plans for a Monday wedding had been thwarted by Mrs. Gardiner, who had caught some kind of infection in her lungs. Elizabeth had been quite alarmed, but the doctor had assured her the condition was not serious; however, he had advised her aunt to remain at home for the day.

In between bouts of coughing, Mrs. Gardiner had insisted that Darcy and Elizabeth wed without her, but Elizabeth could not imagine a wedding without her aunt, and Darcy had agreed. They hoped Mrs. Gardiner's health would improve sufficiently that they could perform the ceremony tomorrow.

Darcy told himself there was no need to rush. His father would cut off his allowance before or after the wedding; it made little difference. However, a niggling doubt in the back of his mind warned that somehow his father would find a way to prevent the marriage itself. He would not rest easy until Elizabeth was his.

His servants had served the first course, a soup, but no one had yet commenced eating. Darcy stood, feeling unaccountably dry-mouthed. Chatter around the table died, and everyone's eyes turned to the head of the table. "Welcome to Darcy House," he told his guests. "I am pleased you are here and will be even more pleased to have you all as guests at our wedding." He gazed fondly at Elizabeth, and she smiled.

"Hopefully soon," Richard chimed in.

"Yes, indeed," Darcy smiled.

"To Darcy and Lizzy!" Mr. Gardiner raised his glass in a toast. Everyone clinked their glasses and sipped the wine. Even Mr. Bennet seemed to be amenable to the match if not precisely enthusiastic. Soon the guests were eagerly devouring the soup.

The dining room's main door opened. Who would be arriving now? All of the guests were present, and the butler would have turned away any callers.

In the doorway, Briggs had a stricken expression upon his face. Darcy stood immediately, even as Briggs intoned, "Mr. George Darcy and—"

Darcy's father did not wait for the butler to finish the announcement but pushed past him into the dining room, almost causing Briggs to lose his balance.

George Darcy's clothes were rumpled and dusty from travel, and he looked haggard with exhaustion. He must have browbeat the coachman to have arrived so quickly from Pemberley. Behind their father, Georgiana hovered uncertainly.

Darcy managed a smile, hoping his father would be civil before his guests. "Father, Georgiana, this is a surprise! Would you like to join us for dinner?"

His father's gaze traveled about the room and he sneered. "I think not. This is not my idea of good company."

Darcy gritted his teeth against an angry reply. During the awkward silence that followed, Georgiana quietly seated herself next to Richard and waited while the servants brought her a table setting. *Good for her.*

Darcy kept his voice level. "Then perhaps you could rest upstairs, and we will speak later—"

"I did not come all the way from Pemberley for social niceties!" George Darcy expostulated. "I came to stop you from marrying that wench!" He pointed to Elizabeth where she sat on Darcy's left.

Georgiana gasped, and Mr. Bennet shot to his feet. Mr. Gardiner blustered at the insult to his niece, "Now see here—"

"You will not speak of my daughter that way!" Mr. Bennet was not precisely shouting, but his voice cut through the other noise in the room.

Darcy's father regarded Mr. Bennet with narrowed eyes, his features twisted into an expression of hatred that Darcy had never seen before on his father's face. "How long have you been plotting this, *Tommy?*" George Darcy sneered. "You would like to get your hands on the Darcy fortune. Well, I will not let that happen!"

Mr. Bennet snorted. "I did not even learn about this—" he gestured between Darcy and Elizabeth. "—until yesterday. I was not best pleased, but my daughter assures me your son's character is far superior to yours."

George Darcy was shaking his head even before Mr. Bennet finished speaking. "You might have fooled Fitzwilliam with that act, but I can see through your machinations. You have maneuvered them into this whole betrothal!"

Mr. Bennet's face was red, all the way to the tips of his ears, but he marched up to Darcy's father and faced him despite their six-inch height difference. "If you believe that I have spent thirty years scheming how to get hold of the Darcy fortune, then you seriously overestimate your importance in my life." Darcy fought the urge to applaud. "And if you believe that he could be taken in by such a scheme, then you seriously underestimate your son!"

George Darcy's mouth fell open. He could hardly have expected an impassioned defense of his son from Thomas Bennet. But Elizabeth's father was not finished.

"You do not know Elizabeth, so you would not understand how she is incapable of such deceitfulness. But you should know your own son's character. He has remained unmarried for many years; would anything less than the deepest love convince him to wed now?"

Despite the situation, Darcy's heart warmed. It was almost worth the mortification of his father confronting him over the dinner table to hear such an impassioned defense from a man who had distrusted him the day before. Mr. Bennet clearly held his daughter's judgment in high regard.

"You were always so sure of your own rectitude," Darcy's father scoffed. "No doubt your daughter dresses up her ambitions in the clothing of respectability as well."

Mr. Bennet opened his mouth for a scathing retort, but Darcy interposed himself between the two older men and encouraged Elizabeth's father to return to his chair. He addressed his father. "Perhaps—"

George Darcy regarded his son with disgust. "I did not come here to feud with Bennet! I came to prevent you from marrying that chit."

Darcy felt his blood pound that much faster at this insult. "Then you made the trip for nothing." He took Elizabeth's hand in his and pulled her toward him, staring defiantly at his father. "I love Elizabeth, and I will marry her—with or without your blessing."

George Darcy laughed grimly. "If you marry her, you will be making do with a lot less than my blessing."

Darcy stood a little straighter. "I know that you might cut off my allowance, and I am prepared for those consequences."

This time his father guffawed. "Cut off your allowance? Boy, that is the least of your troubles. If you marry that chit, I will have you disinherited."

Elizabeth gasped, turning white as a sheet. Georgiana looked as if she might swoon. Richard shot to his feet. "You cannot do that!" Darcy's mind took a moment to absorb the words. Disinherited? The possibility had never entered his mind.

George Darcy turned a challenging look on Richard. "I can, and I will. Pemberley is not entailed. I may bestow it on any family member I choose."

Some of the tension left Darcy's shoulders. "So Georgiana—"

His father scoffed. "A woman could never run Pemberley." Darcy spared a sympathetic glance for his sister, whose eyes remained fixed on her uneaten soup. He said a silent prayer that Georgiana would not take their father's cruel words to heart.

"Besides," George Darcy continued, "she will marry, and the estate would pass out of the Darcy name."

Darcy's brows knit together as he regarded his father. "So who would inherit Pemberley then?"

"John Darcy," his father said triumphantly.

Darcy felt a bit dizzy and wished he could sit. John Darcy was a distant cousin whom Darcy had met only once. Five years older, he owned a small estate in Cornwall. Widowed with two sons, he seemed sober and industrious. Darcy had no reason to believe John Darcy would not treat Pemberley's tenants well, but his cousin's estate was small—smaller even than Longbourn. Could his cousin manage the demands of a large estate like Pemberley?

More importantly, could Darcy give it up? Just considering the possibility made him reel. He had been prepared for exile from Pemberley during his father's lifetime, secure in the knowledge that he would inherit it upon George Darcy's death. But to lose it entirely... Becoming a barrister would then be a necessity. And what would become of Georgiana? If she did not marry, where would she live after their father's death?

Unfortunately, Darcy also had no difficulty imagining the ensuing scandal. The Darcys had one of the biggest fortunes in England. If he were disinherited, the *ton* would talk of it for months, —if not years. Of course, without his fortune, he would no longer be a member of the *ton*, so the gossip would not touch him so directly. Still, any of his friends would regard him with pity or judgment in their eyes.

And what would Elizabeth think of such a sacrifice? She had turned white and was trembling—in rage or fear? She had been prepared for deprivation after marrying Darcy, but she had not expected to wed a veritable pauper. Would she even want him under those circumstances? But then keeping his fortune meant losing her.

Elizabeth squeezed his hand. "William, you cannot give up Pemberley." Her unselfishness left him awestruck. She would surrender her chance at happiness so he might keep the family estate she knew he loved. Those sentiments themselves proved her worth. How could he relinquish such a woman? He would never find another.

Darcy surveyed the faces around the table. Richard glared daggers at George Darcy, who pretended not to notice. Mr. Gardiner looked appalled while Mr. Bennet appeared disgusted by his father's very presence. Georgiana's hand covered her mouth as her eyes traveled between her father and brother. It warmed Darcy's heart to know he and Elizabeth had the support of everyone at the table, but his father still held all the cards.

He gazed again at Elizabeth. Despite the sheen of tears in her eyes, they were still quite fine. He loved her more in this moment than he ever had before—something he would not have thought possible.

He supposed he could ask her to wait for him until his father's demise, whereupon they could marry with impunity. But his father was hale and healthy. It could be another ten or twenty years before Darcy inherited. He could not in good conscience ask Elizabeth to remain unmarried for so long. And then there was the question of his own marital state. His father had already demanded that he wed and provide an heir; he would not allow Darcy to delay marriage.

Darcy could easily imagine that future. He would enjoy the privileges and luxuries of Pemberley and continue his life as it had always been. Run the estate, take care of tenants, attend balls, ride his horses—alone in the echoing halls of Pemberley, or worse, shackled to a wife he did not love. All the while he would know what he had sacrificed to achieve that security. His brief, shining moment of happiness with Elizabeth would need to sustain him for the rest of his life.

This future unfurled before him. If he bowed to his father now, he could never defy him again. His father would threaten to disinherit him at every turn for the slightest infraction. It would be the sword of Damocles hanging over his head.

Examined from that perspective, Darcy's decision was easy. He looked back at his father. George Darcy wore a grim smile as if he knew he had already triumphed. "No," Darcy said simply.

George Darcy blinked. "No? No to what?"

"No, I will not give up Elizabeth. I will marry her, and you may disinherit me if you wish."

Georgiana gasped, and Mr. Gardiner grumbled something under his breath.

His father turned white. "You cannot possibly be serious!"

Darcy smiled, baring all his teeth. "Try me."

"*I* am not bluffing," his father warned. "I will follow through with my threats."

Darcy nodded. "I know." His father never bluffed.

"William, you cannot!" Elizabeth's voice was low and hoarse.

"Think about what you are giving up!" Mr. Gardiner frowned at him. "This is a decision you cannot undo." Even Mr. Bennet's expression had gone from defiant to uncertain.

Darcy's gaze returned to his father's. "I have decided, and I will not change my mind. Elizabeth and I will wed tomorrow."

His father flinched, Darcy noted with some satisfaction. He truly had expected his son to back down. "But how will you live?" George Darcy's voice had grown plaintive. "I am well aware that Miss Bennet has no dowry."

"We will live. That is not your concern."

"I will give you the night to think about it," his father said with the air of someone granting a concession even though one had not been requested.

"I do not want the night. I have made my decision." Fortunately, Darcy's emotional turmoil was not reflected in his voice—it was strong and steady.

His father puffed out his chest. "Then I will go to my solicitor's in the morning and sign the paperwork."

Darcy could not deny the pang he felt at these words, but he refused to be deterred. "Perhaps you will return in time to greet us upon our return from the church."

"You will not go through with it!" George Darcy's tone was now far less certain than before.

Darcy shrugged. "Believe what you will. But remember, I am your son. Everything I learned, I learned from you."

His father frowned as if he did not grasp Darcy's meaning, but then he shook his head. "I will stay here at Darcy House in the master's bedchamber." Darcy nodded; he had expected nothing else. "Let me know when you have come to your senses," his father spat. With that, George Darcy turned on his heel and marched out of the room.

There was a moment of stunned silence, and then— almost as one—all the eyes in the room turned toward

Darcy. He gestured to the table and seated himself. "Shall we finish our meal? It may be my last one at Darcy House."

Georgiana made a stricken noise. Darcy smiled apologetically. "I am sorry for the joke, my dear. It was in bad taste."

She gave him a wan smile. Darcy focused on conveying an air of calmness; he would not have the night before his wedding marred by obsessive discussions about his father. However, he could not help considering how much of his life was now undecided. He would need a profession and a place to live. No, *they* would need a place to live. And they must husband their meager resources carefully. Good Lord, there was much to consider!

"What will I do without you?" Georgiana wailed.

"You will not lose me. I will always be your brother." At his sister's uncertain look, Darcy stood, walked to her seat, and gave her a reassuring hug.

"But father will not let me visit you—"

Darcy nodded. "Perhaps, but we will discover ways to communicate. We can meet while you are in London."

She glanced up at him with watery eyes. "Will you live in London?"

Good Lord, I have no idea. "We shall see," he said and returned to his seat.

The servants finally arrived to remove the soup that almost no one had eaten and supply plates for the next course.

"Surely he will not follow through!" Richard exclaimed. "He is not that big of a fool to put Pemberley in the hands of an untried and virtually unknown cousin."

A footman placed a delectable-looking piece of beef in front of Darcy; he wished he had an appetite. "My father never makes idle threats, Richard."

"So you think he will disinherit you?" His cousin's tone was incredulous.

"I have no doubt," Darcy replied, attempting to remain outwardly calm as he cut his meat. "You know how ruthless he can be when he feels someone has wronged him."

"But you are his son!" The words burst out of Richard as if he could not contain them.

Darcy picked up his wine glass, wishing he could down it all in one swallow. "Yes, but we have been at odds for a long time. No doubt he has always considered disinheritance to be the ultimate trump card to force me to do his bidding."

Everyone at the table looked rather aghast at this pronouncement, but Darcy knew his father. He would lay odds that George Darcy had long held this threat in reserve. Darcy took a sip of wine and cut a piece of meat that he had no stomach to eat.

"William." Elizabeth's voice was soft. "I wish you would reconsider. I do not wish to be the cause of your ruination."

There were various different ways in which one's life could be ruined, Darcy realized. He took her hand in his. "I am not ruined. This is merely a change in direction for the course of my life. I *would be* ruined if I allowed him to dictate the terms on which I live. If I capitulate now, my father will never cease his demands. I refuse to live my life under his thumb."

"Do you think he will throw you out immediately?" Richard asked.

Darcy had not considered this. Damnation! There were so many details. "I do not know." He tried to imagine packing trunks with all of his clothing and other belongings. Where would he take them? Could he take his valet with him? Could he afford to pay the man? Could he take his horse? How would he feed and care for it?

"You are welcome anytime at Gracechurch Street," Mr. Gardiner said stoutly.

Darcy's first impulse was to ask if the Gardiners' house had room for a horse and a valet and then almost laughed at the thought. *Get ahold of yourself, Darcy!*

"Thank you." Darcy focused his gaze on his plate. What if he were turned out of Darcy House tomorrow? A wedding night at the Gardiners was not quite what he had envisioned, particularly given how small the rooms were and how much sound undoubtedly traveled. But suddenly an inn seemed an unnecessary expense. To think he had originally considered taking Elizabeth to Scotland for a wedding trip! He must grow accustomed to a new way of thinking.

Mr. Bennet cleared his throat. "Yes, and you will always be welcome at Longbourn."

Darcy was grateful to have such allies. "I thank you. We must consider our options." Even as Darcy spoke, he wondered which household would be worse. The Gardiners were far better company, but their house was small and full of noisy children. Longbourn had more space, but it came with Mrs. Bennet and the younger sisters. Perhaps Bingley would lend Darcy Netherfield for a time. But then there was the question of earning a living…and no matter which friend or family member they imposed themselves upon, Darcy and Elizabeth would be living on charity. His pride bristled at the thought although not quite as much as it rebelled at the idea of bowing to his father's will.

Was this truly what his life had been reduced to? He glanced over at Elizabeth; she was not even pretending to eat her dinner. They would need to talk in private so he could be certain she was comfortable with this decision. She had claimed she would marry him under any circumstance, but the realities of being a pauper were something else entirely.

Mr. Bennet cleared his throat. "Have you…have you considered what you will do, er, for money?"

Georgiana's eyes grew wide as if it only now occurred to her that her brother must work for a living.

Darcy watched the wine swirl in his glass. "I have a friend who is a barrister here in London. I thought I would talk to him about the possibility of joining his firm." Of course, when he had considered that possibility, he had thought it would be a temporary measure until he inherited Pemberley.

"Do they have sufficient clients to take on another partner? One with no experience?" Mr. Bennet inquired.

Good question. Darcy had never considered it. "If not, perhaps he will know someone he can recommend." Was he being too blithe about the prospect of employment? What if he could not, in fact, support Elizabeth—and a family?

He swallowed, meeting Mr. Bennet's eyes. "Are you considering withdrawing your permission for us to wed?" That would be another unwelcome obstacle. Would it be enough to give Elizabeth second thoughts?

To Darcy's surprise, a corner of Mr. Bennet's mouth quirked up in a smile. "Not at all. In fact, I am more convinced than ever that you are the right man for Elizabeth."

Elizabeth turned her stunned gaze on her father. Darcy nodded an acknowledgement to Mr. Bennet. "I thank you for your faith in me; I will endeavor to deserve it." *Hopefully, he will not one day believe his faith was misplaced.*

From the corner of his eye, Darcy noticed Elizabeth watching him. Was she marveling at the meagerness of his plans and already regretting her decision? Would he live with her regrets for the rest of his life?

He took a gulp of wine, wishing he had something stronger. Would this dinner never end? They were only on the second remove, and already it felt interminable.

"And you will wed tomorrow?" Georgiana asked.

Darcy cleared his throat. "If Elizabeth is amenable." She nodded without hesitation, and a golden bubble of happiness formed in Darcy's heart. Maybe this lunatic scheme would work. He took Elizabeth's hand in his as he continued to answer Georgiana. "I have spoken to the vicar at St. Michael's Church; he was prepared to perform the ceremony today, but when we learned Mrs. Gardiner was ill, he said he could easily do it tomorrow. I will send him a note in the morning. I hope you all will accompany us to the church?"

There was a general chorus of yeses. Warmth spread through Darcy's chest. They might face an uncertain future, but they were surrounded by people who loved them. "I thank you for your support." As he clasped Elizabeth's hand more firmly, he tried not to think how much they would need it.

***

George Darcy's hand shook as he poured more brandy from the bottle into his glass. He cursed as some spilled onto the papers on the desk. Oh well, most of the papers were Fitzwilliam's anyway. Serves him right if his correspondence was drowned in brandy. Since Darcy had spent little time in London recently, his son had commandeered the study for his own use. That, like so many other things, was about to change.

Truthfully, he was not looking forward to the prospect of resuming day-to-day management of Pemberley and the Darcys' other holdings. He had been pleased to surrender those tedious details to Fitzwilliam when he came of age. The elder Darcy would grudgingly concede that his son had done an excellent job of managing those holdings, but he had done it before, and he would do it again. It would only be for a short while until John Darcy could take over.

"Damn the boy!" George Darcy muttered into the empty room. Why did Fitzwilliam need to be so stubborn? The chit was not worth it. *No woman* was worth it!

Being related to Thomas Bennet…it made Darcy's skin crawl. He would not allow that man to have the last laugh—his daughter living off Darcy wealth and his grandchildren inheriting Pemberley. Darcy could not imagine how Bennet had contrived this "love affair" between his daughter and Fitzwilliam, but somehow she had used her arts and allurements to get her hooks into him. Damn the boy for not seeing through her schemes!

Or perhaps it was all Fitzwilliam's doing. Was it possible his son hated him that much? Had he encountered the daughter of George Darcy's most hated enemy and thought to marry her for revenge against imagined slights from his childhood? Darcy pondered this as he stared at the opposite wall. No, in that case, Fitzwilliam would have conceded defeat immediately upon the threat of disinheritance. His son would only stand by that woman if he had been fooled into believing he was in love. She really had wrapped him around her finger.

Darcy gulped down the remainder of the brandy in the glass. Perhaps Fitzwilliam would come to him before Darcy visited the solicitor in the morning. Maybe he would admit he was wrong and beg for another chance. Darcy sighed, relishing the vision.

George Darcy would not be the one to change his mind. If he did, Fitzwilliam would always expect to have his own way. But maybe Fitzwilliam would come to his senses and forget about the marriage before Darcy was forced to follow through with his threat. Fitzwilliam need not abandon the Bennet chit; she could be his mistress. Darcy chuckled at the delicious irony of that idea.

Darcy scowled as he poured another glass and drank it down almost as quickly. He did not relish the prospect of giving Pemberley to a distant cousin and cursed Fitzwilliam for putting him in this position. He barely knew John Darcy and was sure the man had done nothing to deserve the windfall of the Darcy fortune.

Having passed all his life in Cornwall, John Darcy had one of those appalling accents and manners that were a far cry from those acceptable in the *ton*. But Darcy could shape John as necessary. The man was soft and malleable—and would be eager to do anything to keep his unexpected inheritance—unlike Darcy's stubborn son.

Darcy savored another mouthful of brandy. Perhaps it was all for the best. He would exchange a difficult heir for one who was far more biddable—and who would be eternally grateful for the opportunity to better his station in life.

George poured himself more brandy, not spilling a drop. Yes, perhaps this would be for the best after all.

***

Darcy pulled on his cravat again. Today of all days, why did the damn thing have to choke him?

"William!" Georgiana admonished. "Stop fussing with your cravat. It will lose all its starch, and Harrison will be so unhappy with you!" Her voice echoed off the marble tiles in the elegant front hallway of Darcy House. She reached up to smooth one of the loops in the complicated knot his valet had created. *It hardly matters; soon I will be a pauper without sufficient funds to afford a valet—or probably even starch.*

He shook his head to banish such maudlin thoughts. Truthfully, he did not regret his decision, and today was not the day to brood about what he was losing. It was a day to focus on what he was gaining: a lovely, clever wife.

He wanted to look his best for her. Watching his reflection in the front hall's large mirror, Darcy inspected his attire. Was his right cuff slightly askew? He tugged on it. Now it was too long! He pulled on the sleeve of his coat to compensate. Now the sleeves were not even.

"Stop worrying your clothing!" Richard clapped him on the back. "You look impeccable. Everything a bridegroom should be, and I am certain your bride will be lovely."

At this thought, Darcy went completely still. When they had first arrived in London, Mrs. Gardiner had taken Elizabeth to a *modiste* who had rushed to create a white silk dress and matching bonnet for the wedding.

He imagined her walking down the aisle of St. Michael's, a smile on her face—a smile that she reserved only for him. Marrying her was not a mistake. He had searched for years and never found a woman who could hold a candle to his Elizabeth. Soon she would be his in the eyes of the church and the crown. And he would be hers—in every way. Everything else was unimportant.

Darcy ran a hand through his curls and then, realizing he had disarranged them, patted them back into place. "Are we late?" he asked his cousin. "We cannot be late to the church!"

Richard checked his pocket watch and chuckled. "If we leave now, we will be half an hour early. What possessed you to be already dressed and ready to go?"

"We cannot be late."

Georgiana and Richard exchanged exasperated glances. "We will not be late, William," his sister assured him.

Richard rubbed one of Darcy's shoulders. "Calm yourself! You are marrying the love of your life today."

If she has not changed her mind, Darcy thought darkly. But they had spoken last evening after the dinner, and she had been quite firm about her desire to be wed.

He frowned at Richard. "But what if it is a mistake? To marry her with such uncertain prospects? What if that means I am not the right man for her?"

"Is she the right woman for you?" Richard asked.

"Yes," Darcy responded without hesitation.

His cousin lifted one eyebrow. "Then have faith that you are the right man for her."

Huh. Darcy had never considered the question in that light, but his cousin's words had a certain logic to them. He thought back to their first encounter in the Berwicks' garden. How close they had come to never meeting at all! Had that been divine intervention? A sign that they were meant for each other? That thought was somewhat reassuring, but... "Are we late? What time is it?"

Richard laughed and exchanged a knowing look with Georgiana. "Perhaps we should just go to the church. It might cure your pre-wedding anxiety."

Georgiana nodded. "I will fetch my reticule." She slipped into the drawing room while Darcy again fussed with his right cuff.

His attention was caught by movement on the elegant, grand staircase. His father clutched the banister as he stumbled down the steps. Most definitely not attired for a wedding, his father wore a limp cravat and unevenly buttoned waistcoat. Even his hair was uncombed. Had he dressed himself without his valet?

When George Darcy finally reached the bottom of the staircase, he simply stood, holding the newel post and swaying slightly. *Good Lord, my father is foxed!* His father did imbibe upon occasion, but this kind of overindulgence was rare. He must have been drinking copiously and into the early hours of the morning to still be showing the effects now.

"Good morning," his father mumbled, the words slightly slurred. "Off to the church, are you?"

Darcy nodded stiffly, restraining the urge to prop the older man up. "As you see."

"Well, you do what you must, and I will do what I must."

"You cannot visit your solicitor's office in such a state!" Darcy exclaimed.

"Why not?" George Darcy took a step toward his son but then grabbed the post again to steady himself.

Richard interceded. "You should have some breakfast first." Darcy nodded agreement. Food might absorb some of the alcohol if he did not vomit it up.

"You think I am foxed!" His father stalked toward Darcy in an outrage, poking his outstretched finger into Darcy's chest. "I am not foxed. I merely had a couple of glasses of brandy last night."

Darcy doubted his father was in any position to recall how many glasses he had imbibed.

"Uncle George." Richard took his arm, allowing the older man to lean on him. "You seem tired. Why not return upstairs and rest before setting out?"

George Darcy wrenched his arm from Richard's grasp. "You are on his side." He pointed a shaking finger at Darcy. "You hope to prevent me from visiting my solicitor."

"Nothing of the kind!" Richard declared in a vexed voice. "But I do think you should comb your hair and obtain a new cravat before venturing out in public."

Darcy's father ran a hand over his messy head. "Nothing wrong with my hair. I must get to the solicitor's office. They close at two!"

Georgiana emerged from the shadow of the drawing room door; she must have been observing this little farce. Placing an arm around her father's waist, she tilted her head up to look him in the eye. "Papa, there is plenty of time for that later. You do seem unwell. Perhaps you should rest."

"I do not need any God damned rest!" He stamped his foot, causing him to lose his balance and grab

Georgiana's shoulder. "I am visiting the solicitor this morning, and you will not stop me."

"At least drink some coffee before you leave," Darcy suggested. "There is no harm in that."

His father regarded him with narrowed eyes. "You are up to some trickery, I can see."

Richard rolled his eyes, and Georgiana smothered a snicker. Darcy spread his hands wide. "No trickery, I swear! I am merely concerned about you."

Then he heard the distinctive sounds of horses' snorts and jingling harnesses outside the door. "Good, the carriage is finally here," his father declared. "I called for it hours ago."

Darcy rather doubted that. "At least take another footman to help you," he said.

His father lifted his chin. "I do not need a keeper, Boy! And you will not send someone to spy on me."

Darcy sighed in exasperation. "I have no intention of—"

"There is a footman with the coach—and the coachman, of course. That is enough." George Darcy straightened his posture as best he could and turned toward the house's grand front entrance. The butler opened the door and handed his master his walking stick. "When next you see me, you will no longer be my son!" His father shouted over his shoulder and laughed—until he tripped on the threshold, cursing it for being in his way. The door closed behind him, and he was gone.

Richard, Darcy, and Georgiana exchanged looks. "He would hate anyone to see him like that. How mortifying!" Georgiana exclaimed.

"I am more concerned for his safety. No one should be gadding about London in such a state," Darcy muttered.

Georgiana took her brother's hand. "He has two able-bodied servants with him; he will be fine."

Richard shrugged. "You can do little else. He will make his own decisions."

Darcy rubbed a hand over his face and sighed. "Yes, I know. He gets foxed upon occasion, and it has always been fine. But customarily he remains at home."

"Well, if he makes a public spectacle of himself today, perhaps he will listen to you in the future," Richard said.

Darcy sighed. "I will no longer be his son."

Richard clapped Darcy on the shoulder. "Have you forgotten it is your wedding day?" Darcy felt his lips curve upward on their own accord. "Now that is what I like to see!" Richard grinned. Then he glanced at his watch. "Now it really is time to go to the church."

Darcy's eyes slid to Georgiana. "So, Sister, does my cravat meet with your approval?"

Her reply was drowned out by a frantic pounding on the door. Briggs opened it hastily. Darcy recognized the man who tumbled in as Taylor, one of the house's footmen. He staggered to his feet, and his eyes found Darcy. "Mr. Darcy, come quickly! We need you!"

Chapter Twenty Two

Elizabeth smoothed the front of her elegant silk gown while the maid finished arranging her hair. Glancing in the dressing table's mirror, Elizabeth realized she did indeed look like a bride. It felt strange to be readying herself for a wedding a second time, but at least the day had finally arrived. Despite the senior Mr. Darcy's behavior, at least he could do nothing to prevent their wedding today.

"You look beautiful," her aunt assured her from her seat on the bed. She was pale but had recovered almost completely from her fever.

The Gardiners' housekeeper bustled into the bedroom. "Miss Bennet, here's a message for you. The boy ran all the way from Mayfair!" Elizabeth stood quickly to take the letter.

"It is from William." Elizabeth had an immediate sense of foreboding. Why would William send a letter when she would see him in less than an hour? She pulled it open impatiently and quickly scanned the contents. "Oh!" Elizabeth sagged back into her chair.

"What is it? Elizabeth?" Her aunt stood, apparently ready to fetch the smelling salts.

"I do not know for sure," Elizabeth replied. "William merely writes that we should not leave for the church, and he will be here soon to explain."

"What could that possibly mean?"

Elizabeth shrugged, her finger worrying the edge of the letter. "Perhaps he had a change of heart? He has decided not to marry me after all. There are many good reasons against it."

"Oh, Lizzy!" Her aunt pulled Elizabeth into a standing position and then enfolded her in a comforting embrace. "That man is so in love with you that he would face down wild tigers to say his wedding vows."

"But he will be sacrificing so much. How could I possibly be worth it?"

"No one could convince a man so violently in love that he felt otherwise," her aunt declared.

Elizabeth hunched over as if warding off a blow. "He must be having second thoughts, Aunt. What else could it be?"

Aunt Gardiner guided Elizabeth to the bed where they could sit side by side. "Any number of things. Perhaps the priest needs to visit a sick or dying parishioner. Perhaps Mr. Darcy tore his jacket and needed to wait while it was mended. Perhaps the wheel on the carriage is broken, and they are undertaking repairs." With each suggestion, Elizabeth's shoulders lowered slightly. "Perhaps a rogue band of pirates has taken over Darcy House." Elizabeth giggled.

"But if it were something simple like that—well, aside from the pirates—why would he not write it in the letter. Why all this secrecy?"

"Perhaps he did not have time to write a longer explanation."

"Perhaps." Elizabeth knew her doubts were written all over her face. It was not like William to be so mysterious. If he did not offer an explanation, it was because he did not want to. Another doubt assailed her. What if he did not come at all? What if she waited in a wedding gown for a groom who never appeared? She could think of little that would be sadder.

Elizabeth slid off the bed and commenced pacing the length of the small room. "Could we send a messenger to Darcy House?"

Aunt Gardiner shook her head. "We do not even know if he is there, dearest. An emergency could have taken him somewhere else. We *do* know that he will soon be arriving here. You need only exercise some patience, and all will be revealed.

Patience! Elizabeth feared she possessed that commodity in scarce supply today. She longed for William's reassuring embrace, but what if she never felt his touch again?

"We should go down to the drawing room. The others will wonder why we are not ready to depart yet." Her aunt stood.

Elizabeth nodded although she had no heart to make conversation with her father and uncle—and tell them that she had possibly been left at the altar, or abandoned before she ever reached it.

With the sense that she was walking to her doom, Elizabeth descended the stairs after her aunt. Before they reached the drawing room, however, a great knock sounded on the front door.

Elizabeth froze. It must be William. She both longed to see him and dreaded what he might tell her. She heard the housekeeper open the door and the low murmur of voices, then the sound of footsteps approaching, William's sure, even stride. He appeared in the doorway with Colonel Fitzwilliam hovering behind him.

His appearance did not allay her fears. His hair was in disarray, his cravat was mostly untied, and his expression was grim. He did not look like a man who was planning to marry. Elizabeth felt like a fool for not having immediately replaced her wedding gown with something simpler.

William strode right up to her and took both her hands in his. "Elizabeth, dearest. There is no easy way to say this: we cannot get married."

***

Darcy felt Elizabeth's hold on his hands slacken suddenly, and her eyes fluttered closed. Was she about to faint? "Elizabeth!" He grabbed her arms to prevent her from falling. Her eyes opened halfway.

Behind him, Richard's voice chided. "Today! Darcy, you left out the most important part. You cannot get married *today*."

"What?" Elizabeth's voice was groggy and her eyes unfocused.

"Darling, you had best sit down," Darcy said.

By this time, quite a crowd had gathered in the hallway, including Mr. and Mrs. Gardiner and various children and servants. Darcy half carried Elizabeth into the parlor where he laid her gently on a sofa. Mr. Bennet sat on the opposite side of the room, glaring at Darcy. "What are you up to now, Boy? I knew you would be trouble!"

Darcy was not sure how to respond, so he remained silent and focused on making Elizabeth comfortable and seating himself next to her. He was vaguely aware of the Gardiners and Richard arranging themselves around the room.

Elizabeth's face had lost all color, but she seemed more alert as she rubbed her cheek with one hand. "What has happened, William?"

"My father is dead."

Elizabeth's hand flew to her mouth. "Oh!"

Mr. Bennet's voice sounded from across the room. "What? How?"

Darcy's gaze did not waver from Elizabeth's. "The official cause of death is a carriage accident. The truth is a bit more complicated." He swallowed convulsively. "He was foxed, having imbibed excessively last night. This morning we warned him not to venture out in such a state, but he was determined to reach the solicitor's office."

Elizabeth sat up, her eyes soft with compassion, making it easier to tell his tale. "The coachman had stopped to fix a problem with the harness. Apparently, my father opened the door and disembarked from the carriage.

We do not know why. He rushed into the street and was struck by a carriage traveling in the opposite direction. It was not far from Darcy House. The footman hurried back to find us. We brought him into the house and immediately sent for a doctor, but there was nothing he could do."

"I am so sorry, William." Elizabeth's hand squeezed his gently.

Darcy felt his eyes sting. She understood. Even though he had been at odds with his father, he was still devastated by the man's death. She knew, and she did not question it.

"So there cannot be a wedding today or any day until the mourning period is over."

"Of course not." Elizabeth's voice was rich with compassion. "I do not mind waiting as long as I may marry you someday."

He nodded, grateful that she was not unhappy at the delay. Occasionally, Darcy himself had the bitter thought that his father had found a way to prevent the wedding after all. But he vowed that it was only delayed, not prevented.

"You are not disinherited?" Mr. Gardiner asked.

Darcy turned to look at him, feeling the weight of his grief. "No. My father never arrived at the solicitor's office, so he never followed through on his threat."

Mr. Gardiner cleared his throat. "I am sorry for your loss, but I do believe that is the proper result. I think you will be an excellent master of Pemberley."

Darcy nodded. "Thank you, sir. I will endeavor to be so."

"And Lizzy will be an excellent mistress of Pemberley," Mrs. Gardiner chimed in.

Elizabeth blinked at this pronouncement as if it only now occurred to her.

Darcy took his beloved's hand and raised it to his lips. "Yes, she will be indeed."

Epilogue

Darcy gazed around Pemberley's grand dining room, scarcely believing this day had finally arrived. It was good to see the room full of people. After his mother's death, his father had few friends and fewer guests, so any dinners in this room had been sparsely attended. However, today the huge table could barely accommodate all the guests.

Everyone seemed to be enjoying themselves. Jane and Bingley were, as usual, caught up in their own little world. Their wedding had been four months ago, and already Bingley was talking about giving up Netherfield and moving closer to Pemberley—and farther away from Mrs. Bennet.

Kitty was flirting outrageously with Richard, but he appeared to be enjoying himself. Mary Bennet was engrossed in an earnest conversation with John Darcy, who had graciously traveled from Cornwall for the occasion. Georgiana smiled as she discussed books with Mr. Bennet; they had discovered a mutual taste for ancient history. Mrs. Bennet was talking with great animation to no one in particular, a state Darcy thought might have been fueled by the free-flowing champagne. Mr. and Mrs. Gardiner were speaking with each other and holding hands, a couple still very much in love.

Elizabeth squeezed Darcy's hand. "Everyone is having a wonderful time. No need to fret." Darcy smiled ruefully at her; she knew him so well.

His breath caught once again at the sight of her. He could see her a hundred times in this dress and would never grow weary of it. The white satin complemented her complexion perfectly. And her elegant hat framed her face beautifully; Darcy had already envisioned removing it from her head later that evening.

"I just want to make sure all of my—all of our—guests are enjoying themselves," he explained.

Their wedding had been delayed by six months while Darcy and Georgiana observed a formal mourning period for their father. Darcy had chafed at every one of those days, counting the hours until he could bring Elizabeth home. Elizabeth and her mother, however, had used the time to plan a wedding celebration worthy of Pemberley. Once Mrs. Bennet had learned of Pemberley's grandeur, she had readily acquiesced to holding the ceremony in Derbyshire.

Elizabeth bit her lip. "I suppose they are my guests as well now."

"You are officially the mistress of Pemberley," he observed. Her eyes sparkled with happiness. *I have helped to bring that expression to her face.* Darcy permitted himself a moment of pride.

"Yes, I am." Her smile could not have been broader. "I spoke with Mrs. Reynolds the other day about redecorating the whole house in the latest Egyptian style."

Darcy choked on his champagne. *The whole house?* But when he turned his disbelieving expression on Elizabeth, he saw that she was laughing. Ah, this was part of her campaign to bring more teasing into his life.

He set down his champagne glass carefully. "Absolutely not. I insist on an Oriental style." But he ruined the effect by allowing a corner of his mouth to quirk upward, provoking more of Elizabeth's laughter.

"Now that I am mistress of Pemberley," Elizabeth said with a mischievous gleam in her eye, "I intend to start a new tradition."

Darcy lifted an eyebrow. "And what would that be?"

"A midsummer masquerade ball." Her smile was teasing. "I know someone who looks very handsome and mysterious in a mask."

Darcy chuckled. "I like that idea far better than the Egyptian décor, my love. It is time Pemberley enjoyed more celebrations."

"And every year I would like to invite all of your family and all of mine."

Darcy's eyes widened. After all the trouble his family had caused her, she wanted to see them on a regular basis?

But as he watched Kitty and Richard, Mary and John, Georgiana and Mr. Bennet, Darcy realized that the Darcys and the Bennets did seem to be getting along. In fact, they seemed to enjoy each other's company.

Elizabeth squeezed his hand and smiled at him. "You did this. You brought everyone together."

Darcy shook his head. "No, *we* did."

The End

Thank you for purchasing this book.

Your support makes it possible for authors like me to continue writing.

Please consider leaving a review where you purchased the book.

Learn more about me and my upcoming releases:

Website: www.victoriakincaid.com

Twitter: VictoriaKincaid@kincaidvic

Blog: https://kincaidvictoria.wordpress.com/

Facebook: https://www.facebook.com/kincaidvictoria

Please enjoy this exclusive excerpt from Penelope Swan's novel *Darcy's Wager*

Darcy's Wager

A Pride and Prejudice Variation

By

PENELOPE SWAN

When Elizabeth Bennet discovers that her sister, Lydia, has risked her reputation by staking a wager against one of London's most notorious rakes, she races to prevent a scandal before shame and ruin befall her family. But saving her own sister could mean sacrificing another: the sister of the handsome, aloof Mr Darcy. Can Elizabeth make a choice between her family and the man she loves?

From the pleasure gardens of Vauxhall to the gambling dens of Piccadilly, join Darcy and Elizabeth as they banter, dance, and fall in love in this Regency romance for Jane Austen fans everywhere.

DARCY'S WAGER is a sweet, clean, full-length standalone Pride and Prejudice variation romance, inspired by Jane Austen's novel.

EXCERPT

Elizabeth stepped into the main hall and walked slowly towards the nearest shelves. She reached up to run her fingers reverently along the spines of the leather-bound volumes, inhaling deeply of the rich aroma of paper and calfskin. *There is no smell as wonderful as that of a book,* she thought. Her gaze strayed upwards and she spied a volume on a higher shelf which looked particularly intriguing. Stretching up on tiptoe, she attempted to pull it out, but her fingers could not quite reach their target.

"Allow me, Miss Bennet."

Elizabeth spun around and found herself face to face with a tall gentleman.

"Mr Darcy!" she said in surprise.

Clad in an elegant coat of dark blue superfine, with his long legs encased in pale buckskin breeches and gleaming Hessian boots, Darcy cut a fine figure. Though he was not as fashionably dressed as many of the other gentlemen in the room, he easily overshadowed them all— just as he had done when he had accompanied his friend, Bingley, to the society events in Hertfordshire. His handsome face was as austere as Elizabeth remembered from their meetings there, though she fancied she saw a warmth in his eyes as he looked down at her.

Darcy made her a slight bow, then reached up and extracted the volume from the shelf, handing the book to her.

Elizabeth accepted it and dropped a belated curtsy. "It... it is a pleasure to see you, sir."

"I had not realised that you were in town, Miss Bennet," said Darcy.

"Yes, my aunt and uncle have invited us to come and stay with them for a while at their home in Cheapside," she said, darting an impudent look at him and wondering if he would recoil from the mention of such a lowly address.

To his credit, Darcy did not react but merely said, "That is most generous of them."

"Indeed," agreed Elizabeth. "Though it is also a fortuitous arrangement, as my uncle has had to make a trip to inspect his ships at Plymouth and is away for several weeks. Thus my aunt is glad of our company as well."

"And are you enjoying your time in town?"

"Oh yes, though I own…" She looked at the shelves of books around them, her eyes shining. "Today's visit is the highlight of my stay so far."

Darcy raised a sardonic eyebrow. "I would have thought that the highlight of most young ladies' stay in London would be a visit to the fashionable *modistes* of Bond Street."

Elizabeth waved her hand. "We have certainly been patronising many of the stores and bazaars in town. My younger sisters have a fervent love of fashion, gowns, and accessories, but I confess…" She gave a wry smile. "I grow tired of looking at shawls and pelisses. I would much rather pursue the pleasures of a book." She looked around and sighed dreamily. "Would that I had a library of such proportions at my disposal! I am sure I could want for nothing more."

Darcy looked at her in amusement. "I had not realised your worldly aspirations were of such a literary bent. Most young ladies would long for fine jewels or expensive carriages that they could show and flaunt—"

"I am a selfish creature," she said with a laugh. "I do not care about giving pleasure to others, therefore I do not seek to entertain and impress them."

Darcy regarded her thoughtfully. "Do you care naught for the opinions of others, then?"

Elizabeth shrugged. "Perhaps. If they are worthy of being heeded. But most who would give you an opinion are not worth listening to."

"That is a cynical view for so young a lady," observed Darcy.

"Oh, I know you would have me say that those who enjoy advising others speak from a position of wisdom—so that you might have the pleasure of despising my naiveté; but I always delight in overthrowing those kind of schemes and cheating a person of their premediated contempt. I have therefore made up my mind to tell you that I think those who speak with the most authority often have the least knowledge. Now despise me if you dare."

"Indeed, I do not dare," said Darcy, with a teasing smile.

She looked at him in surprise. When he smiled like that, with a twinkle lighting up his dark eyes, he seemed almost a different person. For a moment, Elizabeth felt a tug of liking for him. Then she pushed the feeling aside as she reminded herself of Darcy's arrogant behaviour back in Hertfordshire and his haughty manners—not to mention the way he had snubbed her the first time they met at the assembly ball in Meryton.

"It has been a delight to meet you again, Miss Bennet, and to have had the pleasure of your lively discourse," said Darcy, still smiling. He bowed, then turned and strode away.

Elizabeth stared after him for a moment. She was surprised to find that her heart rate was slightly unsteady and she wondered why this should be the case. Surely she did not find the company of Mr Darcy exciting! With great resolve, she put the gentleman from her mind and turned back to the shelves in front of her.

The time flew by. Elizabeth had spent almost an hour in the store, browsing the many shelves and selecting a few volumes to purchase, when she glanced up guiltily at the clock on the wall.

Heavens! Was that the time?

She had to leave directly, else her aunt would become worried. She had already been out all morning. After accompanying her mother and younger sisters, Kitty and Lydia, for a morning of shopping in Bond Street, Elizabeth had persuaded them to return to the Gardiners' without her. She had been desperate to visit the Temple of the Muses and had insisted that there could be no harm in her taking a hackney coach back by herself. However, she knew that had her aunt been one of the party, she would not have been allowed to come unchaperoned—for her aunt had stricter notions of propriety than her mother. Mrs Gardiner would certainly be fretting now and Elizabeth did not want to cause her aunt any more distress than necessary.

As she stepped out of the front door of the bookstore, she noticed that a light rain had begun to fall. Clutching her bundles to her chest with one hand and picking up her skirts with the other, Elizabeth hurried to cross the street, keen to reach the hackney coach stand on the other side.

But she had barely stepped into the road when a sudden shove sent her reeling. Something—somebody—yanked at her reticule. She tried to hold on but it was torn from her grasp. She lost her balance and cried out, dropping all her parcels and tumbling backwards into the road.

Elizabeth hit the ground with a jolt which knocked the breath from her body. She lay stunned for a moment, then looked around in fear. She was in the middle of the road and vulnerable to any carriage that might pass. She heard the sound of hoof beats approaching and felt a surge of panic.

"Miss Bennet!"

Suddenly, strong arms grasped her and helped her to her feet. A tall, male body shielded her from the oncoming carriage as she was gently ushered back to the side of the road. Her heart still racing from the recent shock, Elizabeth took a deep breath to calm herself.

"Miss Bennet—are you unharmed?"

Elizabeth realised that the gentleman supporting her was Mr Darcy. She flushed as she also realised that he had one arm around her waist, the other holding her hand. Slowly, he released her as she stepped away from him.

"Yes, thank you, sir." She looked around and gave a shaky laugh. "I was warned about the dangers of the capital—the street peddlers and pickpockets and footpads…"

"The street hawkers are often associated with the criminal poor in London but they are mostly just honest folk plying their trade and trying to earn a living," said Darcy. "The pickpockets and footpads, however, you do need to be wary of. They do not normally attack in broad daylight—you must have been extremely unfortunate." He frowned. "Did he take anything?"

"Only my reticule, but I did not have much money left in it," Elizabeth assured him. She had regained her composure now and was able to give him a weak smile as she dusted herself off, then began retrieving her parcels.

Darcy stepped forwards to help her, and together they collected the scattered parcels from the road. By this time, the rain had begun to fall in earnest and Elizabeth was dismayed to see that several of the packages had been torn open and one in particular had fallen into a puddle. It was now soaked and the book was damaged beyond repair.

"Oh!" she cried in disappointment as she picked it up gingerly. "This was my favourite selection and the one I had been most looking forward to reading."

"Perhaps you would like to return to the store to purchase another?" asked Darcy.

Elizabeth hesitated, then shook her head. "I cannot. My aunt is expecting me back home and I am already delayed. What is more…" She paused awkwardly, her cheeks reddening. "I have spent what allowance I can afford on my purchases already."

Darcy inclined his head. "In that case, may I escort you back to your aunt's residence? My own curricle is stationed nearby and I should be pleased to offer you a ride."

Elizabeth hesitated again. The last person she wanted to accept a ride from was Mr Darcy. On the other hand, the rain was getting stronger by the minute and she did not fancy the prospect of standing in the wet, clutching her many purchases and waiting for a hackney to become available. She could see the coach stand beyond Darcy's shoulder and there was already a considerable queue waiting, with no carriage in sight. As was often the case, once the rain started, all available means of transport seemed to disappear!

She turned back to Darcy. "Thank you, sir," she said. "It is very kind of you. However, I should not like to give you any trouble and I am sure that—"

"'Tis no trouble at all," said Darcy smoothly, putting a gentle hand under her elbow and guiding her towards the side of the square.

"Oh…" Elizabeth said as they arrived next to the vehicle and Darcy held his hand out to help her up. She was dismayed to see that there was no tiger perched at the back.

"Is something the matter?" asked Darcy.

"No… That is, I had not expected you to be driving it yourself," said Elizabeth lamely.

She did not add that the prospect of being alone with him in the vehicle made her heart beat unaccountably fast. She had expected there to be a groom or some other servant to chaperone them.

She cleared her throat. "Would it… would it not seem improper for us to be driving together without a chaperone…?" she trailed off.

Darcy surprised her with a chuckle. "Miss Bennet, for a young lady intrepid enough to roam the countryside alone and bold enough to come to the bookstore unchaperoned, it surprises me that you should be so concerned with propriety in this instance."

Elizabeth flushed. He was right—her concerns did appear hypocritical given her usual independence. It was really the thought of being alone with Darcy that unsettled her. She had never really spent any amount of time alone with him. Even during her stay at Netherfield Park when Jane had taken ill—though there had been the occasional half hour when they had been alone together in the library or drawing room—she had never really felt the intimacy of it, for there were others in the house ready to join them at a moment's notice. Now, however, although they were on the streets of London surrounded by the public, it felt as if they were much more alone.

Darcy gave her a dry smile. "If you are concerned about propriety, I feel that we would be absolved in the present circumstances. You have recently had an unpleasant fright and I am escorting you back to your aunt's residence. We are driving in an open vehicle, in public, and it is not uncommon for a gentlemen to take a young lady for a ride about town—as you see daily during the fashionable hour in Hyde Park."

His words made sense and Elizabeth was also conscious of the fact that they were standing in the rain, getting wetter by the second. She felt foolish prevaricating further. She took his hand and mounted the steps to seat herself in the curricle, looking away as he climbed in after her and settled himself beside her. Darcy raised the hood, so that they were well shielded from the rain, then picked up the reins and set the horses in motion. The pair of beautifully matched bays twitched their ears and tossed their manes as they broke into a sedate trot

READ MORE:

www.penelopeswan.com

About Victoria Kincaid

As a professional freelance writer, Victoria writes about IT, data storage, home improvement, green living, alternative energy, and healthcare. Some of her more…unusual writing subjects have included space toilets, taxi services, laser gynecology, bidets, orthopedic shoes, generating energy from onions, Ferrari rental car services, and vampire face lifts (she swears she is not making any of this up).

Victoria has a Ph.D. in English literature and has taught composition to unwilling college students. Today she teaches business writing to willing office professionals and tries to give voice to the demanding cast of characters in her head. She lives in Virginia with her husband, two children who love to read, and an overly affectionate cat. A lifelong Jane Austen fan, Victoria confesses to an extreme partiality for the Colin Firth miniseries version of Pride and Prejudice.

Victoria Kincaid's other books:

When Mary Met the Colonel

Without the beauty and wit of the older Bennet sisters or the liveliness of the younger, Mary is the Bennet sister most often overlooked. She has resigned herself to a life of loneliness, alleviated only by music and the occasional book of military history.

Colonel Fitzwilliam finds himself envying his friends who are marrying wonderful women while he only attracts empty-headed flirts. He longs for a caring, well-informed woman who will see the man beneath the uniform.

A chance meeting in Longbourn's garden during Darcy and Elizabeth's wedding breakfast kindles an attraction between Mary and the Colonel. However, the Colonel cannot act on these feelings since he must wed an heiress. He returns to war, although Mary finds she cannot easily forget him.

Is happily ever after possible after Mary meets the Colonel?

Mr. Darcy to the Rescue

When the irritating Mr. Collins proposes marriage, Elizabeth Bennet is prepared to refuse him, but then she learns that her father is ill. If Mr. Bennet dies, Collins will inherit Longbourn and her family will have nowhere to go. Elizabeth accepts the proposal, telling herself she can be content as long as her family is secure. If only she weren't dreading the approaching wedding day…

Ever since leaving Hertfordshire, Mr. Darcy has been trying to forget his inconvenient attraction to Elizabeth. News of her betrothal forces him to realize how devastating it would be to lose her. He arrives at Longbourn intending to prevent the marriage, but discovers Elizabeth's real opinion about his character. Then Darcy recognizes his true dilemma…

How can he rescue her when she doesn't want him to?

Pride and Proposals

What if Mr. Darcy's proposal was too late?

Darcy has been bewitched by Elizabeth Bennet since he met her in Hertfordshire. He can no longer fight this overwhelming attraction and must admit he is hopelessly in love. During Elizabeth's visit to Kent she has been forced to endure the company of the difficult and disapproving Mr. Darcy, but she has enjoyed making the acquaintance of his affable cousin, Colonel Fitzwilliam.

Finally resolved, Darcy arrives at Hunsford Parsonage prepared to propose—only to discover that Elizabeth has just accepted a proposal from the Colonel, Darcy's dearest friend in the world. As he watches the couple prepare for a lifetime together, Darcy vows never to speak of what is in his heart. Elizabeth has reason to dislike Darcy, but finds that he haunts her thoughts and stirs her emotions in strange ways.

Can Darcy and Elizabeth find their happily ever after?

The Secrets of Darcy and Elizabeth

In this Pride and Prejudice variation, a despondent Darcy travels to Paris in the hopes of forgetting the disastrous proposal at Hunsford. Paris is teeming with English visitors during a brief moment of peace in the Napoleonic Wars, but Darcy's spirits don't lift until he attends a ball and unexpectedly encounters…Elizabeth Bennet! Darcy seizes the opportunity to correct misunderstandings and initiate a courtship.

Their moment of peace is interrupted by the news that England has again declared war on France, and hundreds of English travelers must flee Paris immediately. Circumstances force Darcy and Elizabeth to escape on their own, despite the risk to her reputation. Even as they face dangers from street gangs and French soldiers, romantic feelings blossom during their flight to the coast. But then Elizabeth falls ill, and the French are arresting all the English men they can find….

When Elizabeth and Darcy finally return to England, their relationship has changed, and they face new crises. However, they have secrets they must conceal—even from their own families.